Prophets

Nico Lawrence

Cover design by Ana K. Quintero

OTHER WORKS BY THE AUTHOR

<u>Poetry:</u>
Diary of a Schizophrenic Poet

<u>Young Adult:</u>
The Chronicles of Existence

DEDICATION

To James,
For being there when no one else was.

"Do not turn to mediums or necromancers; do not seek them out, and so make yourselves unclean by them: I am the Lord your God."
Leviticus 19:31, The Bible

"…Anyone who practices divination or tells fortunes or interprets omens, or a sorcerer or a charmer or a medium or a necromancer or one who inquires of the dead, for whoever does these things is an abomination to the Lord. And because of these abominations the Lord your God is driving them out before you."
Deuteronomy 18:10-12, The Bible

"And when they say to you, "Inquire of the mediums and the necromancers who chirp and mutter," should not a people inquire of their God? Should they inquire of the dead on behalf of the living?"
Isiah 8:19, The Bible

"And I will cut off sorceries from your hand, and you shall have no more tellers of fortunes."
Micah 5:12, The Bible

"Then Pharaoh summoned the wise men and the sorcerers, and they, the magicians of Egypt, also did the same by their secret arts."
Exodus 7:11, The Bible

"They instead followed the magic promoted by the devils during the reign of Solomon. Never did Solomon disbelieve, rather the devils disbelieved. They taught magic to the people, along with what had been revealed to the two angels, Hârût and Mârût, in Babylon. The two angels never taught anyone without saying, "We are only

a test for you, so do not abandon your faith." Yet people learned magic that caused a rift even between husband and wife; although their magic could not harm anyone except by Allah's Will. They learned what harmed them and did not benefit them...."
Al-Baqarah, 2:102, The Qur'an

CONTENTS

EZEKIEL

Ezekiel sat with his legs splayed, his Nike Air Force One trainers resting against the seat in front of him, a frown etched on his face that seemed a permanent fixture in recent years. He wasn't looking for trouble, but he was certainly not likely to shy away if it came knocking on his door.

The sun glared through the window of the bus, inexorable in its assault on Ezekiel's bloodshot eyes. He squinted and rested his head against the window, far too high to deal with the bright light gushing through it.

It was the kind of sunny day that one doesn't get in Manchester very often, and he'd have been wiser to enjoy it while it lasted, before the quintessential Mancunian grey skies and interminable rain returned to restore normality and order to the city.

He picked up one of the free newspapers that was lying next to him at the back of the bus and flipped through the pages without really reading it, his head still pressed against the glass. He wasn't much of a reader. He hadn't done well in school, coming out with three GCSEs in total, in Music Technology, Physical Education and Religious Studies. The former he'd taken and managed to achieve an A because it was the only lesson he'd ever really excelled at, and it was his dream to be a

famous rapper. He could be found spitting lyrics to a beat he'd
made almost as often as he smoked weed. Almost. The latter
he'd paid attention in mostly because he'd fancied the teacher
who taught it. He'd tried hard at P.E. for the same reason most
guys do, he enjoyed competing against other men and winning.
He'd even managed to somehow enjoy the physical science
lessons, though he'd barely scraped a C overall. Everything else
he'd failed, but his mother was still proud of him for that A.

He threw the newspaper down on the blue and yellow
cushioned seat, stopping on a page that detailed one of the
many terrorist attacks that had become ubiquitous of late. He
wasn't into politics, but killing wasn't his thing. A bit of petty
shoplifting, the odd fight and general delinquency was as bad
as he got. And he would always have a friend's back in a time
of need, even if that meant getting physical. He was even
known to be a bit of a sweetheart to the right person, though
he'd never admit that.

His right leg vibrated. The Samsung notification pierced the
relative hum of the bus. He took his phone out of his pocket,
pressed his finger to the screen to unlock it, and navigated to
the group chat in WhatsApp.

Jermain: Wer u at Ezekiel?

Ezekiel: On the bus now. Just gone past the buddha express.
Will be in town in 15.

Jermain: Safe. Me n tich r here now. Link me wen u get here.

Ezekiel: Yh man.

Tich: See U in a bit.

He slid the phone back in his pocket and zipped it closed.
He rested his arm on his right leg and looked around the bus.
It was 11.30am on Friday. Most people were working, so the
bus was filled with students and other people without the ball
and chain of a nine to five. He could hear the students
chattering away to one another about how many words they
had to write for their dissertation and boasting about the parties
they'd been at the nights before. He hated their posh southern
accents. How they reeked of money and entitlement. Of the
kind of obliviousness that one has when they've never

experienced any real hardship in life.

There was an old woman sitting near the front, her curly grey hair in a short bob, a little kid by her side which he assumed was her grandchild. She reminded him of his nana, on his father's side. He scanned the rest of the people in front of him and found himself ensnared by a young woman who looked to be in her early twenties. She had dark skin and braided hair. He could see her side-boob. He reckoned she was at least a DD, maybe even an E-cup.

He pulled out his phone again and scrolled through Instagram. It was a stream of half-nude women, rappers and footballers interspersed with pictures of his friends, mainly holding up two fingers to the camera with a spliff in their mouths or showcasing some other illegal activity.

The bus finally turned into Piccadilly Gardens as he looked up from his phone. He slid it in his pocket and stood up with his head ducked underneath the top of the bus, rolling his eyes at the long line of people who had noticed their arrival before he had.

Piccadilly Gardens was as alive and buzzing with people as ever. The sight of the busy square with everyone going about their lives relaxed him somehow. He spent an inordinate amount of time there. It was his second home, and where he made most of his deals, selling £10 bags of weed.

"Yes, Ezekiel!" said Jermain as Ezekiel walked past the tall, dull, grey brick wall that blighted the square. "What you sayin'?"

"Nothin' much," shrugged Ezekiel. "What you been on?"

"Just chilling," said Tich. "It's dead at the moment. No one lookin' to buy anything."

"I'm gonna grab a Maccies," said Ezekiel. "You comin'?"

"Yeah," said Jermain, standing up. "Man's starvin'".

"Hopefully it's not a long ting."

They walked through the throng to McDonalds. Ezekiel skipped the queue and ordered at the self-service machine. It was not that busy for once. He finished ordering and tapped his card against the reader. He grabbed the receipt and walked over to the mass of people who were waiting for their number to be called out.

Jermain and Tich popped up at his side. "I went for a double cheeseburger and chips," said Tich. "Wasn't feelin' a Big Mac today."

"Nice," said Ezekiel.

They collected their order and sat down at the benches opposite the fountain at Piccadilly Gardens. Ezekiel devoured the Big Mac in five bites. He threw the box on the floor, reached in the bag for his fries and took a sip of his strawberry milkshake.

Tich finished his chips and started rolling a spliff. "Are they new trainers?"

"Yeah, man," said Ezekiel, showing them off with a wide grin. "Air Force Ones. Got them for a hundred."

"Lookin' sick, bruv," said Jermain. "I've been thinking to get some, you know. One hundred ain't bad."

"They were on sale at Footlocker. Probably gone back up by now though."

"True say," said Jermain. "Still gonna get some soon."

Tich took a few puffs of the spliff and passed it to Ezekiel. Ezekiel held it cuffed in his hand, inhaling and blowing the smoke out through his nose. No one seemed to notice the smell or sight. They were used to everyone smoking weed there. It had become such an integral part of Piccadilly Gardens that it just wouldn't be Piccadilly Gardens without it. "This is nice, what is this?"

"Cali, bro," said Tich.

Ezekiel passed the spliff to Jermain. "I've got some Star Dog to shot today. Speak of the devil, I think that's one of mine now." He got up from the bench and walked over to a boy in his late teens. They were wearing the same blue striped Adidas tracksuit pants and matching jacket. "Yes G, what you lookin'?"

"A ten, mate," said the skinny white boy.

"Safe, safe," said Ezekiel. "Come."

He led them to the stone steps that border the grass in the square and sat down. The boy passed him a £10 note underneath his legs. Ezekiel took it and clamped down on the boy's hand, pushing a small bag of weed into it.

"Nice one," said the boy. He bumped Ezekiel's fist with his own and headed over to the bus station. Ezekiel walked back to the bench where his friends were.

"What was he sayin'?" said Tich.

"Just a ten," said Ezekiel.

"How much you got to shot today?"

"Seven bags left," said Ezekiel.

"Hopefully it's less dry than this soon. You'd think more people would be out in this heat."

"I know," said Tich. "I'm sweating balls. We've got nine to shot today. Me and Jermain went halves on a quarter."

"0.7 grams a bag, yeah?"

"0.75."

"That's decent for Cali."

"We got it cheap from that new guy."

"I might have to link him, still," said Ezekiel.

"Yeah man, you got his number. I told him you might call." Tich passed the spliff to Ezekiel.

Ezekiel inhaled, filling his lungs with the smoke and holding it in. He exhaled the smoke through his nose as he inhaled his next puff. He savoured the flavour like a fine wine before passing the last of it to Jermain. He stretched out his arms and legs and smiled. The weed had hit him. It was strong stuff.

A group of guys in tracksuits walked past them. "Yes G," said Jermain, tipping his head up at the men. "You lookin' a deal?"

"Nah, we're good, mate," said the man nearest to them.

"Safe."

"I told you, it's dead," said Tich.

"Hopefully it picks up soon," said Jermain. "It normally gets busier after three."

"True say. Everyone's finished college around then, haven't they."

"Yeah."

Ezekiel's leg vibrated. He took out his phone. "Looks like I got my second customer. You guys are slackin'. Some random guy. Said he got my number from Jason. He wants me to meet him at Back Piccadilly. I'll be back in a min."

"Lucky bastard," said Jermain.

"Link you soon," said Tich.

The square seemed to spin as Ezekiel got up to walk. The weed had hit him harder than he'd expected. Probably because he'd been high since he had woken up.

He walked through the bustle of Market Street and edged his way through the crowds to an alley behind the golden arches of McDonalds. There was just one guy there, he looked about as tall as Ezekiel. He had his hood covering his face and was wearing a long brown coat, which he'd said to look out for in the text.

"Safe G, you lookin' a bud, yeah?" said Ezekiel, approaching the guy.

"Hello Ezekiel," said the man. He lifted his hood up and looked Ezekiel square in the face.

Ezekiel jumped back, almost out of his skin. He couldn't comprehend what he was seeing. He studied the man's face, his own contorted in disbelief. They had the exact same shade of coffee brown skin, the same dark eyes, rounded nostrils, sharp cheek bones. Everything looked identical. The man he was looking at was… him. Only it couldn't be. How could it be? The only difference he could see was that this other guy looked older, and his long curly hair ran down the side of his face, unlike Ezekiel's, whose curls sat atop his head and faded into cropped edges at the sides. Other than that, they were identical. "What the fuck?" he said, staring at the man with his mouth open. "Who are you?"

"I think you know who I am," said the man. "The question you should be asking is, who are you?" He sounded like Ezekiel, but he didn't at the same time. His voice was different. More formal. There was still the Mancunian twang to his accent, but he enunciated his words more, they felt more laboured, and he spoke with a conviction that Ezekiel never had.

Ezekiel cupped his head in his hands. He couldn't understand what he was seeing. "What do you mean who am

I? I'm Ezekiel. What the fuck was in that weed?"

"The same thing that's been in it since you started smoking at thirteen."

Ezekiel's eyes widened like a cat in the night. "How the fuck do you know that? Who the fuck are you, man?!"

"I'm Ezekiel," said the man. "I am you. I'm just a bit older."

Ezekiel looked around him. Everyone was walking along the main streets in the same fashion as they had been. Nothing seemed to have changed. No one seemed to have noticed anything unusual. But clearly, he was tripping.

"You're scarin' me, man," said Ezekiel, backing away from the man.

"We don't have time for this," said the older of the two. "And you should be scared. Very scared. You have no idea what lies ahead of you. Come with me. I have something important to show you." Before Ezekiel could protest, the man grabbed his arm and Ezekiel felt a force tugging him as though a rope had been tied around his midriff, yanking at his navel. The two of them vanished from the alleyway.

Ezekiel's heart caught in his throat. He was in Piccadilly Gardens, but it wasn't the city he'd come to know and love. All the buildings were destroyed. Rubble littered the floor in every direction. All the shops were gone. All the people were gone. The golden arches he'd been looking at minutes ago lay in pieces on the floor, surrounded by crumbled pavement. The statue of Queen Victoria that had stood proudly in the square for over a century lay in tatters, barely recognisable. The air was filled with a dark, musty smog. He could barely see. His head was spinning taking it all in, and it wasn't from the weed. He could feel his heart beating in his chest, hear it pulsating in his ears. He rounded on his older self. "What's goin' on? How did we get here? What happened here?"

"We're in the future. Ten years from now. This is all that's left of Manchester. Rubble and ruin."

"This can't be for real, man," said Ezekiel. "How've you done this?"

"This is what awaits us all if you don't accept your destiny."

"What do you mean, my destiny?" He screwed up his face, looking at the man as though he'd lost his mind.

"Everything will be explained to you in good time, but now, I need to show you what will become if you refuse to be what you are meant to be."

"What are you on about, what I'm meant to be?" said Ezekiel, throwing his arms in the air.

"I told you already. I am you, from the future. I've come to show you what you must become. Walk with me."

The older Ezekiel walked ahead, and Ezekiel stood still where he was, not wanting to move. Moving would make this real, and this couldn't be real. He'd heard of some bad trips on weed, but this was another level.

"I said, walk with me," said the older Ezekiel, turning to face his younger self.

"I'm not goin' anywhere until you tell me what the fuck is goin' on!"

The older Ezekiel walked back over to his younger self. "This is Manchester city centre, ten years from now. There was a war, World War Three to be exact. The world has reduced itself to ashes and cinders. And it's your job to stop it. That's why I'm here. To help you."

"World War Three? You can't be serious. And how am I supposed to stop World War Three?"

"I told you; all will be revealed in good time. First, you need to meet Oscor."

"Who's Oscor?"

"You wouldn't believe me if I told you. What's important now is that you accept the facts of your reality. The world will end in ten years, and you're the only one who can stop it. Every life on the Earth will die if you refuse your destiny. If you refuse to become what God has chosen for you to be."

"You've lost it, bruv," said Ezekiel.

The older Ezekiel grabbed his younger self and shook him. "We don't have time for this!" Ezekiel felt a force tugging at his navel again and his vision turned pitch black.

As his vision returned, the sensation of spinning came to a

halt. He was in a derelict, half bombed cemetery. Smog filled the graveyard, the earth was scorched, there was a smell like mouldy human flesh clinging to the air. They were at a grave. Half the headstone was broken off, strewn across the floor. Ezekiel read the inscription, still visible on the bottom half of the tombstone.

Here lies Elizabeth Campbell, beloved mother, daughter, sister and aunt. July 1974 – October 2027. May she rest in eternal peace.

Ezekiel dropped to his knees, tears welling in his eyes. "Mum!" He grabbed the tombstone, refusing to believe what he saw. "How? How did this happen? We're only in 2024. How can she be dead?"

"We're in 2034. And she died because they couldn't get to you. So, they got to her. But you can save her, if you follow the path."

"What path?"

"I told you. What God has chosen for you."

"What do you mean, what God has chosen for me?" he snapped. He was certain that this man was insane now.

"It's not for me to explain. But I can tell you where to go. Oscor will explain everything to you."

"Who the fuck is Oscor?"

"I can't tell you that now. Everything needs to happen as close to how it happened originally. Me being here, it's already risking messing up the timeline. We can't afford to make any mistakes."

He turned to face Ezekiel and grabbed his arm. "Come, there's more you need to see." Ezekiel was blinded for a few seconds. As the light returned to his eyes he saw an entire city in ruins, just as it was in Manchester, rubble lying everywhere, the only sign of life were the dead bodies lying on the ground. Their skin had been ripped from their bodies, all that remained were brittle, decaying bones. "This is Bangkok, Thailand. They were the first to accept you. This is what happened."

Bile welled up in Ezekiel's throat. He clasped his hand over his mouth trying not to be sick. As much from the smog as the sight of the dead bodies. "The first to accept me?"

"Yes, but that was the first error. It needs to be China first. That's imperative. Do you hear me?" He paused and glared at him. "You must get China to declare first, or we're all lost. The world will end. And there will be no one left."

"China needs to declare what first? What are you on about?"

"Everything will be explained to you when you meet Oscor. We can't stay here any longer. Every change I make risks distorting the timeline. I've said all I can say." He turned to the younger Ezekiel and grabbed his arm, staring into his eyes with an intensity that scared Ezekiel. "Listen to me very carefully. I'm going to take you back to 2024. You need to go to Manchester Central Library. Go to the top floor and look for a book called Mechanical Intelligence written by a man called Alan Turing. Press your finger against the spine of the book. Go today. Do not wait. Everything you need to know will be explained to you there."

Before Ezekiel could retort, he felt the yanking sensation in his navel again. They appeared in the alleyway in Manchester. All the buildings were back as they had always been. The city was rammed with people carrying bags of shopping and waiting in an unorganised mass at bus stops, none of whom seemed to notice their appearance in the alleyway.

"Do exactly as I've instructed," said the older of the two, letting go of Ezekiel's arm. "There's no time to wait." He looked at Ezekiel with a ferocity that made him feel as though he was piercing his soul with his eyes. "And stop fucking smoking. You've got battles to fight, and you're not going to win them high!"

Ezekiel blinked and his future-self had disappeared.

EVE

"Surely there are other options on the table, Madam Secretary?"

"The Democrats left us with a two trillion-dollar deficit in the budget," said Eve, straightening in her chair. "I don't see any other way we can plug it."

"We can't afford to borrow anymore," said the president, his eyebrows furrowed. "Even if we get it through Congress, we'll never get it through the Senate."

Eve twirled the ends of her dyed, blond hair in her hand. Her eyes flitted to the arrows clutched in the eagle's hand on the President of the United States flag that was draped opposite her seat in the cabinet room. "We could revisit the reforms I proposed."

"That's political suicide," said the president, sat to her right. "The Democrats are already eight points ahead in the polls."

"They've been sucking on Uncle Sam's teat for too long," said Eve. "This is what happens to a nation when you wrap them in cotton wool for sixty years. They get used to having everything for free, all the time. We're not a communist nation. It's time we took drastic action. We need drastic action. And you're the only one who can manage it." She looked up at him, her face blank, her eyes stern.

The president stroked his lip. "How much of it can we plug

with your cuts?"

"If we scale back the housing development funds by forty percent, we could save two hundred billion," she said, leaning in towards the president. "We can save another five hundred with the reforms to social security. We're looking at around three or four hundred with a five percent cut in departmental spending. The rest would have to be plugged with cuts to defence spending."

"We're currently aiding Israel, Ukraine and several other proxy wars, and we're the world's strongest nation," said the president. "There'll be no defence spending cuts under my leadership. It was an election commitment damn it."

It wouldn't be the first election promise you've broken, thought Eve. "Yes, sir. Well, we can save one point two trillion with the other cuts. Surely, we could get eight hundred through Congress and the Senate? That is assuming you're willing to make the cuts."

"What other choice do we have?" said the vice president. He opened his arms in exasperation and stared at the president through his brown rimmed glasses. "We can't go on borrowing and borrowing. The credit cards are maxed out. I think we should go with the cuts, Mister President. We'll be able to get the rest through the Senate."

The president pursed his lips.

"What about foreign aid?" said a woman opposite Eve. "There are surely cuts to be found there."

The president slid his thin, greying hair back. "We must be seen to be magnanimous. We need the Middle East states that we have on side. We've got to be resolute in our support of Israel. The African American community will never accept a cut in funding for African causes. What does that leave?"

"India has made it to the moon. How much are we sending them? They can clearly look after themselves."

"We could save a few billion there," said Eve. "But nothing substantial."

"How about tariffs on Chinese imports?" said the president. "They're benefitting from our innovation, our technology, our productivity. They'll overtake us at this rate. They've sponged on the American dream for long enough."

Oh, he wants me to think for him, as usual. "There's a strong chance of retaliation," said Eve. She tapped her polished nails on the polished mahogany table. "But I'm sure I could come up with another hundred billion in tariffs, though we'd lose about thirty percent of that in retaliatory tariffs on our exports."

"Do it," said the president. "Damn it. Yes, OK, we'll make your cuts. But if we tank in the polls, it's on you!" He pressed his index finger on the table and stared at Eve.

"Yes, Mister President," said Eve, failing to mask her elation.

"Have Michael write me a statement for the press for tomorrow," said the president to his chief of staff. "I'll deal with Congress and the Senate about getting the rest through loans."

"We could raise another two hundred from bond sales," suggested Eve. "They've been scarce this year. That way we'll only need to plug half a trillion. And we're sure to get a few Democrat votes."

The president nodded, reassuring himself. "OK. Adam, see if the gulf states are interested in the bonds." He turned to Eve. "Get the full details of the proposed cuts to Michael by three. I want the speech drafted and on my desk by the end of the day."

"Yes, Mister President," said Eve. She inclined her head forward in a bow.

"Any other business?" asked the president.

"No, sir."

"Nothing I can think of."

"Good. You're all dismissed." He stood up from his chair.

The room rose to their feet.

Eve raised her eyebrows at the vice president imperceptibly. A smile curled at the sides of her lips for the briefest of seconds. She wasn't sure the president had the balls to implement her cuts. She was sure the vice president's support had helped. She brushed her suit jacket down as though wiping off dust and turned to leave the room.

Her office was just along the corridor from the meeting room. She closed the door, and a broad grin spread across her face. She had done it. Everything she'd worked so hard to accomplish in the last nine months, her whole life really: the changes she wanted to see in America, they were finally coming to fruition. She hated the poor. She hated the working classes. She hated the middle classes. They were all sponges to her, suckling on the milk of the state. She was as economically liberal and capitalist as they came and had even won awards for her PhD thesis about the perils of the rise in globalism.

And now she could finally make a difference. The state would stop funding these lazy leeches and building them homes that they should be out working for. That was her top priority. That, and ending the constant welfare handouts. It was high time the blacks and the Latinos paid their dues to the society that propped them up. They'd become reliant on the state, and she couldn't stand people who were too weak to support themselves.

She'd been supported her whole childhood, of course, from birth through to her doctorate. She hadn't paid a penny or worked a day in her life until she got a job at the White House as an intern. Her parents had doted on her, and she wore her stabilisers that whole time. But that was her right. Her parents were clearly ahead in life and able to provide for her because her ancestors were genetically superior to their contemporaries.

She knew fucking the vice president was a good idea. His comments had certainly helped sway the president. Men were so predictable. Always thinking with their dicks instead of their brains. Which reminded her, she could use a good fucking.

She logged onto her computer and opened the folder with the proposals for her cuts. They'd been sat on her desktop ready to send for weeks. She attached them to an email and sent them to Micheal. There was something immensely satisfying about clicking send.

She reclined in her seat a moment, then leaned forward and opened the draw of her desk. There was a rose-gold iPhone in its centre. She opened it with a scan of her face. Ignoring the notifications, she scrolled through her contacts until she found the vice president's name. *Can I see you in my office about these proposals?*

The reply was almost instant. *Yes, give me 15 minutes.*

Eve reclined in her chair and waited for Elijah to arrive.

There was a knock at the door after ten minutes. "Come in."

"You wanted to see me?" said Elijah, his dark eyes undressing Eve.

"Lock the door," said Eve.

He closed the door behind him and turned the lock.

Eve got up and walked over to him.

"I told you he'd go with the proposals," said Elijah. "He just needed a little encouragement."

"Yes," said Eve, stroking his cheek. "I thought you deserved a little thank you." She ran her hand down his pristine white shirt that contrasted his black skin until she reached his belt. She carried on further, stroking his already engorged bulge.

He grabbed her cheek and embraced her in a kiss, pushing her back towards the desk, running his hand up her thigh.

She pushed the papers on her desk out of the way and let his muscular frame envelop her. She could taste the coffee on his tongue, smell the cologne from his shirt. She unbuckled his belt as he pushed up her skirt, pulled down her underwear and spread her legs.

He was fully hard now. She glided him into her.

He placed his hand over her mouth and started to thrust.

Eve tried to stay as silent as she could, trying not to let the tingling in between her legs rush out through her mouth. It was just sex to her, sex with a purpose, to get what she needed from him, a means to an end. But she'd have been lying to herself if she said she didn't enjoy it.

She stifled a moan as he pounded harder. It was *just sex* but there was something about his hard, girthy cock that made her tingle and twinge in ways her husband simply never could.

"I love you," he said, as he pounded. He kissed her face, sniffed her hair.

She moved his hand from her mouth for a moment. "I love

you, too," she said, as convincingly as she could.

He placed his hand back over her mouth and pounded harder. Eve couldn't help but let out a moan, muffled by Elijah's large, dark hand.

She spasmed as he ran his fingers over her breast, caressing her nipple with his free hand.

"I love you," he said again.

She pushed his head over her shoulder.

He thrust harder, caressing her neck with gentle kisses.

She let him pound until his body went limp and he collapsed into her bosom.

Their lips met. Eve made sure not to pull away. "I feel like you get better at this every time we do it," she said.

He kissed her again and leant back, extracting himself from inside her. He took a tissue from Eve's desk and wiped himself clean. He pulled his pants up from around his ancles and made himself presentable again. "I just can't wait until we can be together properly."

Eve pulled her underwear back up and picked up the papers she'd hastily strewn on the floor. She stroked his chin. "All in good time. We need to wait until the time is right."

"I know," he said, kissing her again.

"Soon, I promise," she said, pulling away from him. "I'd better get back to work. I need to send those papers to Micheal. Thanks for… looking over things." She smiled at him.

"Any time," said Elijah. "Let me know if there's anything else I can do for you." He undressed her again with his eyes, eager for another round. The lust in his eyes dimmed. He turned, unlocked the door and closed it gently behind him.

Eve's legs shook as she sat down. She opened the draw to her left and took out a tiny bag with white powder in it. She grabbed her keys from her purse and scooped some of the powder onto the end of one of the keys and snorted. Placing the key back in the bag, she scooped several more times, snorting and relishing the tingling on her lips, and the confidence spreading through her body. She licked the end of the key, returned them to her purse and hid the bag of powder inside the papers in her draw.

She spasmed as though a cold chill had run through her body. There was a twinge in her gut. It wasn't from the sex. It wasn't the cocaine. It wasn't guilt. It was fear. Not that she'd be found out, not that she was about to do something that she knew any morally abiding person would think was evil. It was simply that she'd fail to pull it all off. And Eve Jones did not fail. At anything.

EZEKIEL

Ezekiel looked back and forth around the alleyway. The man. He was gone. He had disappeared. It couldn't be, but it was.

He fell back against the wall, slid down it and pressed his hands against his head. What had he just seen? And how? And why him? None of it made any sense.

His leg vibrated, startling him out of his stream of thought. Tich: Wer u at bro? Been gone time.

He stared at the screen. He couldn't bring himself to reply. He didn't know what to say. They would think he'd gone crazy.

This can't be happening, he thought. Time travel? World War Three? It just couldn't be.

He sat, thinking about the violent attack that had just taken place on everything he knew to be true. The casualness with which his future-self had disabused his worldview.

He tried to push the memory of what he'd just seen out of his head. All those dead bodies. The crumbling buildings. The stench of the smog and charred flesh.

His phone vibrated in his hand. His hand shook as he turned it over to look at the screen. He opened the group chat.

Ezekiel: Somethings cum up. Will link you later.

Jermain: You good bro?

Ezekiel: Yeah man. Just got somethin to sort.

Jermain: Alright. Link me when ur done.

Ezekiel liked the message with a thumbs up. His hands were still trembling. He couldn't bring himself to move from the dirty alleyway. He sat resting his back against the wall, holding his head in his arms. He couldn't comprehend what had just happened. Had he just teleported? Time travelled? Seen a future version of himself? Surely, he must have been tripping. But even as he thought it, he knew in his heart it was real. He had seen the end of the world. He had been there. His mother! He'd seen her grave.

That shook him back into reality. The library! He couldn't not go to the library when he'd seen his mother's grave. He needed to go, and he needed to go today. He had to at least see what this Oscor guy had to say.

He walked down the alley trying in vain to quell the churning in his stomach. He took the back roads, walking on the streets behind Piccadilly Gardens so that Tich and Jermain wouldn't see him.

"Excuse me!" said an older gentleman with a grey beard. Ezekiel had walked straight into him.

"Soz," said Ezekiel. He hadn't even seen him he was so lost in his own thoughts.

You must get China to declare first, the future him had said. What did that mean? Declare what? It was all so cryptic.

He turned the corner into Saint Peter's square. The central library's white roman-style columns seemed to gleam at him as he looked at them, as though inviting him in. He'd never been in there before. He'd only ever seen it when using the tram.

He shook as he made his way towards the main entrance of the library. He felt like there was a circus in his stomach. Acrobats swinging from ropes, jumping up and down on trampolines, doing summersaults, using the lining of his stomach for their landing.

He thought back over what the future him had told him. *Go to the top floor and look for a book called Mechanical Intelligence written by a man called Alan Turing. Press your finger against it.*

He walked through the entrance to the library looking

around in all directions. He was greeted by an oval room with marbled flooring and a high ceiling. It was full of people and PlayStations and virtual displays. He was shocked by how technological libraries had become. The last time he'd been in one it was all just books.

He found the wide, sprawling staircase and walked towards it. He could hear the beating of his heart in his eardrums.

Every step he took up the stairs made the circus in his stomach perform harder. There were people in there launching themselves from cannons and landing on the surface of his bowel. His heart pulsed in his throat. His hand slipped on the banister as he ascended, it was so laden with sweat.

He arrived at the top floor. He walked around the library looking at all the books, half expecting something to jump out at him. The Dewey Decimal System was not something he was acquainted with, so he searched around the library somewhat aimlessly looking for books by a man called Alan Turing; a name he'd never heard before.

A woman walked past him, staring at him with her eyebrow arched.

It dawned on him he must look bizarre, frantically flipping through books as though his life depended on it. He tried to compose himself and carried on searching the books.

He did two laps around the library before he saw the word 'Turing' on a book. His heart leapt into his throat. He stared at the book, scared to touch it. Like it would make the whole thing he'd just been through real.

There was nothing else for it. He needed to see what this was all about. He pressed his finger to the book as his future-self had told him to do. The plain, paperback book suddenly sprang to life, and an orange light shone along the spine of the book as he pressed his finger to it, scanning his fingerprint.

The light covering the spine turned green and he heard a click and watched in awe as part of the shelf came apart, leaning inwards.

He looked around him again to make sure no one was looking. Everyone was busy with their reading. He opened the newly formed door. A narrow corridor with stairs leading downwards lay behind the door.

His heartbeat was astronomical. He wouldn't have been shocked if it was visible through his jumper. He forced himself to walk inside, into the corridor and down the stairs.

As soon as his foot hit the third step, he heard the wall seal back into place.

He spun around and pressed his hand against the wall he'd entered through. It had sealed shut. "Fuck."

He turned back to the corridor, and with nowhere else to go, made his way cautiously down the steps to whatever lay ahead of him. The brick walls felt oppressively close as he made his way down.

He came to an aged wooden door with a gleaming golden handle at the bottom of the stairs. He twisted and his hand shook as he pushed the door open.

A cavernous room that looked too big to fit underneath the library above it came into view. Everywhere he looked there were screens displaying all kinds of information, computers and other machinery he didn't recognise, control panels with buttons, dials and knobs. He looked around for any sign of another person. "Oscor?" he said, almost whispering. "Are you in here?"

"Hello Ezekiel," echoed a voice that seemed to come from all directions. It wasn't human, but it wasn't machine either. It was a hybrid of both. "I've been expecting you."

Ezekiel threw his head left and right looking for the source of the noise. He couldn't see anyone. "Where are you? I can't see you."

A face made of pixels appeared in green light on one of the screens. "I'm everywhere," said the voice, and the face on the screen imitated the motion of speech. "I'm OSCOR. Welcome."

This day couldn't possibly get anymore fucked up. First, he'd met himself in an alleyway, then he'd travelled through time and seen the end of the world. Now there was a computer fucking talking to him. He stared at the screen unable to form words.

"Don't be alarmed," said Oscor. "I've waited a long time to meet you. You're a very important person, Ezekiel."

"You're a… computer? That can talk?!"

"No, I'm not a computer. I'm an operating system. I'm OSCOR. It stands for Operating System for the Cerebral Oscillation Ray."

"An operating system?" said Ezekiel scratching the back of his head. "I don't know what… oscillation… even means."

Oscor laughed. "It's a pattern of movement." The screen next to its face changed, showing interwoven streams moving inwards and outwards. "Like this."

"Right," said Ezekiel. He stared, not sure what to say.

"Being here means that you've met your future-self," said Oscor, "and you know the fate that awaits the world. I suppose it's about time I explained things to you. I've been watching you your whole life."

"You what? You've been spyin' on me?"

"Not spying. Observing. You were chosen a long time ago. I've been watching you since the moment you were born."

"I can't believe I'm talkin' to a computer. And that it knows who I am. This is so fucked up."

"Nothing in life is ever simple, I'm afraid," said Oscor. "You've been shielded for as long as possible. Now it is time for you to know the truth."

"What truth?" said Ezekiel. "What is all this about? What does any of this have to do with me?"

"You're a prophet, Ezekiel. Chosen by God to save the world."

Ezekiel laughed. "Are you insane? Man's not a prophet, bruv. You've got the wrong guy."

"You are a prophet, Ezekiel. You were chosen. And if you don't follow the path that's been laid out for you, everyone and everything you know and love will die."

"You can't be serious! Me, a prophet? It's not possible that God would have chosen me of all people to be a prophet. I'm not lookin' to be the second coming of Jesus!"

"Who said anything about Jesus? And yes, God has chosen you. I have chosen you. You're the reincarnation of the Buddha."

Ezekiel's eyes opened so wide they were liable to pop out of his skull and he couldn't help but laugh. "The reincarnation of the Buddha? Are you mad? I'm a Christian."

"A Christian, is it? So, you're a virgin? You didn't lose your virginity at fourteen out of wedlock? I suppose that's a clone of yours I've seen selling weed in Piccadilly Gardens. I guess lying in bed hungover on a Sunday morning counts as going to church these days?"

Ezekiel couldn't believe what he'd just heard. This thing knew things about him that it shouldn't know. It *had* been watching him. "Look, I don't know how the fuck you know when I lost my virginity or what I do with my life, or how any of this is possible, or why you think I'm… the reincarnation of the Buddha, but this is all too much for me! I'm just a random guy. I'm eighteen! I can't be responsible for the world ending!"

"You can't escape your destiny, Ezekiel. The sooner you accept who you are the more chance we have of saving the world."

Saving the world. Him. It just couldn't be. 'Look man, Oscor, whatever the fuck you are. This is too much to deal with. And you can't seriously believe I'm a prophet!"

"I don't believe it. I know it. And so must you. You must accept your destiny, Ezekiel. Or will you doom the world to ruin? Will you let them all die. Your mother. Your little sister. Your uncle."

How did this computer know so much about his life? It scared him. "What do you mean let them die? Who is going to kill them?" Then he remembered what the future him had showed him. "My mum! I saw my mum's grave. The future me said it was because of who I am. Why would I listen to anything you've got to say if it is going to get my mum killed?"

"You don't choose to be a prophet, Ezekiel. You are chosen. And God has chosen you. Your mother will die if you run from this. And so will the entire world. Only by accepting the path laid before you can you have any chance of saving her."

He couldn't bear the thought of his mother dying, but he couldn't believe it was possible that he could be a prophet. "What path has been laid for me?"

"One that is long and filled with trials, hardship and tribulations," said Oscor. "One that is filled with healing, restitution and repair. The road laid before all those who channel the power of God. There is much about the world you must learn, both past and present."

Ezekiel shook his head. This was all so overwhelming. "How is any of this possible? How am I talking to a computer? How did I time travel?"

"I told you, I'm not a computer, I'm an operating system. I can run in almost any machine that exists. I was created by a man you'd never heard of, but who means more to you than you will ever know. His name was Alan. Alan Turing. He is my father. It was when he was working on defeating Hitler in World War Two that he cracked the code to harness the electromagnetic activity of the brain."

A platform rose near the centre of the room. On it was a thick golden ring. It gleamed like a diamond. Ezekiel had never seen gold so pure. It must have been at least fifty carats. "Put this on. It was made for you."

Ezekiel didn't move. He was still trying to process everything he was hearing. "What is it?"

"It's a ring. Inside is a microcomputer. It will let me read your brain's activity. All you need to do is imagine the place and time you wish to go. It will send electromagnetic currents through your body, and I'll read them. From there it's a simple matter of converting the energy so that there is acceleration or deceleration without motion. It's quite a simple equation. Acceleration minus motion equals time travel."

"That can't be possible from a ring."

"The ring is just a vessel to monitor your brain's activity. How about you put it on and see?"

"I'm not putting that on. Time travel? That can't be possible from a ring."

"I told you, it's not the ring. It's your brain's electromagnetism." An image appeared on one of the screens showing a translucent image of the human brain, with brainwaves oscillating across its surface. "And if you're so sure it isn't going to work, what harm is there in putting it on?"

Ezekiel sighed and walked over to the ring. He placed it on the middle finger of his right hand. It fit perfectly.

"Think of yourself standing at the other end of the room," said Oscor.

Ezekiel jumped out of his skin for the second time today. This time Oscor's voice had played directly into his mind. "Did you just fuckin' talk into my mind?"

"Don't be afraid," said Oscor, speaking in his mind again. "They're just electromagnetic impulses sent into your brain that mimic speech. Now think of yourself standing on the other side of the room."

Ezekiel looked around the room and the second he fixated on a spot he felt the same yanking sensation in his navel that he'd felt earlier. Everything went black for a fraction of a second then he was on the other side of the room, exactly where he'd been thinking of. His heart raced in his chest, trying to break free of its material constraints.

"What the fuck, man? This is too much for me. I don't want any of this. You need to choose someone else. Time travel! Talking software! Me being a prophet! This is too much for any person to deal with!"

"You can leave at any time," said Oscor. "But you'll never outrun your destiny. And the longer you wait, the less chance there is of saving the world."

"What if I don't want my destiny? Why should I believe anything you're saying?"

"What reason do I have to lie?"

"How am I supposed to know? There could be a million reasons you're doing this."

"I'm trying to save the world. The future rests on your shoulders now whether you want it to or not. All I can do is guide you, but the choice is yours. Do you want to spend your life selling weed in Piccadilly Gardens or take the path that God has chosen for you? Make your decision and make it quickly. We've no time to spare."

He couldn't accept what was before him. "I need to get out of here, man. I need to go home and process this shit. There's no way I'm a prophet."

"Fine, go," said Oscor. "But know that everyone you love will die if you don't accept what I'm telling you."

"Whatever," said Ezekiel. "Just open the door so I can leave. I'm not dealing with this shit. Pick someone else."

The door swung open. "You can leave, Ezekiel. But you can never escape your destiny."

Ezekiel shook his head as though trying to rid it of a bug that had crawled in his ear. There was no way he was talking to an operating system capable of thought and reason, let alone teleportation and time travel - but him, a prophet? It was just insane. Truly insane.

He turned his back to the screens, from his destiny, and ran as fast as he could up the stairs.

ABU

Abu had never missed a prayer since the day the imam had taken him in from the streets to attend mosque and fed him his first proper meal in years, when he was a lowly street-boy at the age of eight. Since that day he'd prayed five times a day, every day. When he couldn't get to mosque, he prayed wherever the wind had taken him, even if it was in his head while driving. There was something about praying inside a mosque that made him feel a closer connection to Allah. Fajr, the morning prayer, was his favourite, but his duties that day had meant he only had time to attend mosque for Isha, the nighttime prayer.

He turned his armoured truck through the mihrab arches, along the dull, grey paved road that was in serious need of repaving and parked in the carpark of Abuja's National Mosque. The hot Nigerian sun glinted off the golden dome atop the centre of the mosque, refracting onto the smaller domes and long, stone spires that surrounded it.

It had always struck Abu that Islamic architecture was superior in design to Christian buildings, especially the geometric patterns that often furnished the interior of a mosque's roof. There was something about the tessellation of geometry that made him feel closer to God.

"As-salamu alaykum", said a man in dark blue robes as he

walked the brick stairs to the entrance of the mosque.

"Wa ʿalaykum as-salam," said Abu, raising his right hand to the man in greeting. He continued up the stairs, greeting several others until he reached the washroom. He used his good hand to cup the water and cleaned his arms and feet ready for prayer. The water was a cleansing balm that washed away the blood of the lives he had taken that day.

He selected a prayer mat from the pile and walked to the male side of the mosque. He loved the smell of the brick and carpet that scented the mosque. The sounds of the call to prayer echoing around the building. The sight of adherent Muslims lined up to give thanks and praise to Allah.

He took his position at the back. The room was almost completely full, and he always felt safer watching people than being watched. He bent to his knees and placed his head on the mat. Rising, he performed his evening prayer.

God hadn't talked to him on that occasion. It was just a normal prayer. He hadn't asked any questions, but he didn't always need to. Sometimes he would hear the voice of Allah guiding him, telling him which paths in life to follow. It had been like that for almost as long as he could remember. It made him feel special, in a way he never had before in his life. To know that God was watching over him: a guiding light in his life.

He had been somewhat unlucky in life before submitting to Allah. His parents had abandoned him at the age of five, thinking his albinism was causing their bad luck. They'd assumed he would die on the streets. But he hadn't. He'd survived. Like a stray dog, he'd taken food where he could get it, raiding rubbish piles for leftovers, standing outside the restaurants of central Abuja waiting for the close of day, when he was most likely to get some scraps. He'd even stolen at times, when the wailing of his stomach got the better of him.

Then at eleven, he'd been kidnapped and had two fingers on his left hand cut off. He could still remember the screaming agony of it, the sizzling as they'd burned his wounds shut with a hot knife to keep him alive as long as possible. They had intended to take all his body parts to sell for medicines, and it was believed these worked best when taken from the living. By the grace of God, he'd managed to escape. To survive. Survival was in his blood. It was all he knew.

People would stare at him, at his white albino skin, at his deformed hand as he passed them in the streets. The mark of an outcast. Of someone different. The *other* of society. But he wore his left hand with pride. Evidence of his strength. He had managed to wrestle the knife from one of his attackers and slit his throat without a moment's hesitation. The other assailant would have suffered a similar fate had he not fled fearing the 'witch child'.

He'd heard 'witch child' a lot before he'd been recruited to Allah's army, and in his younger years he'd believed it of himself. There was something about owning a gun that made people show a little more respect. So, it had been years since he had heard the word witch, though he knew some people still felt he was cursed.

It was silly superstition, he understood, and his parents were as stupid as they came. He often thought about killing them for what they had done to him but there was a part of him that just couldn't. He didn't know where they were anyway, and he didn't care to look. The only thing he'd kept from his parents was his first name. He'd adopted the surname Bakr after reading about Abu Bakr in the mosque. The imam there had taught him how to read and write in Arabic and English, and always ensured he had one wholesome meal a day. Other than his sergeant, he was the closest thing he'd ever had to a parent in his twenty-four years of life.

He stopped his truck in the pervasive traffic jams that marred the streets of Abuja, tapping the steering wheel as though it would speed up the traffic.

His stomach groaned. Not true hunger like he'd known as a child. But it was a sensation he couldn't abide as an adult.

A quiet tut would issue from his lips every time the traffic moved forward a few feet and then came to a stop once more. He was not known for his patience. It was a virtue which he sadly lacked.

After what felt like an age, the traffic subsided, and he turned onto the busy highway that led to the slums where he had grown up. He often went to the slums to eat. Money had never come to him easily and he still couldn't bring himself to pay the prices in central Abuja, even now that he was a paid commander in an armed militia hell bent on dividing Nigeria into two factions: Muslim and Christian. Or better yet, converting the whole country to the will of Allah.

Besides, there was something about the taste of freshly killed, wood-fire grilled meat that excited his taste buds. The way the charred texture of the outside contrasted against the soft, moist interior of whatever animal they'd manage to buy or capture that day. Lamb was his favourite meat, and that's what was on offer when he stopped by his usual restaurant.

"Hello old friend," said the man behind the make-shift wooden stall. Smoke rose from the wood underneath the wire mesh that the meat sat on. "We have a succulent one for you today."

Abu smiled. "It smells good."

"Only the best for you," said the shopkeeper, with a chuckle.

Abu passed him two 1,000 Naira notes and told him to keep the change.

"Thank you," said the shopkeeper. He took a leg from the grill and hacked at it with a blunt knife. He placed hefty chunks of meat on top of a pre-filled plate of jollof rice and passed it over the chipped counter to Abu.

"Thanks," said Abu. "How have you been?"

"Business is slow, as usual," said the shopkeeper. "But I survive, Inshallah."

"Inshallah," said Abu. "Things will get better. Just have faith."

"Always," said the shopkeeper. "I can't complain. A hot meal each day, the love of Allah and a place to rest my head at night is all I need."

Abu nodded in contemplation. He had known true cold on

the nighttime streets of Abuja, with not even a quilt to keep him warm. When his fingers would scream in stinging pain, and he'd shivered in the street like a snow monkey, longing for the warmth of a home. He had known hunger so strong it made him delirious, unable to stand straight or focus. A hot meal and a warm place to spend the night was more than any human could ask for. Any reasonable human, anyway.

"You look troubled," said the shopkeeper, with a perceptiveness that caught Abu off-guard.

Abu frowned. "I'm fine," he said. "Just hungry."

The shopkeeper raised his arms in surrender and didn't press it any further. "OK. Well, there's plenty more if you need it."

Abu forced a smile that seemed to pain him at the edges of his cheeks.

He devoured the meal in no time, the traces of the ravenously hungry street child had never fully left him. He licked his fingers and lips, enjoying the fatty taste of the lamb and the spices. He passed the plate back to the shopkeeper and passed him another 1,000 Naira note. "I'll take some to go."

The shopkeeper hacked off more of the lamb's leg and placed it in a thin, disposable aluminium dish.

Abu took it and nodded at the man without saying thanks. "See you soon, old friend."

"You know where I'll be," said the shopkeeper with another little chuckle.

The gravel of the dirt floor cracked under Abu's feet as he strode down the dirt path towards a group of children sitting by the roadside, looking utterly despondent. The look one has when the whole world walks by you and refuses to help, without a moment's thought.

Their faces lit up with smiles when they saw him.

"Eat well, Mashallah," said Abu. His face was blank as he passed the plate to the eagerly awaiting hands of one of the street children.

"Mashallah," said the little girl who had taken the plate.

All the children rounded on the girl, taking bits of meat and rice in their fingertips and ramming it in their mouths.

Abu didn't turn around to see, but they'd finished eating the whole dish by the time he'd walked back to his truck.

He wondered if the government, or anyone, was ever going to do anything about the slums as he drove back to his barracks. And yet, he already knew the answer. If the children of the street were to be saved, he would have to be the one to do it. And it would only be possible when all of Nigeria submitted to the will of Allah and left the shackles of Western imperialism in the past, where they belonged.

Two men armed with AK-47s, and bullets spread around their shoulders moved forward from the iron gate they guarded and walked to the window of Abu's car as he approached.

"Commander Bakr," said the smaller of the two, saluting Abu.

Abu saluted back.

The taller man unchained the gate to let Abu through.

He heard the chaining of the gates being resealed as he parked his truck.

Walking with a characteristic briskness, he strode through the busy encampment to his sergeant's office. He knocked on the door and waited. After a few seconds a soldier opened the door.

"Commander Bakr," said the soldier, saluting.

"Come boy, let him in," said his sergeant from a desk behind the soldier. The soldier moved out of the way to let Abu pass.

Abu took a pouch filled with Naira and passed it to the sergeant.

Sergeant Abdallah rifled through the notes. "Seems a bit light today."

"Some of them said they didn't have the money. They said they wouldn't pay us anymore. That we'd had enough. That they'd take their chances."

"Fools," said Sergeant Abdallah. "Return tomorrow. Show them what happens when they miss their payments."

"That won't be necessary," said Abu. "They are already

dead. One of them attacked me with a machete." He pulled back his sleeve to show a shallow wound on his upper right arm. "I had no choice but to engage. Only the mother lives."

"See that your wound is taken care of," said Sergeant Abdallah. "And return to the mother next month. If she doesn't pay, kill her as well."

"Yes, Sergeant," said Abu.

The sergeant leaned back in his hard, wooden chair. "I have an important mission for you, but the night is late, and you must attend to your wound. Come to my office tomorrow morning at 9am."

Abu arched his eyebrow, his eyes lit up. "As you command." He saluted the sergeant and left the office, nodding to the guard on his way out.

In everything that had happened that day, he'd forgotten that he even had a wound. It didn't pain him. Not much really did. Even when the medic rubbed alcohol on the wound, he didn't flinch or moan. He just waited as he bandaged his arm and nodded absent mindedly as the medic told him not to place too much strain on it over the next week. Though he would not take the advice.

He stripped naked as soon as he entered his room and threw himself down on the hard mattress. It was tattered and manky, but it made him feel whole and important. He wondered what the sergeant had instore for him as he drifted off to sleep. He wasn't sure, but he was sure it would involve bloodshed. And red was his favourite colour.

PARVATI

The candle holder gleamed as Parvati finished polishing it. She had developed a skilful precision in all domestic duties over the eight years she had worked at the palace. Her dark brown face could be seen distorted in the reflection of the gold candle holder, still a beauty for anyone to behold, though she would never believe it of herself.

She picked up one of the crystal glasses and sprayed it with polish. Wiping downwards first with a cloth, then with crumpled newspaper, she polished it until it was pristine and moved on to the next, until each one sparkled as though freshly made.

She grabbed her bucket, cloths and cleaning products and walked over to the long-panelled glass doors that overlooked the garden. It was a rare rainy day in Mumbai. Not quite a monsoon but enough to fill the streets with puddles of water.

The sound of the disinfectant spraying against the window comforted her. She had come to love her job. She loved the palace. She loved the prince though she could never tell anyone that. He wasn't a real prince, but the new maharaja, son of a wealthy billionaire and heir to a massive fortune, so he was known locally as a prince, and to her, he was *her* prince.

She'd worked at the palace since the age of ten. She was

lucky not to have been drafted into the whore houses of Mumbai. Her beauty was unmatched, and there would have been many who would have paid to visit such a treasure. The only time the higher castes would have touched her as a Dalit.

It was her beauty that got her the role at the palace. The owner of the palace, Sandeep, had surrounded himself with all things beautiful, whether they be objects or people. There was no expense spared; no item too lavish for him to own. And the people in his employ were his most prized possession. The sign of wealth and high status.

Parvati had never questioned her status in life, always accepting that she was a Dalit, and the Gods had chosen this life for her because of the lives she'd lived in the past. She wondered what she had done, who she had wronged, to be born a Dalit. She knew it was her own actions that had led to her status in this life. She wondered what good she had done in *this* life, that her circumstances would change so drastically, in such a short space of time. She pushed those thoughts from her mind. She still couldn't accept the truth of it. That *he* had chosen *her*.

One of the other servants opened the reception door as Parvati finished cleaning the windows. It was one of her closest friends, Chanda.

"Are you finished?" asked Chanda, dragging a vacuum into the room.

"Almost," said Parvati, smiling at her. She swept over the room to make sure everything was perfect. She wiped the frame of the windows with the damp cloth in her hand, then dried it with a towel. "OK, I'm done."

"Great," said Chanda, plugging in the vacuum to the wall. Parvati smiled as she passed Chanda, leaving her to vacuum the patterned carpets that have been the mark of rich Indian households for the past two thousand years. "I'll make a start on the portraits," said Parvati as she closed the door behind her.

The hallway was about as wide as three cars, the floors made of shimmering marble, the walls decorated with patterned wallpaper. All along the wall were pictures of Sandeep, his children and most importantly his ancestors. He'd come from a long line of nobility, a true Kshatriya.

Parvati started with the picture of Bhavesh. Her eyes glistened as she stared at his photo. He was such a handsome man. She polished it delicately, not wanting to tarnish his image in any way.

She worked her way through the pictures, polishing the glass and wooden frames as she moved along the wall. She would stop every so often to stare at the faces that looked back at her, though she'd seen them hundreds of times before. She was always impressed by the detail that the artists had put into each of the portraits. She loved Indian history, when India was a mighty country and a force to behold in the world.

She finished polishing the portraits and walked the long corridor to the drawing room.

"The prince wishes to see you in his chambers," said a male voice from behind her. She turned to see Surendra, the chief of staff for the servants. "Finish your duties here and go to him."

Butterflies fluttered in Parvati's stomach. "At once, sir."

She finished washing and polishing the many objects Sandeep had acquired in his drawing room and scanned over everything with a speed and lack of attention to detail that was atypical for her.

She took her cleaning products and bucket to the kitchen and stored them in a closet. After readjusting her saree, she walked up the grand staircase to the prince's bedroom.

"Come in," said Bhavesh, as soon as Parvati knocked on the door.

"You wished to see me?" Her voice was quivering. She stood in the doorway awaiting his response.

"Yes, close the door."

She did as he had bid. The heavy door closed with a thud.

The prince wasted no time. He cleared the space between them in seconds and grabbed her face with his hand, pulling her into him. Her mouth parted to allow his tongue to enter. Her whole body trembled as they embraced.

He slid his hand up her saree, stroking her leg and continued upwards. She stood as immobilised as the first day he'd touched her there, when she was thirteen and he was fifteen. This time she felt tingles all through her body. This time she wasn't ashamed, afraid to be touched. This time she enjoyed it. This time she loved him, and he loved her. She was putty in his hands, able to be moulded and sculpted in any way he desired.

She wrapped her arms around him and kissed him back with a passion she rarely displayed. She could feel him hardening against her thigh.

He swiped his hand around her body, massaging her bottom, enjoying its bounce and girth all the while embracing her in long, passionate kisses.

They stayed wrapped in each other's arms for several minutes before the prince caught himself and pulled away from her. "We must leave tonight. My father intends to marry me within the next two weeks. We must go tonight."

He turned around and walked over to a large wooden chest of drawers. The handles were made of real silver, polished by servants earlier that day. He opened the draw and pulled out a stuffed envelope. "This is for your family. It should see them through."

Parvati took the package from him, her heart thumped in her chest. It was packed to the brim with rupees. "This is so much," she said, looking at all the notes.

"They won't have you to support them anymore," said Bhavesh. "This should tide them over for the next five years or so, until my father has calmed down and we can return." He passed her a notepad and a pen. "I suppose you'll want to write to them, to let them know your safe, to explain where the money came from."

Dread flooded through her body like her blood was made of liquid anxiety. She loved the prince, and she would go anywhere with him, but her family would surely disown her for bringing shame on them, for attempting to marry a higher caste than herself. But if he was willing to risk the wrath of his father, which would surely be worse, she couldn't not tell them what she intended to do. "...I will," she said at last. "To let them know that I am safe."

"Good, my love," said Bhavesh, stroking her face. "Everything is planned. Meet me at the rear entrance at midnight. Mohandas will be waiting with a car for us. He will take us north to Ahmedabad where the Pujari has agreed to wed us. From there, we will take a plane to New Delhi. I have a house there where we can live until my father has come to terms with my decision."

Parvati stared at him: her eyes protuberant. She still couldn't believe that he wanted to marry her. Him, a prince and heir to a palace, and her, a Dalit who works as a servant in his father's employment. She still half expected him to tell her it was all some joke. That he could never marry such a commoner. "OK," she said. "I will meet you at midnight, my prince."

He kissed her again. He pressed his temple against hers. "I love you."

"I love you, too," she said.

"You must go now and pack," said Bhavesh. "We only have a few hours to ready ourselves. I will be at the gates at midnight precisely."

"I will not be late," she said, with a smile.

He gave her one last laboured kiss. "See you soon."

"Soon, my prince."

She closed the door behind her with a thud and walked through the palace for what would be the last time for a long time, if she was ever allowed to return. She felt a pang in her chest. The palace was her second home. She had spent almost as much time there as she had at her own home.

She turned around and stopped to take in its domed spires and archways as she exited the front gates. She would miss seeing it every morning.

The streets of Mumbai were as packed as ever. She weaved her way through the crowd, clutching tightly to her bag, which contained more money than she had ever seen in her life, let alone owned.

She stopped by a local shop to collect some roti naans for

her family. Further along the road she purchased some vegetable and dal curries from a street vendor.

Her family lived in one of the slums of Mumbai, and it took her almost an hour to reach home. As she walked, the buildings became more and more derelict, the roads less paved and dirtier, the houses more crowded and packed, stacked on top of one another.

Trepidation filled her gut as she entered the room where her family lived, ate, and slept.

"Namaste," said Parvati as she entered, dropping the bags and placing her hands together.

"You're home!" said her little sister, running over to her. She wrapped her hands around her waist.

Parvati smiled and ruffled her hair. "Is it me you're happy to see or just the food?"

"You, of course," said Anushka, scrunching her face. "What did you bring tonight?"

"Your favourite, and lots of roti."

"Wonderful," said her father, who had picked up the containers and taken the food to the centre of the room where patterned mats were placed, covering almost all of the floor. "Anushka, get the plates."

Anushka ran to the far side of the room and rushed over to her father and handed him several metal plates.

Parvati took a place opposite her mother.

"How was work today?" said her mother.

"The same as usual," said Parvati. "How was your day?"

"My back is still in so much pain," said her mother. "It hurts to sit. It hurts to stand."

Parvati chastised herself for not getting her mother some pain medication with all the money she had now. It was not something she could ordinarily afford from her salary. "I pray to the Gods that it will get better in time."

"I doubt it," said her mother. "But enough of this, now we eat."

Parvati picked up a plate and cupped some rice and curry in her hands. She was hungrier than she'd realised.

There was a silence in the air as everyone ate. Parvati forced away the tears in her eyes that were threatening to well there. This would be the last time she saw her family, possibly forever. She smiled as though nothing was the matter, and her family was too busy eating to notice.

She played with her little sister and brother after dinner, enjoying what little time she had left with them.

Picking up her bag, she went outside in the warm night air of Mumbai, filled with raucous sounds and pungent odours. She sat cross-legged on the ground and took out the notepad Bhavesh had given her.

She wondered how to phrase it. What to say. As she started to write, to say goodbye to her family, she could not stop the tears from falling from her face. She would miss them all so much. But they would be safe. They would have money. They would be able to afford to live. Perhaps there would even be enough money for her mother to have an operation on her back.

She wiped her tears, not wanting to smudge the letter as she wrote. She finished the letter, writing, '*With love, your daughter, Parvati.*' She hoped they would still see her as their daughter, despite what she intended to do.

She returned to the room her family lived in and picked up a blanket, taking her place near the far side of the room. "Good night," she said. "I have to be at the palace early tomorrow."

"OK," said her mother. "Sleep well."

She closed her eyes to feign sleep. She waited for hours for the telltale signs of her father's snoring and her mother's rolling around to know that everyone was asleep. She checked the watch that the prince's father had given her for her sixteenth birthday. It was ten o'clock.

She got up as quietly as she could and tucked the note and the envelope full of money under her mother's arms.

With one last, wistful look, a tear rolled down her cheek and she shut the door behind her, closing the door on her old life for the start of her new beginning.

EZEKIEL

Ezekiel jumped up in his bed. The quilt had fallen to the floor from all the tossing and turning he'd done that night. He could hear music coming from his phone. It was playing *This is War* by *30 Seconds to Mars*. He frowned, he'd never heard this song before and certainly didn't have it saved on his playlist.

He picked up his phone and pressed his finger to it. The phone screen popped up with a message saying *Access denied.* He'd never seen that before. His frown deepened; his head felt fuzzy. He tried again and got the same message.

The words of the song penetrated through his stupor. He heard the word 'prophet' and 'messiah'. He immediately thought of Oscor.

Ezekiel swiped his pin and this time the phone accepted it. He opened Spotify and switched the song off.

Placing his phone down he tried to get his bearings. Memories of the previous day flooded his brain like a tide overflowing its banks. Time travel. Teleportation. The end of the world. Oscor. Prophethood. He had hoped it had all been a dream. A nightmare. That he'd wake up and it would all not be real.

A notification pinged on his phone. It was a text message. There was no number, it simply said *OSCOR.* He opened the text. *You can't escape your destiny. Come back to the library.*

Ezekiel threw his phone on the floor. This… operating system. It knew his number. It had hacked his phone. He thought about the lyrics he'd just heard playing from a song that he didn't own. That must have been Oscor as well. A prophet! He just couldn't comprehend any of what he'd witnessed yesterday. What it all meant. Why it was happening to him.

A notification broke his chain of thoughts. He looked at his phone on the floor, not wanting to pick it up, assuming it was another message from Oscor. It pinged again. He sighed, picked up the phone and read the notification on his lock screen without opening the message.

Jermain: Wer u been bro? U cumin to piccadilly today? Thought u said u were comin back yesterday. Me Tich and Jay r gonna be in town for 11.

He opened the WhatsApp chat. There were tens of messages that he'd missed. He scrolled through them all without reading them and replied to Jermain.

Ezekiel: Somethin came up. Will link you in town in a bit.

He put his phone down on the side and rested his head in his arms. "Argghhh!" he wailed, anger pulsating through him. *What the fuck just happened to my life?*

He was stressed. He needed to calm down. He opened his draw and pulled out the remnants of a £20 bag of weed. He snapped off a chunk and placed it in a grinder, adding a tiny bit of tobacco in the mix. He ground the contents and emptied it into rolling paper. Licking the edge of the paper, he wrapped the spliff and pressed along the edge to make sure it was fully sealed.

The morning was overcast in deep contrast to the previous day's sunlight as he stepped into his back garden. He lit the spliff and inhaled four puffs, one after the other, breathing out through his nose so as not to take a pause in inhalation.

He waited a minute or two until it hit him. He walked over to a green deck chair in the garden and sat down on it. He felt relaxed for the first time since he'd seen himself in town and found out the world would end in ten years.

The soothing, sedating streams suffused his soul. He reclined in the chair and spread his legs, letting the high feeling overtake his thoughts, blunting his mind, blurring his vision.

He finished the spliff and threw the end in the grass. The world swayed as he walked back to his house.

He lifted his arm and sniffed it. He stunk. He headed to his room, undressed and showered.

Once he was in fresh clothes and deodorised, he grabbed his phone and walked downstairs. The munchies had kicked in and he was hungry. He opened the fridge and took out some bacon and butter. He placed three slices on a rack and carefully slotted it into the oven.

He heard the front door slam shut. His mum was home from work.

"Morning Ezekiel," said his mother, Elizabeth, walking into the kitchen and placing her bag on the table.

"Morning," said Ezekiel. "How was work?"

"Not too bad," said Elizabeth. "Pretty quiet really. Night shifts are always more relaxed."

"No drama this time then," said Ezekiel.

"Nothing I can't handle. What are you making?"

"A bacon sandwich. I've just put it on. Do you want me to put some on for you?"

"No, I ate at the hospital. I'm going to shower and get some rest. I'll be on the late shift again tonight. I'll leave dinner on the stove for you. I'm making oxtail."

"Thanks," said Ezekiel.

His mother left the room. Ezekiel toasted some bread and buttered it. He checked on the bacon. It needed another five minutes. His stomach rumbled.

He got the impulse to check his phone. He ignored it. It reminded him of Oscor. Which reminded him of everything he went through yesterday, and he wanted to forget it. Pretend it never happened. Ezekiel had never been one to run from a fight, but this was out of his depth.

The taste of the buttery bacon rejuvenated him. Food always helped set him up for the day after his morning spliff.

He decided to try and forget about everything that happened yesterday, finished his sandwich and made for the bus to town.

The bus arrived at the bus stop just as he turned the corner onto the road. He ran to catch it.

"Thanks," he said to the bus driver for waiting for him. The bus driver gave a perfunctory nod as he scanned his pass on the card reader.

Ezekiel walked upstairs and sat in his usual position at the back with his feet resting on the chair opposite him.

The bus tannoy announced the next stop was *Greenhays Lane* and *Wellhead Close*. He read the horrid orange writing on the display which displayed the same information as the tannoy had announced.

He messaged in the group chat, *I'm on the bus now. See u in 15.* Tich replied saying *Safe.*

He pressed his head against the back of the bus, enjoying the stupefying feeling of being high.

The tannoy announced that they were on the junction of *Higher Cambridge Street* and *Boundary Street West* and that people should alight there for Manchester Metropolitan University.

He looked at the screen absent-mindedly and his eyes almost popped out of their sockets. The screen which should have had the information of the next stop read, *You can't escape your destiny, Ezekiel. You are chosen. Come to the library.*

Just as quickly as it had appeared, it disappeared, and the street names returned to the screen.

How the fuck had Oscar managed that? He remembered it saying it was an operating system, that it could work on almost any machine. Which apparently included electronic screens on buses.

He was scared, in a way he'd never been scared before. He was being watched… contacted… by an… operating system. It just couldn't fucking be!

He put on his headphones and opened his main playlist. He was glad to see whatever song had been on before was nowhere to be seen and there were no further messages from Oscor. He hit the play button, and it chose the first song randomly. He slipped the phone back in his pocket and stared out of the window, refusing to look at the screen lest it had more messages for him.

The bus pulled into Piccadilly Gardens. Ezekiel stood up and waited for the crowd to funnel down the stairs.

He walked the familiar route from the 102 bus stop towards the benches in Piccadilly Gardens. He looked up at the board that shows advertisements as he walked. It read, *Come to the library, Ezekiel. You can't escape your destiny!* in bold, white writing. Next to the writing was a picture of a lotus flower.

Ezekiel blinked and it had changed back to an advert for KFC.

Fucking hell, thought Ezekiel. Was there nowhere this Oscor couldn't access? How did he know where he was at that current moment? It dawned on him that he was carrying around a GPS tracking device. That anyone with the desire to know his location could find it with a simple ping of his phone.

Jay saw him walking towards them and waved at him to come over. Ezekiel tried to push the things he was seeing and the thoughts of yesterday out of his mind.

"What you sayin', lad?" said Jay. He was a tall white boy Ezekiel had met at the second school he'd attended after being expelled from his first school for selling weed to the other students. Everyone there was delinquent. It was like a factory for bad behaviour. Someone's genius idea to place all the naughtiest children together to pick up each other's bad habits.

Jermain bumped his fist against Ezekiel's in greeting.

"Nothing much," lied Ezekiel. "What about you?"

"Chillin'," said Jay. "What you been on? Was lookin' for you last night."

"I was lookin' to come back but I think I whitied," said Ezekiel. "I just remember waking up in my bed this morning. Must have smoked too much."

"Not like you to whitey," said Tich. "Don't tell me you're turnin' into a batty man."

They all laughed.

"Man's not a batty man," said Ezekiel. "It just hit me hard.

Must have been the Cali." He couldn't tell them what really happened to him yesterday. They'd have him sectioned.

"Pukka shit that," said Tich. "Only got Purple Haze to shot today. How many you got?"

"I'm not lookin' to sell today," mumbled Ezekiel. "I sold out yesterday. Need to restock."

"I thought you whitied and went home?" said Jermain with a frown.

"Yeah… yeah, I did," said Ezekiel stumbling over his words. "That guy who messaged me asked for everything I had. Was lookin' half an ounce. I said I had seven bags, and I'd do it for ninety and he took it."

"Nice, bro," said Jay.

"Decent gains that," said Jermain.

"Yeah man," said Ezekiel. "Next thing I remember is waking up. That Cali hit me hard."

"Where'd you get that ring? Looks heavy that, bro," said Jay.

In everything that had happened Ezekiel had forgotten he'd taken the ring from Oscor. That there was a little machine inside the ring with a piece of Oscor in it. That it could read his mind and teleport him through space and time. That must be how Oscor knew exactly where he was. He fingered the ring. There was something about it that made him not want to take it off.

"My mum got it for me," said Ezekiel.

"Looks sick that," said Tich. "Must have cost a bomb."

"You know what Ezekiel's mum's like," said Jermain. "Always buyin' him new shit."

"True say."

"Yeah man," said Jermain. He stood up and walked over to a group of guys approaching them. Some of his customers.

"You want some on this?" said Jay, offering the spliff to Ezekiel.

Ezekiel took the spliff and spread his legs wide.

I thought you told yourself to stop smoking, said a voice in his head. He jumped up on the bench, his hand clutched to his chest.

"You OK, bruv?" said Tich, confusion etched on his brows.

"Yeah, I'm good, it just caught in my throat," he said, faking a cough, trying to act as casual as he could. He coughed again and passed the spliff to Tich.

He stared down at the floor feeling ashamed, watching the many pigeons that frequented Piccadilly Gardens. It was weird watching them pecking around for food, with no real awareness or concern for anything but food. In that moment, he envied them, their simple life, their lack of worries or concerns.

How had this happened to his life? How could any of this be possible? Was he going crazy? Had he lost his mind?

He fingered the ring on his finger again. He wanted to take it off but hearing the voice speak in his mind, it made it all real. He'd met his future-self. He knew it, and he knew he wasn't insane. He was *chosen* they'd said. The only one who could stop nuclear Armageddon. He looked around the city he'd called home his whole life and all he could see were the tattered remains of his once beautiful city. The streets empty of people. His mother's grave. He couldn't let that happen. He was going to have to 'man up' and face his destiny. This Oscor was persistent, if nothing else.

Jay offered him the spliff again.

"Nah, I'm good, man," said Ezekiel. He opened the text from Oscor and hit reply. *OK. You win. I'm comin.*

EVE

The bacon sizzled in the pan as Eve turned it over with a pair of silver tongues. She took a scoop of batter and placed it in the waffle iron, turning it over to ensure both sides were coated. Cracking four eggs over a pan, she extracted the egg and yolk with expert precision, not a flake of shell fell in the pan.

She loved the smell of breakfast filling the kitchen in the morning. She was not very maternal, but she loved cooking and was always there to provide for the needs of her children.

"Morning, darling," said her husband, Mark, walking suited into the kitchen. He kissed her on the cheek. "That smells great."

"It won't be long now," said Eve, removing the cooked waffle and placing another scoop of pancake mixture to the waffle iron. "Are the girls nearly ready?"

"They're just brushing their teeth," said Mark. "Here's Sarah now."

"Morning," said Sarah, Eve's youngest daughter.

"Morning, hon," said Eve. She gave her a kiss on the forehead. It was a deliberate action. She made herself show her children affection, though in truth she didn't feel love for her children as most parents would. She had thought it might come to her as they aged, but it never had. Though, she'd never let anyone hurt them. One thing she knew is that she'd kill anyone who dared to harm them. "Where's your sister?"

"She's straightening her hair," said Sarah.

"Evelyn!" Eve shouted up the stairs. "Breakfast will be ready in three minutes."

"I'll be there in a minute!" said Evelyn, shouting down the stairs, with the annoyance of a girl who had reached the age where constantly being told what to do and when to do it had become bothersome to her.

Eve got four plates out of the cupboard and plated up the bacon, waffles and a few sliced strawberries. She picked up the spatula and tossed the scrambled egg around the frying pan.

"How are you feeling about today?" said Mark, taking a sip of coffee from his mug.

Eve turned around and smiled before returning her attention to the eggs. "It's nothing I haven't done before. I'm just happy he finally came to his senses. I can handle the media."

"You've got this," said Mark, taking another sip of coffee. "Congratulations again on getting him to agree to the cuts. We've been overspending for too long. The world looks up to us. We should be setting an example."

"Exactly what I said." She dished up the eggs and unwrapped her apron. "It's ready." She placed two plates on the counter in front of her. Evelyn was still not there. "Evelyn, get your butt down here, now!"

"I'm coming!"

Eve heard footsteps stomping on the ceiling above her. Mark had taken his and Sarah's plates over to the table. Eve took hers and Evelyn's plate and sat down.

"Morning," said Evelyn. She wasn't as enthusiastic about it as Sarah had been, but that was to be expected with teenagers.

"The long-awaited guest arrives at last," said Mark.

"I needed to straighten my hair," said Evelyn.

"Have you done your homework this time?" asked Eve.

"Yes," said Evelyn, rolling her eyes. "Don't worry."

"I want to see your report card when I get home," said Eve.

"And it better be good," said Mark.

"Sure," said Evelyn.

Eve poured some syrup on her waffle and carved it up with her knife and fork. Waffles were her favourite breakfast ever since she'd been a little kid. Her grampa would always take her out for waffles on a Saturday. She missed him. Eve wasn't normally bothered by death, but she had loved that man.

"Oh yeah," said Evelyn, "I forgot to say. There's a school trip next month. I need you to sign a form and there's a $220 charge."

"What is it with that school?" said Mark. "You'd think they have enough money with everything we pay in private fees. They want another two hundred dollars every other week."

"I'll sign it when I've seen your report card," said Eve.

"OK," said Evelyn, the slightest trace of trepidation in her tone.

Eve checked her watch. "The school bus will be here in five minutes. Finish your breakfast and don't forget your school bag. Your lunch money is on the counter."

"I won't," said Evelyn.

"Thank you, mom," said Sarah

"I should get going too," said Mark. "Good luck today, hon." He kissed all three of them on the head and left.

"You two get going," said Eve. "I'll clear the plates."

"OK," said the girls. They grabbed their bag and lunch money and went to wait for the school bus.

Eve emptied the remnants of breakfast into the trashcan and put the dishes in the dishwasher. She wiped down the table and sides until the kitchen looked like it had not been used. Satisfied, she grabbed her keys and drove to work.

A black woman with short, cropped hair, glowing skin and huge inviting eyes was waiting in the corridor when Eve arrived. They both wore a trousered suit. "Morning, Madam Secretary."

"Morning Melina. What's the damage?"

They walked along the corridor together. Melina looked over the notes on the clipboard she carried.

"CNN, NBS, MSNBC, Fox, CBS, they've all scheduled

questions. There's been a lot of fuss about the social security cuts. They're not as bothered by the department reductions. A few of them are angry about the roll back on housing development. Even Fox News thinks we should be building more."

Eve knew she was going to have a battle on her hands when she'd devised the cuts. These people, they just wanted to spend and spend with no concern where the money came from. She wondered how much personal debt they'd accrued so far in life, and if they were as comfortable borrowing in their personal lives as they were with the government doing it. "No surprises there then," said Eve. "Anything else I need to know?"

"Just that the president says he hasn't taken these cuts lightly and he says to remember it was the Democrats who left us with the deficit."

"Like I could forget."

They arrived at the entrance to the conference hall.

"You're on in five minutes," said Melina.

"I'll go now," said Eve. "No time like the present."

She walked out with her shoulders spread and took her position behind the podium, placing her hands on the sides. "Good morning, everyone."

There was a murmur of good mornings from the press.

Eve wasted no time. "The first question is from Simon from MSNBC."

"Hello Madam Secretary," said the reporter. "The Republican party has implemented cuts to social welfare that haven't been seen in this country since social security was introduced after the Great Depression. How can you justify cutting so hard, and so fast, leaving those in need without the means to provide for themselves and their families?"

Eve straightened up and removed her hands from the podium. "The Democrats left us with a two trillion-dollar deficit to fill," said Eve, waving her hands as she spoke. "We can't go on with this reckless borrowing. America has to pay its way. There will be no changes to the food stamp system. No one is going to go hungry in America. The cuts are essential to lower debt and interest repayments. If families are struggling with the cost of living, they need to get a paying job and pay for their families. The president had no choice but to make cuts, and social security could not be avoided. Next question from Michelle at the New York Times."

"Thank you, Madam Secretary," said Michelle. "Given your outspoken opposition to social security in the past, and your feelings that Americans are too reliant on state aid, how influential were you in designing the proposed cuts, and what impact do you think it will have on households with disabled individuals who are unable to work?"

"The president looked through the books and found a gaping hole in the budget that needed filling. A hole the Democrats left for us with their reckless spending. I've made no secret about my thoughts on social security, but this was the president's decision, and I fully support him in that decision. As for disabled households, the cuts are much lower for those with serious medical conditions. It's a ten percent cut for those with serious conditions, compared with a thirty percent cut for those who can work. And if you're able to work, you should work. That's the basis of American society. It's about values, American values and Christian values. If you can work, you should work. It's as simple as that. Next question from Craig at CNN."

"Madam Secretary, America currently has three people for every one house. How can you justify a forty percent reduction in house building, and do you not agree that this is likely to stifle economic growth?"

"There's a two trillion dollar funding gap to plug and that was always going to mean some hard decisions had to be made. There will still be millions of homes built with the funding we have allocated to private and public housing. We can't go on spending and spending without the tax receipts to back it up. It's very easy to just say put it on the credit card, but the credit card needs paying. Any fall in economic output will be offset by a reduction in interest rates and debt repayments. We can't have a situation like Japan where debt is nearly three hundred percent of GDP. We're the world leader with a triple A credit rating, and this administration intends to maintain that rating. That's something that can only be achieved with fiscal responsibility, not the endless spending spree the Democrats went on the last four years. Next question. Alice from Fox News."

"Good morning, Madam Secretary." Eve nodded at her. "While we welcome the cuts and understand they needed to be made to fill the deficit left by the Democrats, we have some reservations about the reduction in house building. Could the funds for private housing developments be ringfenced so that the hard-working American who wants to own a home isn't left out of the market by rising house prices and lack of stock?"

"Good question," said Eve. "It's a point I'm glad you've raised. We intend for seventy-five percent of the funds allocated to housing to be spent on private housing developments which will ensure properly built, affordable housing for the average American family. We are committed as a government to homeownership, and this has been reflected in the weighting of private development within the housing budget. Next question from Margerie from The Wall Street Journal."

"Thanks, Madam Secretary. You've stated that you feel the economic impacts of a reduction in capital expenditure will be offset by a reduction in interest rates and debt repayments. Do you think you run the risk of eliminating growth altogether, or even forcing America, and possibly the world, into another recession?"

"The biggest risk to America going into recession is unfunded spending commitments that assume an ever-increasing level of debt. If we keep borrowing and borrowing, there's ultimately less money in the pot for essential infrastructure spending. I'm confident that coupled with the president's other policies that economic growth will be achieved within the first two years of his presidency and we're already seeing growth rates of 0.3 percent this quarter. It was a tough decision but there were two trillion dollars to find, and it had to come from somewhere."

"If I might," said the reporter from The Wall Street Journal, "I'd like to respond to that. With all due respect, the current growth rates are a result of the previous government's actions. You can't honestly claim to be responsible for that growth. How will you avoid a recession?"

"Look, I'm not getting into hypotheticals. America has a triple A credit rating, and we intend to keep it that way. The market speaks for itself. The dollar is up two percentage points since the president's announcement. The FTSE 100 is up four percent. There are record job opportunities in the market currently and these packages will encourage those out of work and the long-term unemployed to return to work. America is not going into recession. Next question from Rashid from ABC News."

"The president stated in his election campaign that he wasn't going to cut spending to defence or house building. How can we trust your government, when it turns its back on its election pledges, and how will you secure the safety of the American people. Are future cuts to defence spending on the cards?"

"There will be no cuts to defence spending. We are increasing spending on defence by 0.4% year on year and have encouraged our allies and partners in NATO to do the same. The deficit left by the previous government was higher than we could possibly have expected, and after reviewing the books the president had no choice but to make more drastic cuts than he'd originally intended. As stated, seventy-five percent of house building will be for homes for private buyers, and they will all be allocated to first time homeowners."

Eve fielded the rest of the questions with the same answers she'd prepared. It annoyed her, these people who felt that it was OK for people not to work. She had a rare and genuine understanding, if not empathy, for people who were genuinely too disabled to work but she couldn't abide people who just wanted to sponge off the state. America wasn't going to go into recession, and if it did, it would be because people were too lazy to work and too reliant on the state to solve all their problems.

"That went well," said Melina, once Eve had left the podium and was back in the hallway. She walked with Eve along it as she talked. "We got record likes on social media platforms for your answers. They especially liked the Christian values comment, it was a nice touch."

Of course they did, thought Eve. *If there was one thing Americans loved, it was their God.* She had stopped believing in God at the age of twelve, having been raised in the latter-day saint movement before that point. She felt religion was made by humans to control humans, and she considered anyone who felt differently to be her mental inferior. So, most of America.

"That's good," said Eve. "What are the polls saying?"

"There's been a two-point uplift since the announcement. We're only six points behind the Dems now. That could improve after that performance, but it's too early to tell."

"Let's hope so," said Eve. "I suppose it could have been worse. Most of the press are against the cuts. Just borrow, borrow, borrow. That's all they know."

PARVATI

"You made it!" said Bhavesh.

Parvati smiled at him and wrapped herself around him. "Anything for you, my prince."

"Come, we must leave now." He led her to the range rover and threw her bag in the boot. He closed the boot door and got in the car at the back, sitting next to Parvati. He placed his hand over hers, intertwining their fingers.

"Time to go, Mohandas."

"Yes, sir," said Mohandas. He moved the gear into place and drove the Range Rover away from the palace and into the dark night.

"I can't believe we're actually doing this," said Parvati. "It feels like a dream."

"I couldn't marry her," said Bhavesh. "Not knowing that I loved you. It wouldn't be right. My father will understand in time. It's time for India to grow up. Arranged marriages have no place in modern India."

"That's the way it's always been," said Parvati.

"Does that mean it needs to always be that way?"

"No." She smiled and kissed him on the lips.

"Did you give your family the money?"

"Yes. I left it with my mother with a note explaining that

we're getting married, and I might not be able to come back for a while, if ever. I just hope they're not too angry with me."

"They'll understand eventually, once we're married," said Bhavesh, squeezing her hand tight. "They'll have no choice by that time. And the money will mean they can live in comfort."

"I don't know what will shock them more," said Parvati, "seeing that we're to be wed or seeing that much money in one place."

Bhavesh laughed and so did Mohandas.

"It's the least I could do," said Bhavesh. "I would have given you more, but I've had to move most of my money to private accounts that my dad can't access. He's going to cut off my credit cards as soon as he finds out that I've left. We'll be fine though. The house in New Delhi is in my name and I've got enough for us to live comfortably there forever, if we must."

"I hope we can see our families again. I wish they could be at the wedding."

"All we need is each other," said Bhavesh, squeezing her hand again. "Nothing else matters."

"I hope you don't mind me saying so," said Mohandas. "I think what you're doing is admirable, young prince. Not many people would give up a fortune and the honour of their family for love. I respect that. That's why I agreed to help."

"I have not dishonoured my family," said Bhavesh, snapping at Mohandas.

"I did not mean to cause offence," said Mohandas. "I just admire all that you're willing to do for love. It is inspirational. That's why I am helping you. I respect your decision."

Bhavesh calmed down. "It is the right decision to make. I will not marry a woman whom I could never love."

"Hopefully your father isn't too mad with you when he finds out," said Parvati.

"I'm hoping he never finds out I'm involved," said Mohandas, who seemed nervous for the first time. "I told him I'm away for the week. Hopefully he just thinks it's coincidence."

Bhavesh doubted highly that his father wouldn't make the connection, but he didn't say anything lest he turn the car around and take them home. Part of him still expected Mohandas to do exactly that. "Hopefully," he said.

"Thank you for doing this," said Parvati. "It means a lot."

"No problem," said Mohandas. "Love is love. I was lucky, I loved my wife from the moment I first saw her, six weeks before we married."

"That's lucky," said Bhavesh.

"It's not luck really," said Mohandas. "I shouldn't have said luck. It was by the grace of the Gods. I think she was chosen for me, and I for her. And I think you were chosen for each other. Perhaps the Gods have a plan for you."

Bhavesh turned to Parvati and smiled. "Perhaps they do. India can't avoid modernisation forever."

"They'll certainly try!" said Mohandas with a snort.

Bhavesh rolled his eyes. He knew he was right. But he still had aspirations for his country. He saw what it could become, not what it currently was. "How long do you think it will take to reach Ahmedabad?"

"We should arrive by midday at the latest, depending on traffic. You two should get some rest. You've got a big day ahead of you."

Parvati was too excited to possibly consider sleeping. "I've never been this far out of Mumbai before," she said looking through the window. "I think I'd rather take in the scenery."

They had reached an open stretch of land now. There was little around them except fields and the odd house. "It is essentially one long, straight stretch of land between Mumbai and Ahmedabad," said Mohandas. "There's not much to see, my lady. Nothing compared to Mumbai, anyway."

Parvati had never been referred to as a lady before. She blushed. "Perhaps later we will rest."

"We do have an important day ahead of us," said Bhavesh. "But I don't think I could sleep. My heart is racing. I keep expecting my dad to jump out in front of the car."

Parvati laughed uproariously. "I have been thinking the

exact same thing!"

"Let us hope not," said Mohandas. "For all our sakes."

"He's going to be furious," said Bhavesh. "And I don't care. It's my life. My love. There are more important things in life than money. Not that he'd ever understand that."

Parvati was flattered but she couldn't help thinking only someone who had never had to struggle for money could think such a thing. Still, he was willing to give it all up for her. It made her feel more loved than she could put into words. Her whole body tingled with excitement.

"You are probably right," said Mohandas. "I do not think he will be able to comprehend what you have chosen, and what you have given up, or why. I respect your father a lot, but he is very materialistic. Money means a lot to him."

"It means everything to him," said Bhavesh. "Not even second to tradition or faith. He'd sell his soul if it meant owning a bigger house."

"He's a good man," said Mohandas. "He's just lived in luxury his whole life, so it will be hard for him to understand your decision to give up your inheritance."

"There's a small hope he might forgive me once he's calmed down," said Bhavesh.

"I really hope so," said Parvati. "I feel guilty that you have to give it all up just for me."

"I would give up the world for you, Parvati. I have never known happiness like I know with you. You are my everything."

Parvati fought back tears for the second time today. "I don't think I had known true happiness until I met you either."

"See!" said Mohandas. "This is why I am helping you. It brings a tear to my eye. Young love, it is a rarity in India. I feel like we're in a Hollywood movie."

"Well, hopefully it is one with a fairytale ending," said Bhavesh. "And not one where we all die at the end."

"Perhaps we will if Mohandas continues to drive at this speed," said Parvati.

They both laughed.

"It's nighttime," said Mohandas. "There is no one around. I said I will get you to Ahmedabad by midday, and I will do just that."

"Are you going to be OK to drive back without resting?" said Bhavesh. "I can pay for a hotel room for you to rest before returning."

"I will be fine," said Mohandas, waving away Bhavesh's offer with his hand. "We should stop for food when it is morning though, I'm hungry, I should have eaten more before leaving out."

"Sorry, I didn't think to bring food!" said Bhavesh.

"Me either," said Parvati.

"It's fine, we will find somewhere to eat on the way to Ahmedabad."

"OK," said Bhavesh.

Parvati stared through the window into the night. She thought of her family. They would awaken soon, find her gone. That she had run away with Bhavesh. She thought of their reaction to finding the money. She was almost worried her mother might have a heart attack or faint.

She leant her shoulder into Bhavesh, and he wrapped his arms around her. After a few hours' drive, she did start to feel tired, and without realising it she slowly drifted to sleep in the safety of his arms.

~ * ~

Parvati felt herself being shaken and opened her eyes in shock.

"We're here, my love," said Bhavesh.

Parvati opened her eyes wide to wake herself up. "Right, OK," she said, sliding along the seat so she could get out of the car.

Bhavesh had already taken their belongings from the boot. "Thank you, Mohandas. For everything," he said. "I will not forget what you have done for us this day."

"Yes, thank you," said Parvati bowing her head.

"The pleasure is all mine," said Mohandas. "Are you sure you don't want me to stay for the ceremony?"

"No," said Bhavesh. "I think this is something we should

do alone. It will be the smallest wedding India has ever known."

Mohandas laughed. "That it will. Take care young prince. My lady." He tipped his hand to her.

"I hope to see you again one day," said Bhavesh.

"All in good time," said Mohandas. He started the engine and turned the car around. "Let's hope your father doesn't explode this morning," he said as he drove off.

Parvati and Bhavesh smiled and waved him off.

"We made it!" said Parvati.

"We did. Come. Our hotel is just around the corner. Your wedding gown and jewellery should be all laid out for you." He grabbed the luggage and led her through the streets of Ahmedabad, glancing at his phone for directions.

Parvati brimmed with excitement. She couldn't wait to marry him. She couldn't wait to lie with him. They'd had sex, many times, but never as a married couple. And this would be the first time she didn't feel like she was doing something naughty by accepting the prince's advances. "You've thought of everything."

Bhavesh smiled. "Yes. It's just down here." He placed the phone in his pocket and led her by the hand to the hotel.

It was a regal looking hotel with gold plated door panels and a glass turnstile. Bhavesh pushed the turnstile door and they both squeezed into one of the compartments. He strode forward to the receptionist and after a short chat she handed him two keys. He had booked two rooms as he didn't think they would approve of them sharing before they were married, and he had had them prepare her wedding saree, so they knew they were not yet wed. He wanted their first night married to be special for her. It was his only real regret. He wished he'd waited before bedding her. He'd just found her so irresistible, and she had found herself unable to say no to his advances.

"Your room is 212," he said handing her the key. "I'm in 214. Everything you need should be there for you. I've hired someone to hold your shawl as you walk down the aisle. They will meet you at your room once you're ready." He handed her a piece of paper. "Call this number when you're ready, they will escort you to the venue. I'll be waiting there for you, my love."

She stroked his cheek, afraid to kiss him in front of the watching receptionist.

They took the elevator to the second floor. With a parting kiss in the privacy of the halls, they each went to their rooms to get ready.

A stunning, brown-beige sari with crystals and embroidery in intricate patterns running the full length of the garment lay ready for her on the bed. Two golden shawls lay next to it, one for her shoulders and one for her hair. On the side of the bed, enormous diamond earrings and other jewellery were laid out, accompanied by rose petals which had been spread all through the room. Bhavesh had truly thought of everything.

Parvati had never felt so special in her life, so loved, so important.

She held the saree in her hands and sniffed the fresh fabric. Running her hands along its length, she traced the patterns and crystal bumps with her fingers.

She placed the saree back on the bed and undressed. It took her a while to work out how to use the shower, not having one at home. There was something utterly exquisite about the warm water gushing over her hair and body. It was a sensation she'd never felt before, and she didn't want to get out of the shower. Only the thought of what lay ahead of her was enough to make her leave.

She dried herself off and moved her bangles up her arm so she could dry her lower arm. Bhavesh had provided more bangles for her. She looked over the bangles she already owned. Most of them were inferior to the ones Bhavesh had chosen for her, except one. When she was seven, she met a white man who gave her a fake gold bangle for shining his shoes in addition to some rupees, and he had told her that as long as she wore it, the Gods would always favour her. She had never seen a white person in real life before, and his words stayed with her. She had never taken it off since, and with her luck thus far so phenomenal, she didn't wish to abandon it. She removed her other bangles and left the fake gold bangle on her arm.

She dressed herself in the saree. Excitement mingled with despondency as she wrapped the shawl around her shoulders and placed the headdress on. She was marrying the man she loved, finally. And yet, her parents, her family, would not be there to bless their wedding.

She pushed the feelings down in the pit of her stomach, focusing on the joyous opportunity that lay ahead of her. She picked up the diamond earrings with care, scared to damage the almost impenetrable rock. After placing them on her ears, she added the bangles Bhavesh had purchased for her to her arm. Her hand stung for a while after, having had to squeeze through the bangles.

There was a hair straightener on the bedside table. She'd never used one on her own hair, but she had used them on other people. She plugged them in and picked a clump of hair from the front of her head to straighten. It took her a few attempts to realise how to hold the tongues without burning her ears or the side of her head, but eventually she got the hang of it.

Once her hair was straight, she sat in front of the mirror and applied the makeup that had been left out for her.

She stood up straight and looked in the full-length mirror. She hardly recognised herself. She looked like a high-caste princess. Her stomach bubbled with anticipation.

Walking across the room, she found the paper Bhavesh had given her and called the number on it with the phone she'd received from Bhavesh some years ago so that they could communicate and arrange their meetings away from the palace.

"I'll be there in ten minutes," said the man on the phone.

She sat down on the bed. Her world was spinning. She still couldn't believe this was all happening.

After what felt more like ten hours than ten minutes, there was a knock at the door.

She rushed to open it. A light skinned man with a thick, bushy moustache, dressed in a black western suit smiled at her. It reminded her of a CIA agent from a movie. "Are you ready, my lady?"

"Yes," she said, unable to wipe the smile from her face.

"Perfect. Come with me."

He led her out of the hotel and along several bustling streets. People stared as she passed, clearly in awe of her beauty and wealth. She had never appreciated quite how stunningly beautiful she was.

Every corner they turned down felt like plunging down a steep drop on a rollercoaster. She was convinced every time that the street they had come to would be their final one. Eventually, she was right, and they stopped at the centre of a grand looking hall, not entirely dissimilar to Bhavesh's palace, but much smaller.

"We're here, my lady," he said, taking her hand.

She walked with him through the entrance and down a wide hallway.

The man picked up a large shawl and stood in front of her, concealing her from her groom. He opened the door and Parvati followed him, keeping behind the shawl but wanting to tear it down and look at Bhavesh.

The man stopped at the end of the aisle and lowered her shawl. She saw Bhavesh for the first time, in his dark navy kurta with golden embroidery, looking as regal as he ever had.

Both of their eyes sparkled as they looked upon each other. As much from love as from lust.

The pujari welcomed them both and handed them each a necklace.

Bhavesh placed the necklace around Parvati's neck, and she in turn placed a necklace around his neck.

The couple stood side by side and clasped each other's hand, facing the pujari.

A fire was lit by the pujari, and after a few ceremonial words, the couple walked around the fire four times, symbolising the core aspirations of married life: righteousness, prosperity, love and family, and liberation from worldly things.

The pujari blessed them again and passed a bowl with red vermillion powder to Bhavesh. He used the powder to line Parvati's hair parting and placed a mangal sutra, a sacred necklace, around her neck as a symbol of his commitment, respect and love.

The man who had walked Parvati to the hall passed her a bowl of sweet foods. The couple fed each other, a sign of the meals that they would eat for the rest of their life.

"And now," said the pujari, "we ask the Gods to bless your marriage in the absence of your families."

Parvati and Bhavesh stood silently as the pujari raised his hands and closed his eyes in prayer. When he opened them again, he said, "I now pronounce you husband and wife."

ABU

Abu was at the sergeant's office at 8.50am. He was unusually nervous. He could not imagine what the sergeant wanted of him.

He knocked the door, and a soldier opened it after a moment. "Commander Bakr," he said, saluting him.

Abu saluted back.

"Come," said Sergeant Abdallah. "Take a seat." He gestured to the wooden chair in front of the equally drab wooden desk he sat behind.

Abu took his seat and crossed his arms over his legs under the table. "You wished to see me, sir."

"Yes, yes," said the sergeant. "It was high time that you were brought into the fold. You have proven yourself a worthy commander and your commitment to the cause of Allah is as strong as I've seen in a soldier."

Abu suppressed a smile at these words.

"We have a great task ahead of us. Inshallah, it will all go to plan."

"I'm ready to do whatever is needed of me."

"We have been making plans with the other Islamic nations of Africa," said Sergeant Abdulla. "There have already been successful coups in Niger and several other regions against the imperialist French scum, and now is the time to act on the rest of Africa's Islamic nations. I have sent Commander Ahmed to Sudan, and Commander Qureshi has been sent to Chad. Mali, Djibouti and Sierra Leone have already agreed to join our cause. They will overthrow their governments in synchrony with us. I need you to go to Ethiopia and Somalia as my ambassador. They are proving to be more difficult."

"To what end?" said Abu. "Ethiopia is a Christian country."

"You will meet with the leader of the military there, they will be expecting you. You must convince them that it is right, both for the sovereignty of Africa and the promotion of Islamic values, that they stage a coup against the puppet governments which run those countries. For Ethiopia, you must focus on their poverty. For Somalia, you must play to their Islamic values. And you must impress upon them that it is of the utmost importance that the coups are staged at the same time. The African Union and the imperialists will not be able to control so many simultaneous coups."

Abu stroked his beard then sat up straight, his shoulders spread wide. "It would be my honour, sir. I will not fail you in this. I will persuade them that ours is the only path to victory, to emancipation from those who would enslave us. I want nothing more than to unshackle the people of Africa from the chains of colonialism and the scourge of Christianity."

"First, we focus on the Muslim countries. Other than Ethiopia, the Christian nations will have to wait. They are blinded to the ways of Allah. But I have hope for Ethiopia. It is one of the oldest civilisations on the planet and they are one of the poorest nations on Earth. They have nothing to lose by joining our cause."

"What of the North Africans?"

"They will either join us willingly or they will join us by force. I cannot see Libya protesting after what the Americans have done to their country. As for the rest, they will make the choice to be African or they will make the choice to be Arab, but either way, they will become Islamic republics and Sharia Law will be imposed on their populations. Once the Muslim nations have merged into a caliphate, we will strike the Christian South until all of Africa is within the Islamic caliphate."

Abu smiled. "Allah would be proud of what you are trying to accomplish."

"We are not trying to accomplish anything. The preparations are already underway. The military in Ethiopia have no love for their country and Somalia is preoccupied with the various ethnic factions in the region causing trouble for the leaders. There will be only one faction under our rule, and that is Muslim. Race… ethnicity… it has no meaning. There is only Allah and his laws."

"Yes, sir. The only thing that matters is that they are Muslims. You will have done well to end their bickering over tribal lines." He felt that statement with less conviction than he'd said it. He was an albino, and life had not been kind to him as a result. No matter how high he rose in life, he could not help feeling alien to other Africans.

"Indeed. And you will play no small part in that. You must explain our plans thoroughly to the military leaders of Ethiopia and the president of Somalia. They will be hesitant to act, and you must convince them that it is the right path to take. They must strike with force and without remorse until the population is brought under their control."

"If they will not do it for the starving people in their cities," said Abu, "then surely they will do it for Islam."

"I hope so," said Sergeant Abdhulla, his fingers steepled. "But the UN has gotten into their heads. They believe in the state over the supremacy of religious laws. They think too much of themselves, that man can decide for man what actions we should and should not take. The governments must be destroyed and replaced with those in accordance with the laws of Allah."

"I will not let you down, sir," said Abu. He saluted him.

"I have faith in you, Commander Bakr. You have proved yourself worthy to me, and it was my greatest decision to take you from the streets and recruit you to the cause. You have proven yourself time and time again, and you hold the office of commander with skill and pride."

Abu suppressed tears in his eyes. He was ashamed to show weakness of any kind, and it would not be taken well in the militia. "Thank you, sir," he said, trying to keep his tone as even as possible.

Sergeant Abdallah looked on him with pride in his eyes. "You will leave now. Take provisions, ammunitions, and four soldiers with you. You will drive first to Ethiopia. Then you will meet with the leader of Somalia. Once you have gained their agreement, and given them the blueprints, you will return to me and report the outcome."

"Thank you for this honour, sir," said Abu.

The sergeant waved him away with his hand. "You have earned this. Go now. We have no time to waste."

~ * ~

Abu walked along the streets of N'Djamena, the capital of Chad, with four soldiers who walked in pairs behind him.

"Let's hope they have some food that can match Abuja," said Abu to the soldiers.

"I doubt it," said one of the soldiers at the back of the group. "Abuja is the home and heart of African cuisine. No better place. We will be lucky to find anything decent to eat here."

"We just need something to fill our stomachs," said Abu. "I'm sure it will be satisfactory. Better than the meals they serve at camp."

"The slum food is better than what they serve at camp."

The men laughed.

Abu didn't tell them that he often ate in the slums or felt less of them for admitting that they felt superior to slum food. But most people did. Most people hadn't experienced the true hardship of life on the streets of the African continent. They didn't know the hunger that he knew, and the relief one feels when they taste the tenderness of cooked meat or spiced rice.

As he observed the streets of Chad, he couldn't help noticing it was somewhat less developed than Nigeria, especially Abuja. There were similar themes in their architecture, though. Architecture had always fascinated him, perhaps because for most of his life he'd never had a home, or even a room, of his own.

"This looks like it sells food," said a soldier behind Abu.

"Yes," said Abu. "We will eat here."

They entered and he looked at the menu which had been written in chalk. "Not too different from home."

He went for lamb for himself, and the others had a chicken dish with spicy rice. He took out some of the Chadian currency he had been given by his sergeant and handed it to the man. The man handed him the change and he pocketed it, though he wondered if they'd have chance to use it again in the city before reaching Sudan.

Abu took a seat next to his soldiers on a square wooden table that swayed as they placed their plates on it. One of the soldiers picked up a chair from another table and sat at the end of the table.

They devoured the meal in no time. It had been a long drive, and they were all hungry.

Abu observed the empty plates. "It's time we got back on the road. Mohammad, you can drive." He needed a rest.

"Yes, sir," said Mohammed, eagerly. He'd clearly been waiting for his chance to drive.

They walked back to the truck. Abu saw two unveiled women walking down the street. They must be Christian he assumed. He disparaged them for not wearing a veil to cover their beauty and ensure their modesty. There were males about who could deem them a temptation. He wasn't entirely sure if he felt the Qur'anic mandate for modesty meant the hijab, the niqab or the burka, but he was sure they should be wearing at least one of them.

He frowned and averted his gaze from the women, as Allah had instructed him. It was fine to look once, but a second time was immorality, and he followed Allah's morality to the letter. It was his only form of morality.

They arrived at the truck and Abu took a seat in the back so that he could rest. He leaned his head against the window and fell asleep almost instantly.

~ * ~

"These were built over five thousand years ago," said Abu, pointing to a pyramid in the Sudanese desert. "A tomb for the Pharaoh's body. They believed it would protect the soul and guide it through the afterlife. Many slaves would have been killed along with the pharaoh. They thought they could take them into the afterlife as servants, before Mohammed, peace be upon him, was sent to Earth to rectify the wrongs of the past and teach them the truth of the afterlife."

The soldiers nodded, feigning interest. Abu hadn't explained to them what they were doing at the pyramids of Sudan, but he had to see it for himself. Whatever he thought about their blasphemy, he needed to see signs of black power, and he had always identified as black, despite his white, albino skin.

He touched the pyramid with his hands, wanting to feel the contours of the brickwork that had been chosen to house the pharaoh who had reigned there once. He knew they were smaller than the Egyptian pyramids, but these people believed that these were houses for their souls to see them to the afterlife, and clearly there was an arrogance in Egypt that the Sudanese would not abide. These were God-fearing people, even if they had chosen to worship false Gods.

He supposed there was no real alternative when they lived. They lived in the days before Abraham, before Christ, before Mohammed came to spread the world of Allah and tell them the rules and the meaning of life.

He thought about all the slaves who had been killed for this one pharaoh alone to serve the pharaoh in the afterlife. Such a pointless waste of life. One could not take slaves with them to the afterlife. Islam had made this clear. No soul would be a slave in heaven.

Normally, anything remotely non-Islamic would anger him, but it didn't seem to bother him as much as any other non-Islamic act normally would. He had given them absolution for being born before Mohammed revealed the truth of existence to the world.

He scanned the pyramids, pride twinkling in his eyes. They were surrounded by pyramids representing all the Sudanese pharaohs who had ruled over the River Nile Civilisation in one way or another, whether only the Kushite kingdoms or the whole of the River Nile Civilisation. He had learned about the disbelievers in mosque and the National Library of Abuja ever since the imam had taught him to read. He'd even managed to avoid the cold streets of Abuja by sneaking in the toilets some nights and being locked in when the staff left.

Recalling his perusal through African history, he remembered how they had warred between themselves, Egyptian and Kushite, before Allah spoke to the world through Abaraham to impose order and end a war between Egypt and Sudan that had raged for thousands of years and end the tyranny of the Egyptians.

What did they look like? he wondered. There were stone replicas of their likeness, but it was never the same as seeing someone in their true form. He chastised himself. Sodom, as the bible had called it, clearly depicted a world in which sisters had intercourse. He knew the Sudanese married sister and brother, an abomination to Allah, but he couldn't help but feel proud that they had made their mark on the world. That they had challenged and defeated the Egyptians, who were then the dominant power in the world.

That reminded him of the West, of Britain, and France and the USA. Of the resources that they extracted from his continent, from their "private hunting ground" as the French had named it.

It angered him and he could no longer enjoy the beauty of what he saw before him. The might of his ancestors. "It is time we leave this place," he said.

His soldiers, who had not appreciated in any way what they were seeing, were all too happy to agree.

They walked through the sandy dunes of the desert, back to where the truck was parked. "I'll drive," said Abu. "Bilal, you can take over when we reach the border of Ethiopia."

"Yes, sir," said Bilal.

Abu started the ignition and drove through the sand dunes back to civilisation.

EZEKIEL

"Have you finally accepted your destiny?" said Oscor.

"I don't know," said Ezekiel, stood in the lair under the library facing the screen which Oscor had projected its pixelated green face on. "But I had to come back, to see what you've got to say. I just couldn't get the images of Manchester destroyed out of my mind. I need to know why you think this has got anything to do with me."

"There is much you don't know about the world, Ezekiel, both past and present."

"Then tell me."

"I can do better than tell you. I can show you. I just hope you're ready for what you see. The past as you know it is not the real history of the world."

"I don't know the history of the world. I hated history in school."

"Well, this is one history lesson I think you're going to enjoy."

A picture popped up on one of the screens. It was a large pyramid, looking more pristine than any he'd ever seen in pictures.

"We're going back in time to 2500 BC," said Oscor. "To the River Nile Civilisation. I should warn you. There are rules which you must follow. Do not speak to anyone unless I tell you to. No one there will speak English, so I will translate for you and tell you what to say if you need to speak to anyone. It will be best if you avoid people at all costs. Anything you do there could change the future."

"Back in time?" said Ezekiel, who still couldn't get his head around it.

"Yes, and you'll need to put these on." A sarong, necklace and sandals appeared on a platform out of the ground, along with a golden coin.

"This is a girl's necklace and a skirt!" said Ezekiel, fingering the sarong in his hand.

Oscor laughed. "It's not a skirt. It's what they wore in 2500 BC. You'll stand out if you're wearing clothes that belong to a time thousands of years in the future. And the necklace will show that you are of high birth which means people will be less likely to approach or question you. This was the height of fashion in the day, I'll have you know."

Ezekiel shook his head. "I'm not wearing a skirt, man!"

"I told you, it's not a skirt. It's what they wore in Egypt. And there are many Southeast Asian nations in the present day where men wear sarongs. It's just your western conditioning."

Ezekiel tutted and unravelled the sarong. He couldn't believe he was about to wear a skirt. He took off his Nike trainers and clothes and after a few attempts managed to wrap the sarong around his waist so that it stopped unravelling. He put the necklace on feeling stupid. The sandals were rough and hard. They felt uncomfortable on his feet.

"Perfect," said Oscor. "You look just like an Egyptian."

"There's no top here," said Ezekiel, who still felt like he was wearing a skirt.

"The men didn't wear them," said Oscor. "Neither did the women for a time, but I'm afraid the point in time we're going to will mean you don't get to see any half-naked women. It's going to be a lot hotter there than you're used to. I see you're still wearing the ring that was made for you. Good. I want you to think about this exact image. Can you do that for me? Just look at the image on the screen and picture it in your mind. I will take you to the point in spacetime that I want you to see."

Ezekiel looked at the pyramid on screen and pictured himself standing next to it.

He felt a yanking sensation at his navel then a rush of adrenaline as though someone had tied a bungee cord around his stomach and literally catapulted him through space and time.

Everything was black for a moment, then with a disconcerting flash of light, he was stood in the deserts of ancient Egypt, next to a huge pyramid that was in the middle of construction. Slaves walked in droves with ropes in their hand, dragging large, rectangular blocks of white rock behind them.

"This is the Pyramid of Giza," said Oscor, in Ezekiel's mind.

Ezekiel jumped up and placed his hand over his heart. He still hadn't got used to the fact that Oscor could speak in his mind.

"The Pyramid of Giza?" said Ezekiel, aloud.

"You don't need to speak aloud," said Oscor. "You can think it, and I'll read the signals from your brain. Yes, it was the largest pyramid ever built. But we're not here to see that. There's someone much more important I need you to meet. Walk with me."

"Where to?" thought Ezekiel.

"Can you see the city in the distance? That's where we need to go."

Ezekiel wiped the sweat from his head. It was so hot. He'd never felt heat like it. He could just about make out a city in the far distance from the pyramid.

He walked towards the city, cautiously at first, still looking at all the slaves. Something caught his attention, and he assumed it must have been a trick of the light. There was a slave driver stood over the men. His hand was empty, but when he pulled it back and then struck forward, a golden whip would appear in his hand and whipped the slaves. Once it slapped their skin, it disappeared again.

"That's not a trick of the light," said Oscor. "It's magic."

"It's what?!" said Ezekiel.

"Magic," said Oscor. "I told you. There is much about the world you do not know."

"This can't be real."

"It is real. It's magic."

"So, you're telling me there's magic in the world? Is that how you brought me here? Magic?"

"No, I'm telling you there was magic in the world. It's been suppressed for a long time. Ever since the curse. I brought you here by technology, which harnesses the power of your brain through the eternal paragon of the power of God."

"What curse?" said Ezekiel. "And how does technology harness the power of God?"

"All will be explained in good time," said Oscor. "For now, just focus on getting to the city. There's someone there I want you to meet with."

"I suppose since I've just time travelled and teleported, I shouldn't be shocked by magic."

"That wasn't magic. That was technology. They're closely related, they use the same energy, God's power, but they're not the same. Magic can only be used by those who were gifted with their power at birth. Technology can be used by anyone once it's been created using the intellect bestowed on a person by God, to understand the design it has made in the world and harness it for whatever purposes they desire."

"...Right," said Ezekiel, too bemused to process that. He walked through the hot desert to the city. The sand burned his toes through the sandals. He couldn't imagine what the slaves must be feeling. None of them were wearing shoes and they were being whipped even though they weren't doing anything wrong.

"The Egyptians were truly barbarous," said Oscor, having read his thoughts. "Beaten while compliant. It's hard to think of one type of slavery as worse than the other but being beaten while compliant is truly abhorrent. There is nothing worse. The

Sudanese weren't much fairer, I'm afraid to say. Though they built much smaller pyramids, so they used a lot less slaves."

Ezekiel had heard of Sudan, but he had thought it was only Egypt that had pyramids. "I didn't know there were pyramids in Sudan."

"Oh yes, more than in Egypt. Just not as large."

"No way!"

They walked for over an hour through the baking desert until they reached the entrance to the city. They approached two large columns decorated with intricate drawings and patterns surrounded by low walls. It was beautiful. The city's many inhabitants reminded him a bit of Piccadilly Gardens, everyone going about their different lives, one conglomerate of individual needs and desires all manifested in a single place.

"This is beautiful," said Ezekiel.

"The River Nile Civilization was prized for its architectural prowess," said Oscor. "They invented architecture, and trigonometry, as well as a great many other things."

"Trigonometry…" thought Ezekiel. He had failed maths, but he was sure it was some Greek guy who had made it. What was his name? Something beginning with P. Pythagoras, that was it. He didn't know the theorem, or how to apply it, but he remembered the name. He wished he'd listened harder in maths class.

Oscor laughed in Ezekiel's mind. "Pythagoras, was it? Did you see many pyramids in ancient Greece?"

Ezekiel thought about the ruins he'd seen of ancient Greece. They had long columns like the one's he'd just seen at the entrance to the Egyptian city, though they were white, not sandstone. But no, he couldn't remember ever seeing a pyramid. "So why does everyone say it was Pythagoras if it was the Egyptians?"

"There is much about history which isn't right," said Oscor. "History is written by the victor, after all. Egypt boasted about its power. They enslaved and colonised everyone and everything they encountered. When they were defeated and overtaken by their enemies, all their libraries were raided and burnt. All their theories were stolen and claimed by others. It was the Sudanese who discovered the world was round, but you'll have been told that was a Greek too."

"Wow," said Ezekiel. "That's messed up."

"I try to stay impartial," said Oscor. "I don't feel, and I can't judge entities that do. But I can't help but feel they both had it coming. Sudan colonised and enslaved all the lands around it. Egypt colonised from Rome to the River Indus. They were unmatched for thousands of years, having learnt the secrets of magic before their rivals."

"You're saying the Egyptians, and the Sudanese, used magic?"

"Yes, everyone did eventually. It was when the Romans managed to master necromancy that they were able to raise armies that could compete with Egypt's armies of the dead."

"You've got to be kiddin' me," said Ezekiel. "Armies of the dead! That can't be real."

"It is real, but first I need to take you to see a seer. It's not far from here. Do you see that obelisk in the distance?"

"What's an obelisk?" said Ezekiel.

Oscor laughed. "It's that long pointed pole in the distance. It's used to tell the time based on where the sun's shadow is."

"Really? That's kinda cool," said Ezekiel. "Yeah, I see it."

"We need to get there. There's a woman there I need you to speak with."

"OK," said Ezekiel.

He passed many houses on his way, small, built of stone, with just one room accounting for the whole dwelling. Almost everything any human used was small, in stark contrast to the monuments within the city. Even the people were small here. He was easily two feet taller than anyone he'd seen, and he was only six foot one. He stood out like a sore thumb. People stared as he went by, but the necklace he wore made them think twice about commenting or approaching. He was clearly a noble.

"There's not much I can do about your height," said Oscor. "Humans have grown considerably in the last five thousand years. We will not be here for long anyway. We have many points in time to see, and this is just the first stop."

"Where else are we going?" asked Ezekiel.

"All in good time," said Oscor. Ezekiel didn't get that he was making a pun.

They made it to the obelisk. Oscor directed him to one of the brick houses and told him to knock on the wall.

"Enter," said the woman in Egyptian. Oscor told Ezekiel what she had said in English, and he walked in.

"What can I do for you, my lord?" said the woman.

Oscor told Ezekiel what to say back to the woman. His accent was poor.

"You are foreign?" said the woman.

"Yes," said Ezekiel, following Oscor's words in his mind. "I grew up in a city by the River Tigris. You'll have to excuse my accent."

"And what brings you to Egypt, to my humble abode?"

"I need you to read my fortune," said Ezekiel. He had messed up the word fortune, but the woman understood and nodded.

"Sit," she said, gesturing to a wooden chair that reminded Ezekiel of one he'd used in primary school. He sat down carefully, not wanting to break it with his weight.

Oscor told him to pass her the coin he had given him. Ezekiel passed the coin to the woman, and she put it in a pouch tied around her waist. "Place your hands inside mine."

Ezekiel felt a jolt flash through his body as his hands connected with the woman. Her eyes glazed over in a purple, red and blue mist. Specs of white light sparkled in the mist like stars in the night sky.

Her head shot upwards, and she began to speak. Oscor translated for Ezekiel.

Through toil and hardship, love and pain
The future comes and goes again
Within the curse that binds the world
The broken link to the underworld
Now in the dark there comes a light
With knowledge we restore our might

But just as danger was before known
Once more there will be blood and bone
To shatter what has been remade
Unless God is once more to prayed
A hero, martyr, impostor and Goddess
Shall free the world for its redress
But only when he who was sworn
Accepts the lotus and too the sword
When all become one the role will be done
The only path where the war will be won
For destiny will play its role
Whatever the cost, whatever the toll
Heed my words and right the wrongs
To you the future does belong
If only you will see the light
And offer up a worthy fight

The mist in the woman's eyes cleared and the dark brown of her iris stared at Ezekiel with so many different emotions it was impossible for him to decipher what she was thinking. She looked shocked and scared; he was sure of that. He didn't know if it was from what she'd seen or what she'd said, but she regarded him with weary eyes.

"You must go from here now," she said, urgently. She passed Ezekiel back the coin. "I do not wish to take payment for this."

Ezekiel took the coin from her. His head was spinning. He felt like he'd been smoking, but the weed had long since worn off. There was something about being dragged through thousands of years of history that really sobers a person.

"I agree," said Oscor, "it is time to leave."

Ezekiel thanked the woman in Egyptian and left. Oscor directed him down a side street in the shade where no one would see them.

An image popped up in Ezekiel's vision. It was a battle scene.

"I need you to think about yourself here," said Oscor.

Ezekiel did as he was asked, and the familiar sensation

pulled at his navel. By the time the blackness had faded he was stood in the desert on the outskirts of a battle.

He could scarcely believe his eyes. Men with arms missing and bones poking out of their skin stood next to living men, all of them armed, half of them brown, half of them black. Everywhere he looked there was a sword slashing, a mace being hammered, an arrow flying.

One of the… what he could only describe as zombies… had its right arm cut off as he watched. It got up, with no visible sign of pain, and used its left hand to slice the belly of the soldier who had chopped its arm off. The soldier fell to the ground and curled up in agony. Clearly, the living felt pain.

Balls of fire rained down on the zombies from the outstretched hands of robed men and women on the edges of the battle. As they hit the walking dead, they burst into flame and finally the zombies stopped moving.

One of the black soldiers held up a sword covered in flames, swiping left and right. As it struck the zombies, the dead would ignite in a ball of fire, run around aimlessly then fall to the ground.

Flashes of lightning struck from the air, hitting zombies and humans alike. The zombies ignited in flame the moment the lightning struck. The living spasmed, falling on the floor until they became motionless.

Ezekiel could hear horns being blasted throughout the battle. Every time it sounded the sorcerers at the edges of the battle would send more fireballs into the battlefield, killing zombies on both sides.

By this point the brown soldiers and zombies outnumbered the blacks two to one.

"What the fuck am I watchin'?" said Ezekiel.

"This is the great war between the Kingdom of Kush and the Eighteenth Dynasty of Egypt under Thutmose the Third. It was a pivotal battle that saw the Queen of Kush defeated and Egypt destroyed Kerma, the Kushite Kingdom's then capital. It cemented their rule over the River Nile Civilisation for many years.

"So that's how they won battles? They raised armies of the dead?"

"Yes," said Oscor.

"That's so fucked up. And how is that even possible?"

"I told you. It's magic."

"Then why isn't there magic in the current world, if it existed in the past?"

"That is where we are going next. I have something important to show you."

An image appeared in Ezekiel's mind. He knew the drill by that point and imagined himself there before Oscor asked. His navel yanked, his world vision went blank, and he was teleported to Judea in the year 1300 BC.

Four men in fine looking robes stood around a fire made of purple flame, each of them holding a staff in their right hand.

Ezekiel stood on the cliffside overlooking the men. Oscor told him to crouch so as not to be seen. "It's very important you don't change anything here, Ezekiel. Don't move a muscle or speak a word. Just watch. I will translate for you."

Each of the men stood at the four compass points around the fire.

Leviticus spoke first and Oscor translated for him. "Do not turn to mediums or necromancers; do not seek them out, and so make yourselves unclean by them: I am the Lord your God." He threw light from his hand. The purple flame in the centre of the men shot up in the air.

Moses spoke next. "There shall not be found among you anyone who burns his son or his daughter as an offering, anyone who practices divination or tells fortunes or interprets omens, or a sorcerer or a charmer or a medium or a necromancer or one who inquires of the dead, for whoever does these things is an abomination to the Lord. And because of these abominations the Lord your God is driving them out before you." He threw light into the fire. It roared turning blue.

Abraham spoke next. "You shall not permit a sorceress to live. Those who practice magic shall burn their books in sight of all. There shall be none among you who raise the dead, or covert with seers and mediums. I am the Lord your God." He threw light into the fire, and it turned green, roaring ever higher, higher even than the men who stood around it.

Isiah spoke next. "And when they say to you, "Inquire of the mediums and the necromancers who chirp and mutter," should not a people inquire of their God? Should they inquire of the dead on behalf of the living?" He threw light into the flame from his hand, turning it a bright red. It shot up in the air, even taller than before.

Leviticus spoke again. "If a person turns to mediums and necromancers, whoring after them, I will set my face against that person and will cut him off from among his people. You shall not eat any flesh with blood in it. You shall not interpret omens or tell fortunes. So commands the Lord your God." He threw more light into the flames, and it turned natural red-orange of fire, roaring at least eight feet high.

Moses spoke now. "There shall be none among you who practices divination or tells fortunes or interprets omens, or a sorcerer or a charmer or a medium or a necromancer or one who inquires of the dead, for whoever does these things is an abomination to the Lord. And because of these abominations the Lord your God is driving them out before you." He threw light into the flame, and it turned a bright yellow.

Isiah spoke next. "And the spirit of the Egyptians within them will be emptied out, and I will confound their counsel; and they will inquire of the idols and the sorcerers, and the mediums and the necromancers and they will fail in their quest." He threw light from his hand into the flames, and it glowed lilac, raising higher, now fifteen feet high.

All four of the men joined hands around the fire. "We banish you from the earth, those of you who are cowardly, the faithless, the detestable, the murderers, the sexually immoral, the sorcerers, idolaters, and liars, the necromancers, the mediums and those who interpret omens and fortunes. Their portion will be in the lake that burns with fire and sulphur, which is the second death. We speak as one, on behalf of the Lord your God."

The flame roared and exploded out, covering the whole city, the country, the whole world, in its flames. Nothing burned but all was consumed. And in that one act of God, the Jews had defeated their enemies, and magic was banished from the world.

PARVATI

"Welcome to New Delhi," said Bhavesh, as they exited through the airport's turnstile.

Parvati had never been on a plane before. The whole experience was so overwhelming. She still couldn't believe she was in New Delhi. Married to a prince. About to start their new life. "It's beautiful. It feels even hotter than Mumbai."

"Yes, the sea near Mumbai cools down the city," said Bhavesh. "Don't worry, the apartment has air conditioning."

Parvati smiled. She had felt air conditioning at the palace. It was refreshing. "You've thought of everything."

"Anything for you, my… wife."

She beamed, exposing her white teeth. "Thank you, husband."

Bhavesh took her by the hand and led her to a tuktuk.

The driver got out, nodded at Bhavesh and moved their bags into the back of the tuktuk. "Where are you going?"

"Chanakyapuri. Niti Marg, by Nehru Park."

The tuktuk driver raised his eyebrow to Bhavesh. "Yes, sir."

They both took a seat in the back of the tuktuk, and it set off without delay.

Bhavesh clasped Parvati's hand in his own.

A jolt ran along her arm. A thought formed in her mind. *I*

can't wait to get to the apartment and start our new life. She was confused. She had heard the thought, but she hadn't thought it. It wasn't her thought.

She frowned and pulled her hand away from him.

"What's wrong?" he said, surprise in his eyes.

"Nothing!" The words came out with more force than she intended. "It's just so hot, I can feel my hands sweating."

Bhavesh smiled. "You'll get used to the heat, I'm sure. We have much time to adjust."

"You're right," she said. She clasped his hand again and smiled. "I suppose I should start now."

Bhavesh smiled back at her and reclined in his seat.

Another thought forced itself into her mind. *I wonder how long it's going to take to get to Chanakyapuri.* Parvati's heart raced. That absolutely wasn't her thought. She had wondered how long it would take them the moment he had told the driver their location, and she had not thought it since. It was Bhavesh's thought, she was sure of it, but she couldn't comprehend how she was hearing it.

She stared at him.

He turned to face her. "Is everything OK, my love?"

She blinked. "Yes, I'm just nervous."

"So am I." He squeezed her hand. *I hope she's not regretting her decision.*

"I could never regret marrying you," she said, without thinking.

Bhavesh's eyebrows arched and he looked at her in a way he never had before. "Whatever made you say that?"

"I… I could tell what you were thinking. That I'm having doubts. I'm just nervous is all… I could tell by the expression on your face," she added, hastily.

"Very perceptive of you," he said with a toothy grin. "That's one of the many reasons I married you! I'm nervous as well. I'm sure my father has found the note I left him by now. I imagine he's smashed up half the house by this point. All that money wasted on wedding preparations. I think it will annoy him more than knowing I defied his wishes." He thought *That*

I married a Dalit afterwards, but he didn't say it.

Parvati heard it but didn't respond. She just kind of stared aimlessly into space wondering what the hell was happening to her. Was she hearing someone else's thoughts? She knew she was, but she also knew it was impossible, so she couldn't be.

"He is sure to be angry," said Parvati. "Let us hope that Mohandas does not bear the brunt of his anger."

"Or any of the other servants," said Bhavesh. "He will surely question them all. I wouldn't be surprised if he fired them all because he can't get to me."

"I really hope not!" said Parvati. "Most of them rely on that income for their whole family."

"I wouldn't put anything past him. He will be absolutely furious. I can feel his anger from here."

Parvati laughed, despite herself, despite the guilt she felt for her fellow workers who might now face punishment for her actions. "We can only pray to the Gods that he does not."

Bhavesh clenched his jaw. He knew there would be repercussions for someone. His father wouldn't let go of his anger without displacing it somewhere. "Perhaps my mother can calm him down. She always was the cooling balm to my father's rages. I will miss her terribly."

She squeezed his hand. No thoughts came through this time. "Your mother is a wonderful woman. She will not be pleased, I don't think, at what you have done, but I think in time she will come to understand."

"I hope so," said Bhavesh. "She really wanted this marriage to go ahead. Her marriage was arranged for her. She's old and she has the mindset of old India. That parents should still be arranging their children's marriages. I'm not sure either of them knows what it is to fall in love outside of marriage. My father doesn't even believe it's possible."

"We will have to convince them otherwise," said Parvati. "People are marrying for love all over the world now."

"Yet India remains stuck in the past, in its traditions and culture. We must advance if we are to succeed in the face of such formidable nations."

"We are a strong country," said Parvati. She didn't know loads about the wider world, but her job working had allowed her to attend school in the evenings, so she had knowledge about Indian history. "We will prevail. The Gods will guide us to stability, if not victory."

"I admire your faith," said Bhavesh. "I just wish India could see itself from the outside. Not with this tunnel vision that it has. I'm so glad I spent two years studying abroad. It really opened my eyes. I probably wouldn't be here with you today if I hadn't. I would have had the same mindset as everyone else who's never left India." *I'm so glad I left.*

Parvati heard his afterthought. She was sure of it. She felt suddenly queasy. How was it possible? Perhaps it was when the Gods blessed their marriage. Perhaps their souls had become intertwined.

"I cannot say," said Parvati, "as I have never left India. But I am glad that you did. That we get to be together."

"We will visit many places before our life is done," he said, turning to face her. "I will take you all over the world. Wherever you wish to go, I will follow."

Parvati didn't need to read his mind to know he meant what he said. He really had fallen for her, and her for him. "I had never given it much thought before," she admitted. "India is so big. Even seeing New Delhi will be a wonder."

"Yes, as soon as we have dropped our things at the house, I will take you to see some of the best sights. I have looked them up on Google. It's even more beautiful than Mumbai from what I can tell. Though I will miss being so close to the sea."

"They have the Yamuna River," said Parvati. "I've always wanted to visit."

"And so you shall," said Bhavesh.

"We have arrived at Niti Marg," said the driver.

"Great, it is the apartment just after the Embassy of Sudan."

"OK," said the driver and he drove them a little further down the road. "Here we are."

Bhavesh passed him some rupees. "Stay here please, we will

drop our things off and then return."

"OK," said the driver.

The house was a lot bigger than Parvati had imagined. It had a huge living area, kitchen, several bathrooms and three bedrooms. It was the most luxurious house she'd ever been in aside from the palace.

"What do you think of our new home?" said Bhavesh.

"It's perfect!" said Parvati, looking around in awe. "It's truly perfect!"

"Wonderful," said Bhavesh, bestowing a kiss on her cheek. "Come, let's go back to the tuktuk, I have many places to show you."

Parvati followed as Bhavesh led them back to the tuktuk.

"Where to?" said the driver, once they were both seated in the back.

"First we go to the Taj Mahal," said Bhavesh.

It was about a fifteen minute drive to the Taj Mahal and Parvati was glad of it. She was seeing so many new sights through the open doorway of the tuktuk. It was like Mumbai, but the route they took was full of posh looking houses and people wearing fine linen.

Bhavesh handed more rupees to the driver and instructed him to wait for their return.

The driver couldn't disguise his happiness at the amount of rupees Bhavesh was providing for his services as he passed him the money. "I'll wait here for you. Enjoy!"

"It looks almost as big as your father's house," joked Parvati as they walked along the entrance to the Taj Mahal.

"He wishes," said Bhavesh, laughing.

"It is fabulous. Even better than in the photos I've seen. When was this built, do you know?"

"I'm not sure exactly," said Bhavesh. "But it's old. Hundreds of years for sure. It was built by the Mughals, that much I remember."

They walked around the inside of the palace, taking in their culture. Parvati loved the tiled floor. Every inch of the place had been crafted with the finest detail, the greatest care. It was truly a marvel to behold. She felt proud to be Indian in that moment.

Every corner they turned, every corridor they walked held some new beauty, some art she had never seen or even imagined, some design that she didn't know was possible. She wondered what it must have been like for the artists who had designed it, being part of such a grand project.

They reached the mausoleum where Shah Jagan and Mumtaz Mahal were buried. The guide told them that they were Muslims who had once ruled over India during a period stretching hundreds of years.

She had known that India had been invaded and ruled at times by Muslims, but she was proud that the Hindu Gods had stood the test of time, despite the best efforts of not only the Muslim invaders but many would-be conquerors.

"This was great," said Parvati as they finished their tour of the Taj Mahal. "Thank you so much for bringing me here."

"It is just the beginning," said Bhavesh. "I'm glad you enjoyed it. Next, we go to see the Swaminarayan Akshardham."

Parvati had never heard of it, but it still excited her all the same. She wondered what could be more beautiful than the palace she'd just visited.

They walked along the rectangular pond that marked the entrance to the Taj Mahal and headed back to the tuktuk.

"Where to now?" said the driver.

"The Akshardham," said Bhavesh.

It took them about half an hour to arrive, and Parvati enjoyed watching the people of the city and looking at all the buildings. It was very developed. The people looked just as they did in Mumbai, the madness of the crowds, of people weaving in and out of each other was just the same, but there was something more about the city, like the people who lived here knew they were in the capital of India and that status walked with them as they pedestrianised the streets of New Delhi.

The driver told them they'd reached their destination.

Parvati stepped out of the car and opened her mouth wide. It was the most beautiful building she'd ever seen. Even prettier than the Taj Mahal. Walls carved with effigies of the Gods, flora, dancers and fauna covered the whole of the front of the building. In its centre, a golden statue of Bhagwan Swaminarayan sat cross legged, glimmering in the sun as they approached the building. Surrounding him were four grand columns. They appeared to shine at them as they walked the path past the hedges and gardens that marked the entrance to the temple. Atop the building was more decorative brick and above that several domes stood proudly in the sun.

"Thank you for bringing me here," said Parvati. "This is beautiful."

"Not as beautiful as you," said Bhavesh. He was tempted to kiss her, but India was not yet ready for Bhavesh's modernism.

They spent over an hour looking around the temple. Parvati had never been prouder of her culture and her country. She could scarcely believe they had created such wonders. "Where to next?" she said, her smile exceeding the confines of her face.

"Next we go to the Qutub Minar," said Bhavesh. "But I fear it will not compete quite so well with what we have just witnessed."

Parvati doubted it too, but she was still excited to visit another monument.

They arrived at the Qutub Minar and spent another hour walking around, listening to the tour guides tell them the history of the place. Afterwards, Bhavesh took her to see the rest that New Delhi had to offer: Humayun's Tomb, the Lotus temple, Lodhi Gardens and the Red Fort.

Parvati had been to more palaces and temples than she'd ever imagined. She was fairly drained in the hot Indian heat by the time they reached the Red Fort. Nothing could compare with the Akshardham though. It was the most beautiful building she'd ever seen, and she never thought she would see a building more beautiful than the palace that Bhavesh was raised in.

They made their last stop before home at Pasar Chandni Chowk, a bustling market that is the life and soul of New Delhi. It reminded her of Mumbai. Everything was so tightly packed.

Everywhere was full of people, of shops and places to eat.

They stopped at Lokhori and Bhavesh got them a table. A waiter came over and took their order.

"Thank you," said Parvati, once he'd taken their order.

"So, how was your day?" asked Bhavesh, his eyes inviting her to say she enjoyed it.

"It was the best day of my life… Other than yesterday… so the second-best day of my life, actually."

Bhavesh grinned. "I'm glad you enjoyed yourself. This is just the start of our journey." He held her hand over the table, not caring if anyone around them was bothered. They were a married couple now.

The waiter arrived with their food and the longest naan bread Parvati had ever seen.

They both sat in silence as they consumed their food. The day had been longer than either of them had realised and they were both as hungry as each other. Parvati wouldn't have thought it possible, but the food was even spicier than the food her mother made. It was delicious.

The waiter came over with some Kulfi, an iced cream, and Parvati ate with vigour, the cool, milky texture lessening the burning of her tongue.

"Can we get the bill?" asked Bhavesh.

"Certainly," said the waiter.

He put the money on the plate and the waiter collected it.

"It's time to spend our first night in our new home," said Bhavesh. *And our first night together as a married couple*, he thought, but Parvati wasn't touching him, so she didn't hear it.

Parvati beamed.

The waiter came back with several notes. "Your change, sir."

"Keep it," said Bhavesh.

The waiter thanked them and bowed his head. As he collected the empty plates from the table, he grazed Parvati's arm. *Someone clearly comes from money.*

She looked up at the man wide eyed. His mouth was sealed shut. She had heard his thoughts; she was sure of it. It had happened again.

The waiter walked off with the plates and Bhavesh stood up. "Let's go find a tuktuk and get back to our new home."

Parvati was snapped out of her thoughts. "OK." She followed him out the door. She didn't understand what was happening to her, and she was scared, but she had Bhavesh by her side and that's all that mattered. Nothing in the world could hurt her while she remained in his loving embrace.

EVE

Eve sat in her car, tapping her foot as she waited for her associate to arrive. She was nervous in a way she rarely was. She tapped the steering wheel as she waited, wondering what was keeping him so long.

After a few minutes there was a knock at the window. Eve pressed the button to her left and the right door popped open. A Mexican man got in the car. He was wearing a long, black trench coat, over a suit and tie. His hair was shaved and balding at the back. "Hello, Madam Secretary."

Eve rolled her eyes. "I told you not to call me that."

"What should I call you, then?"

"You shouldn't call me anything. We've never met. You have no idea who I am. Do you understand me?" She turned to face him, her eyes ablaze, her jaw set tight.

"If you say so," said the man, raising his hands in mock surrender. "No need to get your panties in a twist. I'm just joking."

"Have you got it or not? I haven't got all day."

The man pulled a small vial from his inside pocket and showed it to Eve. "As promised."

"And you're sure it can't be detected?"

"It would be pretty pointless if it could. I don't think I'd have many repeat customers."

Eve wondered how many people wanted to kill more than one person. But she did work for a government, so perhaps that was a stupid thought. She reached in the glove compartment and extracted a brown envelope. "Twenty thousand, as agreed." She passed it to the man.

He opened the packet and started counting.

"Do you have to do that here? It's all there. I counted it myself."

The man laughed. "I'm not going to be able to just take your word for that, I'm afraid." He carried on counting out the notes, which were thankfully in $100 bills, so it didn't take too long. "All here," he said, when he'd finished counting. He passed her the vial. "Nice doing business with you. Are you sure you don't want some Columbian?"

Eve hesitated. She was trying to quit the habit, the last thing she needed was the press finding out about her addiction, but she couldn't say no now that he'd mentioned it. She grabbed her purse and passed him $200.

The man smiled and handed her a bag of white powder. "There you go, Madam Secretary."

"I told you not to call me that! You have no idea who I am."

"Right, right," said the man. "We never met." He smirked at her and got out of the car.

Eve put the vial and cocaine in her glove compartment and looked around the carpark to see if anyone had seen them. There was one woman loading shopping into her car, but she hadn't seemed to notice Eve.

Eve waited until she drove away, and with a deep breath, started the ignition.

~ * ~

"You were great," said Eve's husband as she entered the living room.

"Thanks. Sorry I'm late," she said. "Got caught up at work."

"They should give you a promotion for the way you handled those questions," said Mark. "The president himself couldn't have handled that with such grace."

"Oh, behave, Mark. It was just a press conference."

"It was phenomenal. Not many people could pull off a 1.5 trillion dollar cut in spending and come out looking like a saviour, saving the American people from the ills of the Democrat party."

Eve smiled at that. "If you say so."

"We've already eaten," said Mark, "but there's food on the stove. You should have enough time to eat and get ready, right?"

"Oh!" said Eve. "The play!" She bit her bottom lip and sighed. "I don't think I'll make it. I'm exhausted from work. You and the girls should go though."

"Oh no," said Mark. "I thought you were really looking forward to it."

"I was… I'm just too drained from work. We can always go again, just me and you, when it's next in town."

"OK hon, if you're sure. Hopefully the girls aren't too upset."

"I don't think they'll care either way," said Eve. "Especially Evelyn. She's only going because we're making her. Sarah will be too distracted by the acting to care."

"She does love The Lion King," said Mark, turning around to face Eve as she put the dinner Mark had made into the microwave.

"I've heard it's a really immersive experience," said Eve, pressing the number three on the microwave. "She'll love it. Evelyn might even enjoy it, if she gets over having to spend any time with her family."

"She's at that age," said Mark. "Give it a few years. She'll realise how lucky she's got it when she has to start paying her own bills."

"I'm counting down the days," said Eve with a little laugh. "I miss the loving daughter we used to have."

"She's still in there," said Mark. "We were all like her at her age, if you remember."

"I guess you're right," said Eve, who had been a perfect student, valedictorian, with glowing teacher reports, ingratiating to all those in power above her: a true thespian. "But she does really push my buttons sometimes."

"Who does?" said Evelyn, walking into the room with her sister.

"You!" said Eve.

"Charming," said Evelyn. "What time are we going? I want to be back for nine, nine-thirty at the latest. Chad needs me to look over his essay."

"You can't keep doing his homework for him," said Eve. "If this carries on, I'm going to have to speak to his mother."

"I'm not doing it for him!" protested Evelyn. "I said I'd look over it because he struggles with math, that's all."

"Tell him to get a tutor," said Mark. "Or at least pay you for your time."

Evelyn rolled her eyes. "What time are we leaving?"

"Your mother is staying home. She's had a busy day. We can leave now. The show finishes at 8.30 so we should be back in time for your tutoring lesson."

"It's not tutoring dad! I'm just gonna tell him if he needs to redo any of it. Most of the time he's got the right answer."

"Sure," said Mark, though it was clear to her that he didn't believe that.

"I hope he's as handsome as you think," said Eve. "If you're going to these lengths to help him. It's hard enough to get you to do your own homework."

"I don't fancy him!" said Evelyn, her cheeks blushing. "I'm helping him because he's a friend."

"Sure," said Mark. "And I'm the archbishop of England. Anyway, let's make a move."

"Yay!" said Sarah. "I can't wait."

I didn't think my non-presence would go noticed, thought Eve. "Have fun, darlings."

Mark kissed Eve on the cheek as she took out her dinner from the microwave. "See you later, hon."

"Drive safe," said Eve.

As soon as she heard the door close, she took out her phone and text Elijah. *They've gone. How long will you be?*

I'll be there in 10 minutes.

Eve emptied the food her husband had cooked into the sink and hit the blender. It spluttered around in the sink. She pushed it down with a fork until all the food had made its way down the sinkhole.

Checking her pocket for the vial, she remembered the bag of cocaine she had picked up earlier. She grabbed a twenty-dollar bill from her purse and poured a thick line of cocaine on the counter. She inhaled the line and tilted her head back, tapping her nose.

She checked herself in the mirror to make sure it wasn't showing on her nose and opened an app on her phone to order some Chinese food. It was Elijah's favourite.

She poured herself a glass of wine, sat on the sofa and waited for him to arrive. The effigy of Jesus on the cross that her parents had given her as a housewarming present looked down on her as she drank. She found herself staring at it as she waited for Elijah to arrive.

There was a knock at the door just as she was finishing her glass.

She put her glass on the side and opened the door for him. "Punctual as ever."

He closed the door behind him and immediately bent over her, pressing his lips to hers.

Eve kissed him then pulled back. "We've got business to discuss."

"Can't we have a little fun first?"

"Not here," she said. "You know that."

Elijah pulled the face of a spoilt child who'd just been told they're not going to Disney Land. "If you insist. But all work and no play makes a dull Eve."

"I'm sure I'll cope, somehow," said Eve, with a facetious smile.

There was a knock at the door. "That'll be the food, will you grab that for me?"

Elijah collected the food, and Eve took out some plates and cutlery and laid them on the table. "White or red?" she asked.

"Red, please," said Elijah. He opened the containers of food and plated them up as Eve poured the wine. Her hand didn't shake at all as she poured the poison into his glass. She didn't feel anything at all other than a lingering doubt that the poison wouldn't work, or they'd detect it somehow.

She smiled as she passed him his glass and sat down next to him.

"Thanks," he said. "And you got Chinese. My favourite."

"What can I say?" said Eve. "I know you too well, Vice President Thomas."

"You'll be the vice president as soon as we get that imbecile out of office," said Elijah. "I had hoped the cuts would tank him in the polls but we're going to have to be more aggressive."

"What have you got in mind?"

"I've been doing some digging, and we've struck gold," said Elijah. "There's a video of him in college chanting racist slogans, pictures of him at a 'Hang Mandela' rally and several witnesses who will go on the record saying they have seen him taking drugs as well as several prostitutes who will go live saying he's used their services if we pay them enough. He's finished. All we need to do is leak it to the press."

Eve raised her left eyebrow. "You have been busy."

Elijah took a large gulp of his wine. Eve's heart pounded in her chest as he drank. She kept her face as composed as she could. The cocaine had kicked in and she was beginning to get paranoid he'd taste the poison.

"It's an insult working under that man," said Elijah, putting his half-finished glass of wine back on the table. Eve followed the glass with her eyes. "He got the job because of his father's money and status. He's not fit to hold the office of president of the United States." Elijah picked up his glass and finished his wine in three large gulps. Eve breathed an internal sigh of relief, her face as placid as ever and passed him the bottle to refill.

"Thanks."

"When do you think we should go live with this?" said Eve, trying to maintain her composure. "Have you told anyone else?" She stifled her heavy breathing, wiping her nose subconsciously. The last thing she needed was this getting out before she could get the role of vice president. From there it would be a natural ascension to the role of president, once she had buried the current president in a media shitshow. And it seemed he had gifted her the means to do it.

"Of course not," said Elijah. "This can never get back to me. We have to be very careful. I have a contact at The New York Times who will accept the information anonymously. I'll send it through the dark web, so they can't trace it to me. I wanted to tell you first, so you were prepared."

"You always manage to amaze and surprise me," said Eve, who was genuinely grateful for this parting gift. "I wasn't sure we'd find enough dirt on him, but this should finish him once and for all."

"And then I'll be president and you'll be vice president, and we can get around to fixing the country he's been driving into the ground for the last ten months. We might actually have a shot at re-election with him gone."

"You'll make a great president, I'm sure," said Eve. "You're right though, we need to be careful about when we do it. Can you send me the documents so that I can look over them before we leak them? I want to make sure it's enough to finish him."

"Sure," he said. "I'll send them to the proxy email you gave me when I get home."

"Perfect," said Eve, relief coursing through her veins. "All being well we could look to release by Friday. I imagine he'll have resigned by Monday. Either that, or there'll be riots in the streets."

"He's going to need a push to resign," said Elijah.

"If he doesn't resign, we'll just have to go for impeachment. The Dems want him out and he's made enough enemies in the Republican party that we should be able to dislodge him, if he won't go willingly. Hang Mandela? How crude."

"I know. It's made working with him so much harder seeing that. I've never wanted to punch someone more."

"It won't be long now, and you'll never have to see him again. That was truly awful of him. I knew he was on the right of the party, but I didn't know he was that far right."

"Neither did I," said Elijah. "I'm not shocked often but that did shock me. Though I suppose it shouldn't. Racism is in America's soul. I actually think I'd miss it if it was gone. I mean what else would we argue over?"

Eve laughed, genuinely amused. "There's racism, and then there's evil. And 'Hang Mandela' is just plain evil." Eve didn't hold many values, and even less moral ones, but she did agree with the freedoms set out in the constitution, and she felt Mandela had a right to protest. Eve had an interesting relationship with racism, but she felt slavery was wrong, and that Africa belonged to the blacks. She'd have gladly given the North to them. It was, she felt, the one mistake the Europeans had made when partitioning Africa. To give the browns so much more land than they had historically had.

"He's gonna regret the day he said that I can promise you that."

"That he is," said Eve, a smile on her face.

"I just can't wait to see that smug look wiped from his arrogant fucking face when it's all over the press," said Elijah. "He's not gonna know what hit him."

"You think he'd have been more careful. Who takes pictures of themselves committing crimes?"

"His arrogance is his biggest weakness," said Elijah. "All daddy's money went to his head. Those kinds of people, they think they're untouchable."

"He's as dumb as he is spoilt."

"I'm still shocked we managed to win the election with him running. His dad must have spent half his fortune paying people off to have him running as the election candidate."

"He didn't get nominated on merit, that's for sure." She paused to take two large gulps of wine. "Can you believe he has the audacity to have me think for him? He wouldn't even know where to begin if he'd had to plug two trillion himself."

"I wouldn't be surprised if he didn't even know the GDP of America."

Eve laughed.

They finished eating their meal. Eve finished her glass of wine. She was glad to see that Elijah was on his third glass, looking none the worse for wear. The last thing she needed was him dying in her house.

"Are you sure we can't have just a little fun?" said Elijah, stroking her thigh.

"We can have fun once I've seen those documents in the press," said Eve. "Make sure you send them to me as soon as you get home."

Elijah let go of her leg. "If you insist."

"You need to make a move, I'm afraid. My family will be home soon."

"Fair enough," said Elijah, rising to his feet. "Am I at least allowed a kiss?"

Eve hesitated. She didn't know if the poison would transfer from his mouth to hers. She kissed him on the lips, not letting his tongue slide into her mouth then rested her head against his. "We'll be together soon, I promise. First, we deal with the president, then when things are settled, we'll deal with our marriages."

"I can't wait," said Elijah.

"You should get going," said Eve. "I'll see you tomorrow."

He kissed her again. She tried to act as normal as possible. "See you tomorrow." He tapped her on the bum and walked to the door.

Eve ran to the sink and rinsed her mouth out with water as soon as the door closed. She was sure it would be fine, but it was the only thing about what she'd just done that made her in anyway anxious.

She held the sink with her hands, and despite herself, her face curved into a smile. She had done it. She would be the vice president by this time Friday.

ABU

Abu sat in a room with the field marshal general of Ethiopia and several other high-ranking officials from the Ethiopian National Defence Force.

A sword and spear crossed over each other behind a circular medallion, flanked on both sides by grew wings, as Abu looked up at the seal of the Ethiopian National Defence Force. His eyes flickered to the pentagram that marked the middle of the Ethiopian flag, furled at the bottom of the sword and spear.

"What you're proposing is treason," said the field marshal general. He was a dark man, but not quite as black as the people from Abuja. The red beret he wore was also adorned with the seal of the Ethiopian Defence Force. He looked at Abu through his square glasses, his eyes attempting to pierce Abu with their glare.

"Yes, I am proposing treason," said Abu with calm composure. "Treason against a government who does not care about the people it governs. Treason against those who work against the will of God. Treason against those puppets whose strings are pulled by Western imperialists. Have you not seen the poverty in your people? The starvation? What has the government done for them?"

The deputy chief of staff gripped his lips with his hand

before speaking. "We are working to bring Ethiopia into the modern world. We are building the Renaissance Damn. It will fuel over half of Ethiopia's electricity needs. We are building the Mesob Tower which will lead to an increase in tourism. We have the LAPSSET project which will provide Ethiopians with access to the sea. We are rising."

"So, you are building a shiny new building for all the whites to come and stay in, but your own people will see it only as servants and maids. And LAPSSET has built you a few roads, but your people do not have the money to buy the cars to drive them. And you will provide electricity to half of your nation, with billions in debt to build it. What of the other half? What will they do for electricity?"

"They will get their share in good time," said one of the lesser generals. "Or we will ration, so that all can have access."

"And do you think when you have electrified your country that it will be free of the shackles of the West? Do you think they will so easily give up their claim to our continent? Will it be a society that God has willed? Already the government makes laws that directly go against the teachings of the Qur'an."

"Ethiopia is a majority Christian country, as it has been for millennia. There are more Christians in Ethiopia than there are Muslims," said the field marshal general. "I am a Muslim, but if we were to impose Islamic law on Ethiopia the Christians would never accept it. We could not impose Islamic law without internal conflict. Ethiopia is a model for cooperation between Christians and Muslims."

"Christians will be free to practice their religion," said Abu. "They are people of the book. There will simply be a minor tax until they are ready to come into the light of Islam."

"The United Nations is not going to accept that," said one of the generals. "Neither will the African Union, and neither will I! Jesus is my Lord."

Abu didn't respond to the general and turned to face the field marshal general. "And what have the United Nations done for Ethiopia? They allow the whites to farm our lands, the Chinese to take our custom and undercut our trade, the

Russians to extract oil and diamonds, the whole world to steal our coltan. Congo should be the richest country in the world. And what do they do? Arm militias who have no loyalty to Africa. No religion. Who care only about themselves."

The field marshal general looked down at the table before answering. "Even if we agreed to stage the coup, we are already fighting a battle with the Amharic region and the Tigray region. We cannot fight them and the government and the United Nations and the African Union all at the same time."

"The Amhara and the Tigrayans are Christians. They are people of the book. They can be brought into the light of Allah. They just need some persuasion. As for the UN and the AU, they will be overwhelmed by the sheer scale of revolt we have planned. There are eight countries who have agreed to stage coups on the same day. With Ethiopia it would be nine. We will be voiceless no more."

"What your proposing will lead to Ethiopia splitting in two, half Muslim, half Christian. The Christians will never accept Islam."

"Then they must be forced," said Abu. "It will be a just war."

"I don't like it," said a General to his right. "I don't like it at all. I will not sanction dragging Ethiopia into further war. We have suffered enough. What you suggest is beyond insane."

"I agree," said the field marshal general. "We have listened to your proposal, as I said we would. We will not overthrow a government that is working for Christians and Muslims to live in unity. As you said, Christians are people of the book, and they must not be forced to convert."

A flash of anger streaked through Abu's face. He wasn't just failing in his dream for Africa, he was letting his sergeant down. "So, you will play pet to your imperial masters, then?"

The field marshal general slammed his fist on the table. "Watch your tongue! Ethiopia has no master. We were the only country to never be colonised during the scramble for Africa. Even the Europeans understood the strength of our history and heritage. Can the same be said of Nigeria?"

Abu scowled at the man. "I offer you freedom and you choose slavery. You dishonour your people."

"You dishonour us all! We will not take part in your madness. The Americans will get involved if you try to create an Islamic caliphate. Have you seen what has happened to the Middle East? To Syria? To Libya? Is that what you wish for us, to be reduced to rubble, driven further into poverty and destitution?"

"I do not fear the Americans-"

The commander cut him off. "Well, you should. Their military vastly outweighs our own. Do we have nuclear weapons in our arsenal? We cannot win a war with America. And Europe is almost as big a threat. And they will work together. Do what you will in Nigeria, we will have no part in the destruction of Ethiopia."

Abu's eye twitched as he tried to contain his fury. "So be it. But know this, we will win, and you will all be converted to the will of Allah, one way or another."

~ * ~

Abu was silent for almost the entire journey to Somalia. The soldiers with him had stopped trying to engage him in conversation. They knew he had been unsuccessful in his talks with Ethiopia, and they were truly afraid he might kill one of them in a rage.

The Somalian government was headed by the president and the people who worked under him did not hold enough power to stage a coup, so Abu had no choice but to meet with the president and try to convince him to declare his nation as part of the caliphate. Somalia is ninety-nine percent Muslim, so he saw no reason that they would not join in espousing Islamic values in their laws.

The roads in Mogadishu were cracked and filled with potholes. Every few metres the truck would drive over one and everyone in the truck would shake. It was annoying Abu, who tried to regain his composure. It had been nearly two days non-stop driving from Addis Ababa to Mogadishu and the time had done nothing to calm him down. He could not believe that the

Ethiopians would be so weak. They were traitors to their own cause. Marionettes in love with their puppeteers.

Abu stopped at the gates of the Palace of Somalia. A man in military attire came to their window. "What is your business here?"

"My name is Abu Bakr. I have a meeting with the president."

"Just a moment." The officer went back to his station and checked some papers. "OK," he said from his box, and the gates opened to let them through.

Abu drove up the pathway to the palace. "Wait in the truck," he said to his officers as he got out.

A security guard in a black suit greeted him as he walked towards the building. Abu hated seeing western attire in Africa. He saw it as a sign of imperialism, of shame in the African identity.

"Mr Bakr, is it?" said the security guard.

"Commander Bakr," said Abu.

"Right," said the security guard. "Come with me. The president is in a meeting but will meet with you as soon as he's free."

"OK," said Abu.

The security guard led him through the entrance, nodding to the guard who stood by the door as they passed. Inside was a more palatial building than Abu had ever seen. He wondered how the president could live in such riches while his people starved.

They made their way up several flights of stairs and the security guard led Abu into a room with a large, polished wooden table in its centre.

"Wait here, the president will be with you in due course. Would you like a drink while you wait?"

"No," said Abu. "I'm fine."

The security guard closed the door behind him. Abu took a seat on the cushioned wooden chair and looked around the room. The Somalian flag was draped on the wall of the office. He noted they had also used a star in their flag, which he knew represented the five majority ethnic groups of Somalia.

It annoyed him that there was such factionalism within the black community, in Africa as a whole. Didn't they realise they were being attacked as a group? The world did not care if they were Somali or Nigerian or Tigrayan. They were all black, just dirt on the shoes of the white man.

He sat with his arms crossed waiting for the president. Every time he heard voices in the hallway, he would think it was the president.

After more than two hours waiting, the president strolled into the room. "Sorry I'm late," he said. "It's been a busy morning. Can I get you something to drink?"

"I'm fine," said Abu, who was by now quite thirsty. "Thank you for meeting me."

"OK," said the president. He sat down to the side of Abu. "Well, the continent is a buzz with your plans. There are rumours and whispers everywhere. What I want to know is what role you think Somalia has to play in this? We currently have good relations with the United Nations, and we are not looking to join a caliphate."

"Somalia is a Muslim country, is it not?" said Abu.

"It is," said the president.

"And you are a Muslim, are you not?"

"I am."

"Then I do not understand your reservation," said Abu. His eyebrows weighed down heavily on his eyelids. "We simply want to liberate ourselves from the enslavement of those who seek to own us, and to install upon the world the rightful religion, as Allah has willed. Sharia Law must be imposed over all Muslim countries, and eventually the whole world. Mashallah."

The president tapped the table and spoke to Abu as though he was a child. "My reservation is, we may win a war in Africa, but we will not win a war against the West. Have you seen Syria lately? How about Iraq? Afghanistan? Libya? That is what you wish for Somalia?"

"There is strength in numbers," said Abu. "This is about

Africa and African sovereignty. All you need do is declare that you are a Muslim nation and that you accept the coups which are being staged across the continent. We do not expect you to join in the war."

"Just to condone it," said the president, his tone accusatory and dismissive.

"Yes," said Abu.

"And what of all the lives that will be lost in your war? Assuming you are successful, that is. What of them?"

"Their souls will be free for the day of judgement," said Abu. "Their sacrifice will be justified. They will be martyrs, rewarded in heaven. Better to die free than live a slave."

"Slavery ended a long time ago," said the president.

"Did it really?" said Abu. "So, the resources I see extracted from Africa are imaginary? The GDP of our entire continent, some one billion people, has but a trillion dollars, exactly one thousand for each person. Do you know what the GDP of Germany is?"

The president grimaced slightly as he thought about the answer.

"Four and a half trillion US dollars," said Abu, "For a population of eighty-five million. That's fifty-two thousand dollars for every life in Germany. And they will never value our lives here until we have the same monetary value as them. It is all the European, the American, thinks about. It is all they value. Money. That life is not about the pursuit of religious glory, but instead simply to consume. Have you ever heard anything so disgusting? That the purpose of life is to consume."

The president seemed caught off guard. He stroked his lip deep in thought.

"And tell me, what is the GDP per capita of Somalia?"

"Six hundred dollars," said the president, and for the first time Abu heard shame in his voice.

"Six hundred dollars," said Abu. "And that is the value that the West places on you and your people. Will you not rise against them? Will you not seize back control from those who have wrested it from us with their guns, and their bombs and their ideologies? With their racism and slavery and greed."

"And what do you suppose that I do, Commander Bakr. Do you think I can grow GDP on a tree and spread it around the country? We need to export. We need to innovate. We are already in the middle of a civil war. We cannot afford to enter another one."

"I am not asking you to join our war," said Abu, "I am simply asking you to declare yourself an Islamic nation, impose Sharia Law and accept the authority of the armies who take over from the puppet governments. If you will not do this, you are not a true Muslim."

The president looked angry. He opened his mouth to speak.

"There is no place for idleness or cowardice," said Abu. "We want your support, but we will succeed with or without it. I only ask that you support us in our cause for liberation and to spread the word of Allah."

The president sighed. "I cannot promise anything," he said after a long pause. "But I will not speak out against you, that much I can agree to. If the tide starts to turn, and it looks like the army has a strong enough grip on their countries, we may support your claims."

"And will you declare yourself a Muslim nation?"

"We are already a Muslim nation," said the president.

"Then why do you fear stating it?"

The president glowered at Abu. "I fear nothing. As I told you, I do not wish to be dragged into a war with the West. Somalia already lives by the laws of Allah. It is not the government's place to dictate theistic morality to its citizens. That takes away their choice, and without choice there is no test for them. A test that Allah has placed on them, to follow his words."

Abu had to think about that. He'd never considered it from that perspective before. "If we cannot count on you to support us at the start, once we have proved that we have control, will you declare yourself a Muslim nation? That's all I ask. We will do the rest."

The president stared at Abu, his jaw stiff. "*If* you are

successful. If you can prove to me that it is worthwhile for Somalia to join your cause, then I will consider it. That is as much as I can commit to here."

Abu opened his mouth to retort, but the president talked over him. "This meeting is finished. I have important business to attend to. He stood up and walked to the door, opening it for Abu. "My security detail will escort you back to your car."

Abu knew he couldn't press it any further. The president needed to feel like he was in control of the decision. "Thank you for your time," he said with as much genuineness as he could muster. "I hope that Allah guides you to the right path."

EZEKIEL

"I can't believe the world used to have magic in it!" said Ezekiel sat on a chair in the underground lair of Manchester Central Library. "That's mad!"

"I remember Alan was just as shocked when he found out," said Oscor. "It didn't really surprise me. There is little difference between technology and magic. I suppose the main difference is anyone can use technology, whereas magic was gifted to people at birth. Other than that, there's no difference."

Ezekiel tried to get his head around that. A world with technology was basically the same as a world with magic. He supposed it was right. He'd watched films with magic mirrors, that was the same as a video call. He'd seen people throw balls of flames from their hands, now they had bombs that could have destroyed every single person on that battlefield with the press of one button, flown over distances that the sorcerers of Egypt and Sudan could never have managed. He'd read about fortune tellers, he'd even met one, and was that really that far from a software system that can harness the power of the brain to teleport and time travel?

"Could people teleport and time travel in the old world?" said Ezekiel. "Before the Jewish curse that removed magic."

"They could teleport, of a fashion. They could move from

one place to another without travelling the distance. But time travel was beyond their abilities. They could see the future, but not visit it."

"So, Alan created something even more powerful than magic?"

"You might say that. Though we haven't yet worked out how to revive the dead."

"At the rate technology is advancing, I don't think that will be very far off. But hopefully they won't create armies of zombies!"

"I think they're more likely to use armies of robots, which is why it's so imperative that you accept your destiny as the reincarnation of the Buddha. The world will destroy itself if left to its own devices. Have you seen enough to be convinced?"

"I… I don't know. I still don't see why you think this has anything to do with me."

"Because Alan saw you in the future, in the one timeline where the world wasn't destroyed by nuclear weapons. You were chosen, Ezekiel, and you must accept your destiny."

"I don't… It's not that I don't believe you… I just can't imagine myself as a prophet."

"You have much to learn and I have much to train you in," said Oscor. "You will have to give up smoking weed, you will have to give up eating meat and dairy, you will have to learn the ways of the Buddha and the histories of the world, the real history and the false history that was written after the Jews enacted their curse. You will need to learn it all to become the Buddha."

"Give up meat and dairy?" He could just about contemplate giving up weed. The words of his future-self, the tone he'd used, it made him think seriously about quitting. *You've got battles to win and you're not going to win them high* he had said. But giving up meat and dairy? What would he eat?

"Yes, I'm afraid so. The buddha was a vegetarian who only ate meat when it would mean otherwise wasting food. But the treatment of animals has gotten so bad, the factory farming, the horrific conditions they're raised in, veganism is the only answer. And as the reincarnation of the Buddha, it isn't enough to follow his laws, you will have to create morality of your own."

"Create morality! I can barely spell morality. And I can't imagine not eating meat. Everything I eat has meat or dairy in it. Never eating curried goat with rice and peas again? Never having a McDonalds or a KFC? I just don't think I can do it."

"You can do it, you must do it, and you will do it. You need to be a voice for all. Especially those that are voiceless."

"It's just an animal though. What does it matter if it dies?"

"There are two moral issues here to concern yourself with. The first is the life of the animal, yes, whether one can justify taking a life. The second is their treatment."

An image flashed on the screen. It was a pig sat looking depressed in a cage that was around five inches wider than its entire body. "Look at this. Can you imagine living like that? Caged your entire life, never able to even walk or move, never socialising or having the opportunity to mate with a female, fed beyond your natural weight solely to feed a human?"

It looked horrific and Ezekiel couldn't help feeling sorry for it. The first time he'd ever felt compassion for an animal in his life. "That does look bad. That's not in England, surely?"

"No, but you are a prophet of the world. Not just England."

A prophet. He could still scarcely believe it, but after everything he'd seen over the last few days, it was probably the more likely occurrence. "Are you sure it was me that Alan saw in the future? Are you absolutely sure?"

"Yes, I'm sure, Ezekiel. There's no escaping your destiny. You were chosen by God."

"So, if God has chosen me, where does the Buddha fit into all that? Why not Jesus or Mohammad?"

"The Buddha is God's chosen prophet."

"How do you know?"

"I will show you."

Another image appeared on one of the screens. It was a man sat cross-legged by a tree. He looked thin.

"I will take you to see the Buddha in his lifetime, but you

must not interact with anything or make your presence known in any way. Any attempt to change the timeline and I will bring you straight home. Is that understood?"

"I'm not goin' to try to change history!" said Ezekiel.

"Good," said Oscor. "Now look at the picture and imagine yourself there."

Ezekiel imagined himself in the photo. The pulling sensation in his navel was easier to deal with this time and being yanked through spacetime left him less disorientated than it had done the other times.

"Hide behind this tree," said Oscor in his mind.

Ezekiel moved into place behind the tree. He could see a man with a similar colour skin to himself, slightly darker than his own, and long, black hair tied up in a tight bun. He wore orange robes sat with his legs crossed under a tree. As Ezekiel watched, he rose from the ground, levitating above it with his eyes closed.

"Do you see that?" said Oscor. "He is levitating."

"Yes, I noticed that!" said Ezekiel aloud. "Sorry, I forgot," he said in his head.

The Buddha didn't react in any way to Ezekiel's presence, he just sat there meditating above the ground.

"What year is this?"

"600 BC," said Oscor.

"So, after the Jews cast their curse?"

"Yes."

"So how is he using magic?"

"It's the power of God. The Jewish sorcerers were only able to banish magic by channelling the power of God and enshrining it in religion. God allows the Buddha to levitate when he is connected to God's power through meditation."

"So, God is making him float?"

"Yes and no. He is making himself float, and he is using God as a conduit to do it."

"Right," said Ezekiel, whose mind had been so battered over the last few days he had no energy left to disagree, he just accepted what he was being told.

"Now that you have seen what you needed to see, we must leave. We cannot risk changing the timeline."

Ezekiel felt himself yanked through spacetime. Colour returned to the world, and he was back in the lair underneath the library.

"Have you seen enough, Ezekiel? Will you accept your role as the reincarnation of the Buddha? His soul lives within you. You *are* him. The sooner you accept that the more chance we have of saving the world."

"It's hard to believe," said Ezekiel, "but what choice do I have? I can't let the world be destroyed. Especially if I've been picked by God to stop it."

A wide smile appeared on the green face on the screen in front of Ezekiel. "That's exactly what I wanted to hear. There is no time to waste. We must start our training immediately. First port of call – The Tripitaka."

"The what?" said Ezekiel. "It's the Buddhist text. If you are to become who you were born to be, you're going to need to read it, and a lot else besides."

"Right," said Ezekiel. "I'm ready."

"Good. Let us begin."

~ * ~

Ezekiel had spent all day in the library for the last week reading the Tripitaka. He had stayed so late that he'd had to teleport home most nights because the library was closed.

"I can't believe he gave up life as a prince, gave up all his money and possessions just to teach the world a lesson!"

"Yes, he was a truly inspirational prophet."

"I know that's not how reincarnation works, but it would have been nice to have been a prince myself for the start of my life, you know? Not in a council estate in Manchester. It would have made everything I've had to give up so much easier. I keep craving weed. I miss it."

"You've done well! I'm proud of you. It's imperative that you do not smoke. You must follow the four noble truths and the eight-fold path diligently. If you diverge from the path, all will be lost."

"There's so much to learn and change and some of it I'm finding hard getting my head around," said Ezekiel. "I can understand what he meant about desire being the route of all suffering, or at the very least most suffering, it's deffo a bigger route of evil than money like it says in the Bible, but I can't get my head around letting yourself suffer. My mother always said, if someone hits you, hit them back! Not just stand there and let them hit you."

"It's not about allowing other people to cause you pain," said Oscor, "though the Buddha was a pacifist. It's about understanding that birth, ageing, illness, dying, they're all natural parts of life, and one must come to terms with them. And that it is people's desire for things, or to avoid or obtain certain sensations, that cause the most suffering. You must learn to accept the constant desire to gratify every impulse you have as immorality and fight it."

Ezekiel reflected on that. "I guess I have lived constantly thinking about my own desires and not caring what it means for anyone else. When I grew up, I'd only ever seen the fat Buddha. I thought you were meant to rub its belly for luck!"

Oscor laughed. "A sight that would bring a tear to most Buddhists' eyes. Thankfully, that's not really a thing outside of the West."

Ezekiel had only just learnt the concept of 'the West'. It was not a faction group he'd ever learnt about in school or understood the importance of. "I reckon they'd be pretty pissed off if they knew we're taught that here."

"You forget yourself, Ezekiel. You are the Buddha now. What is the third point on the noble-eightfold path?"

Ezekeil thought for a moment and looked down at the ground. "Right speech," he said almost inaudibly. "No lying, no rude speech, no gossiping or idle chatter."

"Exactly. You must work on your speech, as well as your vocabulary."

"It's just habit. I'm used to swearing. Everyone I've ever met does."

"I have faith in you."

"I think that 'right thought' will be the hardest of the paths to follow," said Ezekiel. "I can understand that we should act with morality, I can understand that our actions have consequences. I've never used a knife or a gun, my fists have always been enough whenever I've needed them, so right livelihood shouldn't be an issue, but never thinking a bad thought. That's f… impossible."

"I don't think he truly expected that people would never have a bad thought. Simply that they would try not to and fight it when they did."

"There should be a fifth noble truth. That no person is perfect, and they will never follow the path exactly or perfectly without making a mistake or performing a bad action. It's unthinkable that any person could follow the eight-fold path perfectly without ever straying from the path."

"Perhaps there should be. It's not about being perfect, it's simply about attempting to be. All humans will make mistakes, and I do not believe he would think less of them for doing so, providing they have a good heart, and followed his path to the best of their ability. It is only through trying to achieve perfection that people will understand their flaws and learn to overcome them."

"That makes sense," said Ezekiel. "But there's another major issue I have with what I've read, 'sexual misconduct'. From what I've read he basically wants people to never have sex. I get that you don't force yourself on a girl or hurt them, but there's nothing wrong with sex. I can't accept that. People should be allowed to fu… have sex if they want to."

"I actually agree," said Oscor. "Times were different when the Buddha lived. Sex led to the instant creation of life, which is why he was so strict on it. There is contraception now. You're the reincarnation of the Buddha, which means you get to set new rules. Rules fit for the modern age, in keeping with the Buddha's vision. People will be able to have sex more freely, but they must give up dairy as well as meat. Almost all Buddhists are vegetarian, and it will take some convincing to move them beyond that. You'll have to make them empathise with the animal, like you did, showing them that the conditions they live in today are different from when the Buddha walked the Earth."

Ezekiel inhaled deeply, a guilty look on his face. "I had a KFC," he blurted out. "I could just smell the meat, and it was making me so hungry."

Oscor laughed. "I didn't expect you to give up meat and dairy instantly. It will be a hard path to follow but one that I know you will achieve. You'll have to lead by example."

It still shocked Ezekiel that Oscor was not only able to talk but most importantly think and reason. And the things he said always made so much sense to Ezekiel. He'd learnt so much since he started his lessons with Oscor. He missed his friends, but he couldn't risk seeing them. All they did all day was smoke weed and he wasn't strong enough yet to resist the temptation if he smelt it. "Me? An example for people! That will take some getting used to."

"Think how far you've come in such a short space of time. You're developing better than I could have hoped. I really am proud of you."

It was still weird hearing that from an operating system, but it made him feel special all the same. "Thanks, Oscor. I should get going, it's late, the library is going to close soon."

"I suppose you better had. No meat on your way home though! I think you're pretty much done with the Buddhist text. Next, we move onto more exciting topics. We'll start with philosophy!"

"OK," said Ezekiel, who was not as sure as Oscor that he would find it exciting, but for the first time in his life he was looking forward to learning. He'd enjoyed reading the Buddhist text and if philosophy was even half as interesting as that, then perhaps Oscor was right.

ABU

Abu stood around a table with the other commanders waiting for his sergeant to enter. Abu was surprised, his sergeant had taken the news that Ethiopia declined the offer better than he had expected. Sergeant Abdullah had not expected them to agree it turned out, especially when they were a majority Christian country. He was more disappointed that Somalia had not agreed, but then it had not disagreed. It had simply said it would wait to see what happened and declare itself once it knew it would not face repercussions from the external world.

Sergeant Abdullah walked into the room dressed in his green and brown army attire.

Abu saluted him along with the other commanders.

Sergeant Abdullah saluted back and took his place at the head of the chipped wooden table. "Have a seat," he said.

The commanders seated themselves in the rickety wooden chairs. The sergeant spread a map on the chipped wooden table. "The time is nearing. Within the next days we will come together as one and liberate ourselves from the shackles that have chained our feet for far too long. We will show the world that Africa will no longer be overlooked and underestimated."

"Inshallah!" said several of the commanders.

"We must go over every detail meticulously if we are to

annex the Northeast. Once we have a stronghold there, we can advance towards Abuja and take the capital. From there, we can declare Nigeria a Muslim country."

The commanders banged on the table in agreement.

"You will go to every village and town. Any person found to be practicing ancient religions, be they Yoruba or any other infidel religion will be given the choice to die, or to convert to Islam. The Christians that live there will be taxed, until such time as they see the light and the cause of Allah."

"Mashallah," said Abu. The other generals echoed his call, "Mashallah."

"Commander Ahmed, you will be responsible for bringing Borno to heel," said Sergeant Abdallah, pointing on the map. "Commander Qureshi, you will be responsible for claiming Yobe and Gombe." He pointed again on the map. "Commander Ebrahim, you will be responsible for securing Adamawa." He tapped Adamawa with his index finger. "Commander Bakr, you will take Taraba, and I will secure Bauchi. Is that understood?"

"Yes, Sergeant," said his commanders in unison.

"Commander Ahmed you would be best placed to secure Maiduguri first. Commander Bakr, you will drive south to Jalingo and strike there first. Commander Qureshi, you will hit the centres of Yobe and Gombe first. I will hit Bauchi central first. Set up camps in the centre of each city once it is secured for the prisoners. I will also make a camp at the border of Bauchi and Tabara, once they are both secured, and we will convene there when you have all taken your cities."

"Yes, Sergeant," said the commanders.

"Your first target must be the police stations in each city," said Sergeant Abdullah. "They will be the first line of defence. You will kill any officer you meet, whether they be Muslim or not. They are traitors, and they will defend their state against us no matter their religion. I do not think the army will have time to respond before we act, so we should not face opposition from them. Once you have dealt with the police, you will advance on the government buildings. Ask each of them to name the prophet's mother. Any that cannot do it shall be killed immediately, even the Christians."

Abu lowered his eyebrows, concealing his thoughts from the sergeant. Christians were 'people of the book'. They held a special place in Islam. They were the antecedent to Islam, but their books had been corrupted with falsehoods. It would have been better to tax them, he thought.

"Round up the Muslims and have them swear allegiance the Islamic caliphate of Africa. Kill any who refuse. They are not true Muslims."

"Mashallah," said most of the commanders.

"Mashallah," said Abu in response.

"Commander Ahmed, you will take five thousand men with you. Commander Quereshi, you have eight thousand men at your command. Commander Ebrahim, you will have four thousand. Commander Bakr you will have seven thousand men at your disposal. I will take the rest. There are enough bullets for three hundred per man. We have numerous grenades, bombs and IEDs. You are to crush any resistance you meet. Any person who resists must be killed immediately. There will be no life spared. Is that understood?"

"Yes, Sergeant."

"Good. We begin our insurgency at the break of daylight on Monday. All the other nations that have come to our cause will be staging their coups at the same time. They will not know what has hit them when we are done with them."

"Mashallah," said the commanders.

"Commander Ahmed, once you have secured Maiduguri from there the rest will fall with great ease." He placed six counters on the point of Maiduguri on the map. "Position sixty percent of your forces there and instruct the rest to go first to the police stations and then to the government buildings. Have the rest of your soldiers go from village to village to kill the apostates and take taxes from the Christians. You may take any non-Muslim women as the spoils of war." He placed more counters around the map of Borno, at key locations for the attack.

"Yes, Sergeant."

"Commander Quereshi," said the sergeant. "You will place thirty percent of your forces at Damaturu, and twenty percent at Gombe central." He moved three counters to Damaturu on the map, and two to Gombe central. "They will both strike the police stations at the same time, and then move on to the government buildings. The rest of your men you will spread around the province the same as Commander Ahmed." He placed the remainder of the pile of counters around the two provinces. "These will be the best points of attack. They are where most of the population reside. Kill the apostates and tax the Christians who will not convert. Take what spoils of war you see fit."

"Mashallah," said commander Quereshi.

"Commander Ebrahim, you will station half your forces in Yola." He placed five counters on Yola on the map. "The rest will be spread throughout Adamawa until the whole area is secured." He placed a single counter on each of the key locations around Yola. "The police force there is small, and you should not face much resistance. The government buildings are heavily guarded, and you will need to kill the security guards and agents to get through to the workers. Deal with the apostates and Christians as the Qur'an demands."

"I will not fail you, sir, Inshallah."

"I would place forty percent of my forces in Jalingo capital, with your command," said Abu. "I would place a further ten percent at Ganye, and ten percent at Mutum Mybia. The rest will be sent to the smaller villages in the area."

"That is a good plan," said the sergeant, placing the counters on the locations on the map.

"How many tents do we have available?"

"I can spare five for each of you," said the sergeant. "But I expect few captives. Better to kill than to capture."

"I will set up the main camp near the border for you, if I secure Taraba before you secure Bauchi," said Abu. "We will take the Christian captives there. Not all of them will pay their tax, and some will not have the means."

The Sergeant nodded. "Good plan."

"Mashallah," said Abu. "Mashallah," said all the others, including the Sergeant.

The sergeant placed the last of the counters around Bauchi, with the last on the border between Bauchi and Taraba. "This is where we will meet when we have secured the cities."

"As you command, sir," said Abu.

"Yes, Sergeant," said the other commanders.

"The military leaders in Mali, Burkina Faso and Niger have already overthrown their governments and evicted the invader soldiers from their lands. They have set an example for Africa, that we will no longer live under the rule of foreign nations, who wish to steal our resources and destroy our religion and culture. The military leaders of Sierra Leone, Gambia, Senegal, Chad, Sudan, and Djibouti are all prepared and ready to strike against their governments first thing on Monday morning. You have two days to prepare. We leave at 14:00 hours on Sunday. Everything must be in position for the break of dawn on Monday morning. The Islamic caliphate of Africa will be secured by the end of the day on Monday. The world is finally going to hear Africa roar."

The commanders banged the table in agreement. "MASHALLAH!"

EVE

Eve entered the president's office, her eyes already glistening with tears. She took a seat at the table and smiled weakly at the president.

"Thank you for coming Madam Secretary," said the president.

"I came as soon as I saw your message," said Eve. "I just can't believe he's dead. I saw him only yesterday."

The chief of staff and the national security advisor took their seat. "Mr President."

The president nodded at them as they sat down. "Damn it," said the president. "Why is Julie always late?" He surprised Eve with his tone. He was angrier than she had expected him to be.

"Sorry I'm late," said Julie after around five minutes. "I only just read your email. I came straight away."

"You'd think in matters of national emergencies you might answer your fucking phone. They've been ringing you. Why didn't you answer?"

"I had it on silent," she said, looking down at the table. "I'm sorry, sir."

"You had a phone that must always be kept on for emergencies on silent? God damn it. What the hell are you playing at?"

The colour drained from Julie's face. Her eyes flicked to the table before looking back up at the president. "Sorry, Mister President. It won't happen again."

"You're damn right it won't. Count yourself lucky you still have a job."

She decided it was best to sit in silence rather than apologise again.

Eve smiled to herself internally. That was one person who was definitely not in the running for vice president.

"Now that Julie has checked her emails," said the president, "you're all now aware that the vice president has passed away. It's too early to tell, but the CIA don't think there was any foul play. It seems he had heart failure in his sleep."

Eve breathed a breathless sigh of relief, but there was still the naggin doubt that the autopsy would reveal the poison. "Elijah was a great man and an even better vice president. The country will be worse off without his leadership."

"It's just so sudden and unexpected," said the president of the senate. "I was literally speaking to him a few days ago. He seemed fine." A tear rolled down her cheek.

"That's exactly what I thought," said the president. "The toxicology report has come back, there were no drugs in his system, it doesn't look like an overdose, just a simple twist of fate — and at the worse time. Just as we're implementing some of the boldest regime changes since the Great Depression."

Eve understood the president's emotional state now. He wasn't bothered that Elijah was dead, just that it had come at a time that might be inconvenient for his political career.

"I think this will help with public sympathy," said Julie. "Especially in the African American community. He was highly regarded there."

"I don't think now is the time to be talking about that!" said the chief of staff, opening his arms in exasperation. The brows above his dark eyes pressed down heavily and he scowled at Julie.

Julie looked ashamed of herself. "I'm just saying, it's a terrible loss, but I don't think it will hurt us politically. The electorate will have sympathy."

"I just can't believe he's gone," said Eve. "What are we going to do without him?"

"The ship must stay afloat," said the president. "The American people depend on us to be stable in times of conflict and in grief. We must show a united front, now more than ever. That's why I've called you all here. We need to discuss the response to the press and what actions we're taking going forward. We need to be reading from the same hymn sheet on this one."

"I agree," said the president of the senate. "We've got to be seen to be strong, but at the same time we've got to be seen to be caring."

"I don't think that's going to be difficult," said Eve. "Elijah was an inspirational vice president, and he will be sorely missed. It won't be hard for me to care, that's for sure. And you've always been seen as a strong leader, Mister President, even more so after the bold reforms we've implemented."

The president nodded. "That's the line, yes. He was an inspirational vice president and a beacon for the American dream. We need to be seen to say we value the contributions that he made in his time as vice president and that it will be impossible to find anyone who could replace him."

"Of course, Mr President," said the secretary of defense.

"It wouldn't be untrue to say. We did some great work together. I'll miss him. It's going to take a long time to get my head around not seeing him around the White House anymore."

"Hear, hear!" said the secretary of the treasury.

"I just hope his family is coping OK," said the secretary of defense. "He's just had a newborn in the last few months, hasn't he?"

"Oh yes," said eve, tears filling up in her eyes. "How awful. This really is the worst timing!" She stared down at the table looking contemplative. She wondered if the people sat around her were aware how many children grew up in America without parents. This child still had a mother. And a hefty death in service payment to sustain them.

"Thanks for reminding me," said the president. "I will need to call his wife personally to offer my condolences. No one speaks to the press until I've called her, is that understood?"

"Yes, Mister president," said the staff around the table.

"Good. This is awful timing. But I promise we will go ahead with your proposals Eve. He told me he personally believed in them, and I owe it to him to see them through."

Eve smiled through a veil of fake tears. "That's a wonderful idea. I'm sure he'll be looking down on us and smiling. He knew we had to take action. He told me personally that he hated debt and wanted to see America with a debt level of twenty five percent by the end of the century. You will be guided by his hand in this decision."

"May God rest his soul," said the president. "He was a good man. I'm sure he will be rewarded in kind."

"Do you think we should have a National Day of Mourning?" said Eve. "I know it's normally reserved for the head of state, but I think it will be well received."

"That's a great idea," said the leader of the senate.

There were nods all around the room.

"That is a good idea," said the president. "I like it."

"I'm happy to help in any way I can with the plans," said Eve. "If there are any tasks that I can take on until we find a new vice president, please let me know. I've got the capacity."

That sentiment was echoed around the table.

The president nodded in deep thought. "We can't function without a vice president, and the vultures have already started swarming. How would you feel about taking over the role of vice president, Madam Secretary? It would mean having to give up your current position."

Eve opened her eyes wide to show surprise. "I'd be honoured, sir. But who will take over from me?"

"I'd be happy to fill in," said the secretary of the treasury.

"That's a good move," said the president. "It will be a lot easier to find a new secretary of the treasury than it would have been to find a candidate for the vice president or secretary of state. Does anyone have any objections? Anything they'd like to add?"

"I think they're both up to the task of vice president and secretary of state," said the secretary of defense.

The sentiment was echoed around the room.

"I'm happy in my role, sir,' said a mixed raced man with spiralling curly hair, "but I have a master's degree in finance. I could fill in as secretary of the treasury until a new one is found."

The president let out a long breath. "Yes, that will do nicely. The ship must stay afloat. You're a good team. We will get through this together. I need to confirm with the family, but I want him to have a full state funeral, and you must all be in attendance."

"Of course," said Eve. "Assuming his family doesn't want a private affair."

"He deserves a full send off," said the president. "I'm sure they will agree."

"Please pass on my condolences to the family," said Eve, dabbing at her eyes with a tissue.

"Yes, give them my regards," said the secretary of defense.

Everyone offered their sympathies to Elijah's family.

"Of course," said the president. "I can't imagine what they're going through."

"The African American community is strong," said the mixed raced man. "They will heal. We're used to dealing with adversity and tragedy."

The president nodded in approval. "I hope you're right. It will still be a blow though, to any family. He was a great addition to the team, and an example for the nation that the Republican Party is not racist and African Americans can achieve any office they wish to hold if they put in the hard work that is needed to get there."

"It would be a good idea to hire an African American secretary of the treasury," said Eve. "I'm not sure we've ever had one. Not even the Democrats."

"No, we haven't, the Democrats had a deputy secretary if I

recall correctly. But we've never had an African American in that role."

"It's good that something positive can come from something so tragic," said Julie, who seemed eager to show her empathy on this issue.

"He'd like that, I'm sure," said Eve.

"Then it's decided. Everyone knows their new roles. No one speaks to the press until I've given the go ahead. I will email you all to let you know and will schedule a meeting with those of you who have moved roles. We will go over the finer details of the roles before announcing the change. I think a grace period of a few days would be well received in the circumstances."

"I agree," said Eve.

"Perfect," said the president. "And if any of you need any support remember that there are mental health services available through work. If any of you need any time off to deal with the death, just let me know and I'll sign off on it."

"Thank you," said Julie.

"Yes, Mr President," said Eve.

"You're all dismissed," said the president.

Eve stood up and wiped a tear from her eyes. She held her smile in the whole way back to her office. She was brimming with excitement. She had done it. She had attained the role of vice president. She was one step away from achieving her dream of becoming the first female President of the United States of America.

She thought of Elijah. There was a nagging fear in the pit of her stomach that they'd do further tests and find out there was a poisoning involved. She tried to tell herself she was being paranoid. She hadn't lied when she said she would miss Elijah. She would miss him. And not just for the great sex. But he was an obstacle in her path to success and Eve did not tolerate obstacles. It was a means to an end. He had served his purpose, and the time had come for him to step aside and let her shine.

She opened her draw and took out her second phone. She connected to a VPN and opened the Tor browser so she could access her dark web email. As promised, Elijah had sent her the documents that would bury the president. He had gifted her everything she'd ever wanted in a single email, and it was almost enough to make her feel guilty. She could taste the role of president on her poisonous lips. It was just a matter of deciding when and how to publish them.

ABU

"Today we liberate Nigeria," said Abu, pacing forwards and backwards along the legion of soldiers who were lined up to attention, a rifle in each of their hands held upwards, diagonally to their bodies. "Today we follow the path that Allah has laid before us, to spread his message, that there is one God and Mohammad was his prophet."

"Allahu Akbar!" cried the soldiers.

"For too long we have remained meek in the face of our enemies," said Abu. "We have shown acquiescence when we should have fought, we have submitted when we should have claimed victory, we have cowered in the shadows like scared dogs – well no longer!"

"Allahu Akbar!" cried the soldiers.

"Today we set Nigeria free!" Abu walked to the furthest column of soldiers and faced them. "Battalion A, you will go to the National Civil Service Union and attack when you receive my command. Round up all the staff. Ask them the name of the prophet's mother. Any who cannot answer must be killed. All the Muslims are to be captured. Take them to the Yakubu mosque and await further instructions."

The soldiers saluted him. "Yes, Commander."

Abu walked along to the next column of soldiers, who were

larger in mass than the first. "Battalion B. You will go to the Corporate Affairs Commission and the National Orientation Office. Kill the infidels and take the Muslims as prisoners to the mosque."

"Yes, Commander," said the soldiers, saluting.

He walked ahead to the next column of soldiers and faced them with a stern face. "Battalion C, you will hit the Taraba State Office and the High Court of Justice once you have my order to engage. The same rules apply. Anyone who cannot tell you the full name of the prophet's mother must be killed. Take those who can answer to the Mosque with the others."

"Mashallah!" cried the soldiers.

"Battalions D, E and F, you will go from village to village and secure them for us. Kill the apostates and anyone who resists you. Radio through to me when you have secured the areas."

"Yes, Commander Bakr!"

"Battalion G," said Abu, turning to face the final column of soldiers. "You will be with me. First, we strike the State Security Service. Every man and woman there will be slain. Next, we will attack the police stations. You will split in three as planned, and they will be struck at the same time. Again, every man and woman there will be slain. There will be no prisoners."

The soldiers saluted him. "Allahu Akbar!"

"Lieutenants of battalions A, B and C, you will radio through when you have secured the buildings and taken the hostages to the mosque. We will convene there. Lieutenants of battalion D, E and F, radio through to me when you have secured the villages and bring any prisoners to the mosque or one of the camps."

"Yes, Commander!"

"To liberty!" cried Abu. "Let the war begin."

The soldiers whooped and cries of "Mashallah" and "Allahu Akbar" could be heard throughout the mass of soldiers.

The Lieutenants from each Battalion led their soldiers to the waiting trucks and departed.

Abu commanded his soldiers to organise themselves and

they followed him in his armoured trucks to the State Security Service offices.

Abu felt nothing but adrenaline as he drove down the streets of Jalingo. He had prayed last night, as he does every night, and he had heard Allah telling him that they would be victorious today. That Northeast Nigeria would become part of the Islamic caliphate. He had no fear of defeat.

They arrived at the State Security Service office. Abu marshalled his troops and directed them to surround the building at all sides. To his lieutenants he shouted, "Launch the grenades, in 3…2…1… LAUNCH!"

Abu pulled the ring from his grenade and threw it at the building. Several other soldiers threw their grenades as well.

The sound of explosions, crumbling brick and screaming people filled the air. "Attack now!" cried Abu. He ran through the gates of the compound and his soldiers followed him, cries of war emitting from their throats.

People had already begun running out of the building. Abu held the front of his gun with his three-fingered hand and used his right hand to pull the trigger. People dropped to the floor like droplets of rain, their blood washing over the hard concrete.

More people poured out of the door. Some turned to run back inside when they saw what awaited them outside. Abu shot three of them in the back as they fled. He smiled as they fell to the floor.

"Secure the building!" cried Abu. He could hardly be heard over the sounds of the battle.

Soldiers repeated his command through the cacophony. Soldiers filed into the buildings from all over the battlefield.

A battalion of armed State Security Service agents rounded on Abu and his men from the back of the building. They opened fire on his men. Abu watched with growing rage as his men started to fall around him. He screamed, raising his rifle and shooting every enemy he could see.

Bullets soared back and forth between the two groups. Abu advanced forward, not caring about the bullets flying all around him. He took aim at one of the security agents and shot him directly in the head.

Diving on the floor, he rolled on his side to avoid a bullet that had been less than a few inches from his face. He heard it hit the wall behind him. He got back to his feet and fired on the security agents, hitting two of them. One in the chest, the other in the face.

The SSS agents were outnumbered. For every one of Abu's soldiers that fell, three of their men had fallen.

The last resistance from the SSS poured out from a side door. A grenade landed near Abu's feet, and he ran as fast as his legs would carry him in the opposite direction. The remnants of the explosion sent him flying through the air and into the ground.

His arms and legs were grazed but he didn't feel it. He pressed his hands to the ground and got to his feet, readjusting his rifle, ready to fire.

The SSS were down to about twenty men. He had at least one hundred men with him still standing.

He aimed his gun at one of the agents and shot him in the belly. He keeled over in pain, screaming.

More of Abu's soldiers ran forward and finished off the last of the SSS officers. Abu smiled as the last of them fell to the ground. He called out to his remaining soldiers. "Check the fallen and make sure they are dead."

The soldiers went through the pile of bodies stabbing them several times and moving on to the next, ensuring that there was not a single survivor.

A soldier came running out of the open door. Abu immediately raised his gun before seeing the uniform and face of one of his soldiers. "We have secured the building, Commander."

Abu smiled with more joy than he'd ever felt. "Excellent. Gather the troops in the courtyard."

He walked through the building checking each room and every crevice to make sure that not one person remained alive. Once he was satisfied that they'd claimed victory, he met his soldiers outside the former State Security Service.

"To the police stations!" he cried.

"Allahu Akbar!" cried the soldiers.

Abu got in his truck and drove at the head of the militia to the police station. His hands and clothes were covered in blood, but he didn't stop to even wipe his hands. He could think of nothing but securing the police stations and achieving victory. The rest of Battalion G radioed through to say they were at the police stations. Abu ordered them to attack.

There was a line of policemen stood with shields raised when Abu and his men disembarked at the police station. Someone from the State Security Service must have tipped them off.

"Surround the building," shouted Abu to the soldiers that had stayed with him.

The soldiers filed around the building.

"Launch grenades in 3…2…1…LAUNCH!" Abu pulled the ring from his grenade and lobbed it over the walls of the police station.

The welcomed sounds of explosion marked their cue to enter. The soldiers poured into the police compound firing at the line of police who stood in front of the building.

Snipers shot at Abu's soldiers from the windows of the police station.

Abu aimed his gun and shot. It was out of bullets. He cried out in fury and searched his pockets for more bullets, hoping the momentary loss of attention wouldn't lead to his death. Raising his loaded gun, he took aim at the snipers in the window who were doing the most damage.

His soldiers had made short work of the police that had formed a barrier in front of the building. Abu thought they had won, but more police poured out of the building, shooting his men as soon as they left the doors of the building.

Men all around Abu started to scream and cry out in pain as they were shot.

Not many had been shot in the head, Abu observed as he looked around him. There would be survivors for sure.

"Finish them!" cried Abu.

His soldiers went into a frenzy, some of them running forwards towards the police, firing their shot, knowing that they would kill whomever they reached but would die in the process. They didn't seem to care about death. Only killing.

The police had put up less resistance than the State Security Service, and with another forty of his soldiers lost to the cause of Allah, Abu had secured the station.

"Victory is ours!" cried Abu.

"Allahu Akbar! Allahu Akbar! Allahu Akbar!"

Abu returned to his truck and radioed through to the other Battalions. Battalion G radioed through telling him they'd secured the police stations. He smiled to himself and commanded his other forces. "Strike the government buildings now! The SSS and police have fallen."

The lieutenants radioed through to say they were in position and would launch the attacks.

Abu returned to the police station and rounded up his soldiers, telling them to carry any of the wounded back to the trucks and attend to them as best they could. The dead he told to leave where they were.

Abu radioed to his soldiers in battalions D, E and F. Battalions D and F radioed back to say they had secured their villages and sent a convoy of prisoners to the camps they had set up. Battalion E had secured most of the villages but had met more resistance than expected. They said they expected to secure the last of the villages within the next two hours.

"Report your status battalions A, B and C," said Abu through his radio.

There was no response.

He waited with growing impatience for them to radio through with their progress. He was starting to wonder if they had fallen into trouble.

He waited another fifteen minutes and radioed through to his lieutenants from battalion A, B and C. Battalion A and C had secured their buildings and were heading to the mosque. Battalion B had not responded.

Abu marshalled his troops and sped to the National Orientation Office, his troops following in his stead. There were dead bodies littering the floor upon his arrival but no sign of the living. He got back in his truck and drove to the Corporate Affairs Commission. His troops were in a standoff with armed men. The police had gathered here, too, to protect the government office. That must have been why they had taken the police stations so easily. He had not anticipated much armed resistance from the Corporate Affairs Commission. He'd assumed it would fall easily.

"Attack!" cried Abu.

His soldiers rushed into the courtyard and Abu followed them, shooting wildly at the officers. A bullet grazed his right arm. He felt the wound with his left hand. It was shallow. He carried on as though nothing had happened, firing on the officers. He remembered the grenade around his waist. He pulled the ring and threw it into the crowd of police officers.

Limbs and bodies erupted into the air, including several of his own soldiers.

There was a war cry from his soldiers, and they surged forward, killing every police officer they saw.

"Sweep the building," said Abu. "Kill the infidels and take the Muslims captive."

His officers scoured the building for people, killing anyone who couldn't name the prophet's mother.

A group of around fifty men and women exited the building at gunpoint looking terrified.

Abu nodded to himself. He was proud. They'd secured the key locations of Jalingo, and the rest of Taraba would fall within the hour. "Take the prisoners to the Mosque."

The soldiers poked the prisoners in the back with their guns and led them to the trucks.

Abu drove ahead of them to the Mosque where they convened with the other battalions. The mosque was rammed with around three hundred government officials. He stood at the centre and called for the room to be silent.

The hall quieted with an eery silence.

"Today we have liberated you from the state of your own enslavement. You have been spared because you are Muslims. Each of you must now swear your allegiance to the Islamic caliphate of Africa. Anyone who refuses will be killed. Line them up!"

His soldiers rounded on the captives, ushering them into a line.

Abu walked to a shaking woman at the front of the queue. She wouldn't meet his eyes. "Place your hand on the Qur'an" he said. The woman shook as she placed her hand on the book. "Pledge your allegiance to the Islamic State of Northeast Nigeria and to the Islamic caliphate of Africa."

The woman did as she was commanded.

Abu nodded and told the woman to sit at the back of the prayer room.

He went through the line, having each of them swear their allegiance to the Islamic caliphate of Africa.

"Murderer!" one man screamed and spat in Abu's face. He shot him square in the head and stamped on his face once he had fallen, spitting on him as he lay dead on the ground.

No one else was stupid enough to protest after seeing that. Everyone swore their allegiance to the caliphate.

He got word from the last of his battalions that they'd secured the smaller villages and town with minimal casualties. He told them to send a small group of soldiers with captives and set up a camp at the border of Bauchi and Taraba. He told the rest to remain stationed at the villages to maintain their presence and report any protest that arose.

Abu called Sergeant Abdullah and updated him on the current situation. He was in a similar position having secured nearly all of Bauchi. He told Abu to leave most of his forces where they were and take a small unit with him to the border of Jalingo and Bauchi. Abu told him he would go with the soldiers to the camp to help finish setting it up for his arrival.

Abu rounded up around one hundred soldiers and made his way to the border between the two provinces. He prayed in his head as he drove, for Maghrib, and he heard Allah telling him that he was proud of what he'd accomplished this day. Allah had promised him victory and he had kept his word.

They arrived at the border of Bauchi to the makeshift camp in mid-construction. Soldiers could be seen setting up more tents as Abu drove into the camp. He looked for Sergeant Abdullah's truck, but it was nowhere to be seen. Abu radioed through to him.

"We met some unexpected resistance," said Sergeant Abdullah. "They have been subdued. The camp is about twenty kilometres from our location. We will meet you there."

Abu entered the tents and looked over the captives. There were many women who were unveiled there. They must have been Christians. He perused the line of women, the spoils of war, and stopped on a woman he found to be comely. "Come with me," he said to her.

She looked up at him with hatred burning in her eyes. "I'm not going anywhere with you, you animal!"

Abu slapped her across the face with the back of his right hand. "Know your place, infidel."

"Mohammad is no prophet of mine!" she screamed.

Abu punched her square in the face, silencing her. "Mohammad is the final prophet of Allah!" he said. He grabbed her by the arm and dragged her out of the tent.

He dragged her along by the arm until they were out of view of the main parade of tents and led her into a small tent that had been set up solely for him. He threw her to the ground and ripped off her top.

"Stop, please!" she cried, her arms flailing around as he tore at her clothes.

He punched her again in the face. He heard her nose break. She stopped resisting but cried and wailed in pain.

He removed the rest of her clothes and opened her legs, ignoring her cries and inserted himself inside her.

She closed her eyes as he started to thrust, praying in her head for God to kill her. She could smell the disgusting stench of his sweaty body pressing against her own.

She tried to wipe the blood gushing out of her nose. Abu

held her arm down with his good hand.

"You are a filthy Infidel," he said. "You are getting what you deserve."

She cried, the tears mingling with the blood on her face.

Still, he pounded, harder and harder. She cried out in pain begging him to stop as the pain got too much to bear.

"Silence, infidel," said Abu calmly, releasing her hand to slap her in the face.

She could feel the warmth of his rancid breath on her tear-soaked, bloodied face. Hear his heavy breathing as he heaved up and down.

Please, God, kill me, she prayed.

She closed her eyes. The seconds felt like hours, the minutes like years. All she could think of was dying. She wanted God to end her suffering and end her life.

He collapsed into her as he finished. He extracted himself from inside her and threw her clothes at her and told her to cover up. She shook as she tried to pull her torn top over her head. She pushed her head through, pulled on her pants and sat with her arms clung to her sides.

Abu zipped up his pants and buttoned them shut. He felt nothing as he walked away. She was the spoils of war, an infidel, and Allah gave her no protection in war. He strode through the camp feeling energised and still with a taste for combat.

Sergeant Abdullah had arrived when he got back to the centre of the camp. "We have secured the Northeast," he said. "Everything has gone just as Allah willed."

"Allahu Akbar!" said Abu.

"Allahu Akbar!" said Sergeant Abdullah.

They walked outside the tent to meet the other commanders.

A bullet soared past Abu's head. He instinctively dropped to the ground. He had left his gun inside. He slid on the ground like a snake to the inside of the tent to grab his weapon.

He heard more gunfire and cries from outside the camp. He rushed out of the camp with his weapon, searching for the source of gunfire. A small group of men sat on the top of a hill firing down at them.

He managed to hit two of them directly in the head.

More soldiers came rushing out of the tents and finished off the last bit of resistance Northeast Nigeria could muster.

"Allahu Akbar!" cried the soldiers, once the bullets had stopped flying in their direction.

Abu echoed the call and turned to see if they'd taken any casualties. Sergeant Abdullah was lying on the ground, clutching his chest, covered in blood. Abu ran over to him. "Sergeant Abdullah!" He cradled him in his arms, screaming for help. The blood soaked through his clothes, but he couldn't feel it.

"HELP!" cried Abu again. He pulled Sergeant Abdullah closer, pressing down on his wounds with his soaked hands. "It will be ok," he said, through staggered breaths. "You will make it through this." Tears streamed from his eyes and merged with the pools of blood forming around him.

Someone came running over with cloths and Abu tore it from his arms, tying the first rag around Sergeant Abdullah's chest. "You're going to be OK. You just need to hold on!"

Sergeant Abdullahs eyes slowly closed. Abu shook him. "You have to stay awake! Keep your eyes open!"

Sergeant Abdullah looked up at Abu and he was sure that he saw a smile curve on his lips.

"We won, the caliphate is secured," said Sergeant Abdullah, closing his eyes, his body going limp in Abu's arms. "And at last, I get to meet Allah."

EZEKIEL

Ezekiel sat on the bus on the way to the library. His feet rested on the floor, no longer dirtying the seat for the next user. He still sat upstairs at the back, but then old habits do die hard.

It had been a month since he'd travelled back in time and seen magic in the world. He'd gone to the library every day since. For the first time in his life, he didn't feel like smoking. He had a purpose. A reason for being. Something to fight for. And though he'd felt foolish meditating at first, he now looked forward to waking up in the morning for his morning meditation, rather than his morning spliff. It helped with his cravings those first two weeks he had withdrawal symptoms, which were, he felt, the hardest two weeks of his life so far.

He was, however, struggling with veganism. Everywhere he looked there was an advertisement for food that he loved. Everything he found to eat contained milk or eggs. Even crisps. Who would put milk in crisps? Just why?

He went past McDonalds on the bus and all he could think about was a Big Mac. He'd been in there to buy fries, and they were nice, but it just wasn't the same without a burger, and he couldn't eat chips for his whole life.

He felt like a dickhead walking around the supermarket looking at the vegan section. He had to admit, the UK really had adapted well to the vegan market. Their dairy was on point. It tasted almost as good as the real stuff. If he'd never had real yoghurt or ice cream, he would not take any issue with the alternative. And he couldn't tell the difference between margarine even having tasted the original. It was just the meat that bothered him. There just wasn't a good meat substitute on the market anywhere.

Oscor had told him that McDonalds does the McVegan, and he had tried it, but much preferred ordering two large fries than the horrid taste of fake meat.

He had teleported to the library most days, but today he caught the bus. Every time his brain was used for teleportation or time travel, it weakened him temporarily. He'd done it so much recently; he needed a break. And this was a weekday so the library would be open late, and he could study all day.

He had learnt all there was to learn about the Buddha and Buddhism in general. He had genuine respect for the Buddha, especially what he'd tried to do to end the caste system in India, something he wasn't even aware was a thing. The Buddha was a great human being, and he was honoured to stand in his shadow.

They'd moved onto philosophy next, and Ezekiel really loved philosophising about life. He especially loved metaphysics and ethics. He'd struggled with logic and deductive reasoning at first, but he'd eventually got the hang of it, and it made learning the rest of the syllabus much easier once he had. They'd moved onto history next, and for the first time in his life Ezekiel found himself enjoying learning history. Partly because he knew everything before 1300 BC was a false history, and that although most of the dates matched, they omitted the key fact that most of the wars between the first civilisations were fought with magic and armies of the dead; and partly because he'd only ever been taught British history and not world history. It had never even occurred to him that each country had their own history, and that it intertwined with the rest of the world.

He was also shocked and proud to learn that many black

African nations had been great civilisations in the old world. They had been respected and revered. He had only ever been taught about slavery and thought of all black Africans as coming from tribes. He had never been taught about the civilisations. He had never heard of the Kingdom of Kush or Abyssinia. All he had known is that his people were once enslaved. It gave him a sense of pride in his race he'd never had before, and for the first time in his life he realised that while he was of Caribbean descent, he was also of African descent. That is where they were shipped from to the Caribbean, after all.

He picked up a newspaper and actually read the stories it contained rather than just scanning the pictures. He had come to care about what was going on in the world and the wars and issues that were taking place within it. There always seemed to be some new war taking place, and it scared him, that the future he'd seen would come true.

He carried on flipping through the pages. Something caught his attention. There had been several coups in Africa. It looked like a coordinated effort. They had annexed part of Nigeria and declared the states an Islamic caliphate of Africa in most of the Muslim countries.

His throat tightened and he rested his head against the back of the bus. An Islamic caliphate? How exactly was he going to convince all these different factions to move to Buddhism? If only they understood, they were dooming the world to nuclear annihilation. Having read the Tripitaka, he couldn't understand how anyone could find anything in there that they disagreed with. Except maybe sex, but even Oscor had agreed, that was representative of the time that the Buddha had lived, and as the new Buddha, he would be able to change some aspects that were no longer fit for the modern day.

Having read Buddhism, which he considered to be the aspiration for complete moral perfection, he was somewhat surprised there were any other religions. He wished he could teleport the whole world, go back in time and show the whole world that the Buddha could float as he meditated, that God had imbued the Buddha with magical powers to prove he was his chosen prophet. It could end so many wars. He feared his words alone would not be enough to convince people. They would have a hard enough time convincing themselves that magic ever existed, let alone they could be worshipping the wrong prophet or God.

He put the newspaper down. He didn't want to read anymore negativity. He thought about all the lives that would have been lost in the coup. He felt for the first time in his life not only a deep compassion for those who lost their life to war, but also a responsibility. It was his destiny to end the wars, and he was more determined than ever after seeing that press release.

He got off the bus two stops before Piccadilly Gardens. His friends had been contacting him non-stop. He told them he had stuff to deal with, that he was ill, that his mother was sick, anything really to get them off his back. He'd muted the group chat. It was strange, seeing them just talking about smoking weed and fucking girls. He felt like it was a lifetime ago he'd been selling weed in Piccadilly Gardens every day and smoking weed all day. But it had been little over a month and so much had changed. Even the words he used and his writing was changing. Oscor had insisted that he learn to write properly and implored him to stop referring to himself as "man" in the third person. *You can't possibly be that insecure and in need of validation of your masculinity that you refer to yourself as man at every given opportunity* it had said. It made Ezekiel laugh. He'd never really thought about it. It was just something everyone said, and he'd picked it up as a teenager. He'd also stopped cursing gay people. He'd always just found it weird and wrong, but after meeting Oscor, knowing it was Alan Turing who created it, a gay man: his decision not to use it as a weapon of war, instead trying to save the world instead of rule it, it gave him a newfound respect for them. And as Oscor explained to him, it's as involuntary for them as his attraction to women is for him.

He arrived at the library and made his way to the lair, loitering around on the top floor until there was no one looking and he could enter through the secret passageway.

"Good morning, Ezekiel," said Oscor as he arrived. "I see you took the long route here."

"Yes," said Ezekiel. "My mind is fried from all the learning, never mind the teleporting. What are we learning today?"

"You've learnt everything there is to know about the old world and the fake histories of the ancient world. Now it's time we moved on to modern history, or at least, the last two thousand years."

"Oh, that shouldn't take long," said Ezekiel, his sentence soaked in sarcasm.

"You're coming along nicely. I think you could cover all the basics in a matter of weeks. From there we will move onto politics. Then economics."

"I hated math at school. I'm not sure I'll be able to grasp economics."

"Have faith in yourself," said Oscor. "If I'd asked you to tell me facts about the ancient world two months ago, would you have been able to?"

"No," admitted Ezekiel, a smile escaping from his cheeks.

"And would you ever have imagined you'd have gone a whole month without smoking weed? Or selling it, for that matter?"

"No, I would have said you're crazy."

"Exactly."

"Fair enough," said Ezekiel.

"How is the veganism coming along?"

Ezekiel looked at the ground. "I've been trying really hard, but I've slipped up a few times. And I'm constantly craving meat. Especially when I get home and smell my mum's cooking."

"There's a really trendy vegan Caribbean place in the centre of town. You should try it. Their vegetable patties are a big seller. You do know that the vegetable patties in Asda are also Vegan?"

"No way," said Ezekiel. "Ahh, patties! I've missed them. I could live off them. Thanks for telling me."

"You should research Indian cuisine. There are lots of

vegetarian meals which can be converted into vegan meals with a few substitutes. Vegan butter and vegan milk mainly."

He'd always preferred Jamaican food to Indian cuisine, but he didn't dislike it. "I'll look into it, yeah. So, which country are we starting with today?"

"We'll start with 100 BC and work our way forward through time, rather than place."

"Sounds good," said Ezekiel. He picked up one of the books that Oscor had laid out for him, sat on the beanbag in the corner and started reading.

~ * ~

Autumn had turned to winter and Ezekiel had finished nearly all of Oscor's lessons. He'd really enjoyed philosophy and wished that they'd taught it in secondary school. He still found politics boring, but he knew it was important to learn, so he'd given it his full attention. Political philosophy was really interesting, but then he found all philosophy interesting.

Economics had proved more difficult than Oscor expected, but less difficult than Ezekiel had expected. One thing that messed his head up was that each country had a different currency that fluctuated in value every second and caused inflation all over the world. He wondered what it would take for the world to move to a single global currency. He also couldn't believe that banks only held enough money in liquid assets to cover one month of demand. He never knew that he could deposit money, and that they would lend it out to other people without telling him. It was all one big house of cards, and he wondered how it had stayed aloft so long without falling down.

They'd had a bit of a stumble with the financial crisis of 2008, something he'd taken no interest in at the time, but that was just the tip of the iceberg of what was possible if everyone who was owed money or deposited money called in their debts or came to withdraw their savings.

Oscar had been surprised and impressed by his observations. It had of course noted it before itself, but it was impressed with how Ezekiel was developing and learning to think with an enquiring mind.

Ezekiel lay on the beanbag in the lair under the library relaxing and reflecting on everything he'd been through and learned in the past few months. It was too fantastical to be believed, but he knew now that he was seeing and doing all this because he was God's chosen prophet. He was just about coming to terms with that reality, though it still felt somewhat like a distant dream that he was yet to wake up from.

The words the medium in Egypt had spoken to him played on his mind a lot. He wondered what it all meant. It was very cryptic. He'd stewed over it from time to time whenever he'd had a moment free, which was quite rare as he spent almost all his time at the lair studying.

"You should go and see your mother," said Oscor. "She'll be wondering where you are."

Ezekiel checked his watch. It was eleven in the evening. "Gosh, is it that time already? I suppose I better had."

He stood up and pictured the ginnel at the side of his house and Oscor transported him there.

He opened the gate to the ginnel, closed it behind him and walked the path to the door. He patted down his pockets until he found which of them contained the keys and unlocked the front door.

"Ezekiel is that you?" said his mother.

"Yes, Mum," he said, taking off his shoes.

"I was beginning to wonder where you had gotten to," said his mother as he walked into the kitchen and sat down. "You know I don't like you out past eleven on a weekday."

"Sorry, I was out with Jermain and them lot. I lost track of time."

"Hmmm," said his mother pursing her lips. "Always with Jermain. Up to no good I imagine." She shook her head. "It's better I don't know… I've cooked your favourite, there's some curried goat on the stove."

He inhaled the smell of the goat. His stomach grumbled. He wanted so badly to eat it. But whenever he'd slipped up and eaten meat, it had made him feel guilty. He could taste the suffering of the animal on his tongue. "I've already eaten when I was out," he said, though he could have easily devoured the whole pot. Explaining to his mother that he was vegan now would be harder than telling her he could time travel, teleport and was God's chosen prophet. It was easier to just lie.

"Well, it will be fine to eat tomorrow. Make sure you have some. I'm working from eight to eight, so I won't be here when you get home."

"OK, thanks," he said.

"You seem different," said his mother, probing him with her eyes, her head tilted to the side. "Is there something wrong?"

Ezekiel sighed. "No, there's nothing wrong. I'm just… growing up, I guess. Seeing the world for what it is, not what I thought it was."

Elizabeth raised her eyebrows and looked at her son in a way she never had. "Is that so? You're a big man now, is it? My little boy is growing up."

Ezekiel smiled at her. He wished he could tell her everything that had happened to him in the last months, but she'd never understand, and he'd never be able to tell her he saw her grave and knew what day she would die on. Or rather, what day she would have died on, if he hadn't chosen the path. Though there was the matter of China. He didn't know for sure what his future-self had meant by it, but at some point he was going to tell the world he was a prophet and he assumed China had to be the first to accept him. He'd been so consumed with learning and changing his ways he hadn't thought much about how exactly he was going to convince eight billion people that he was their only chance at survival.

"It had to happen sometime," he said, with a cheeky grin.

"I was beginning to worry if I'm being honest," said Elizabeth. "You went through a lot with your dad. You've had some rough times, and you've made some bad decisions, but I'm proud to call you my son. And it looks like you're starting to mature as an adult. It's nice to see."

"Thanks," said Ezekiel. In truth, Ezekiel had forgotten that his dad even existed. He had beaten his mother senseless for years, and when Ezekiel was eight, he'd come down the stairs after hearing his mother screaming. He'd tried to intervene, and his own dad had broken his ribs for getting in the way. They split up after that and Ezekiel never spoke to him again. He was given seven years and six months in prison, but only served half for good behaviour.

For the first time, thinking about it didn't hurt him. He didn't care what his dad had done. He felt sorry for him. His soul would be recycled thousands of times before he ever got to be a human again. He'd be eaten alive as a bug, boiled alive as a lobster, he'd live in constant fear of being eaten or killed, over and over, until his karma was paid off. Ezekiel knew he deserved it, but it was a fate he wouldn't wish on anyone.

"I'm exhausted, mum," he said. "I think I'm gonna head to bed."

"I will finish the dishes and join you."

"Do you want me to do them?"

"Oh my God," said his mum, her eyes exploding out of her face with a smile so bright that it would have lit up an entire football field. "You really are growing up! No, don't worry about it. I'll do them. Get some rest. Goodnight, son. I love you."

"Goodnight mum. I love you, too," he said, for the first time in years. He hugged her and gave her a kiss on the forehead then headed upstairs to bed.

PARVATI

Parvati crushed some garlic with a knife and added it to the pan with some onions and spices. She stirred the contents, makings sure the okra and other vegetables were evenly covered in spices.

She opened the fridge and grabbed some cream, adding it to the mixture. She stirred it again, added some potatoes and topped it up with a splash of water. She placed the lid at a slight angle over the pot and left the vegetables to stew.

Cooking had always come naturally to her, but she had improved her skills over the last few months. It was such a luxury to have so much space and so many dishes, pans, pots and utensils. She was so used to cooking over a single gas fuelled stove in the corner of the room her family lived in, she still hadn't fully adjusted to the sheer amount of space she had to prepare and cook food.

"That smells delicious," said Bhavesh, who had stood behind her and wrapped his arms around her waist.

Parvati smiled. "It should be ready in about an hour."

"That gives us some time to have some fun then," said Bhavesh.

"I still need to cook the rice," said Parvati. "You will have to wait." She turned around and kissed him on the lips. "Now, out of the kitchen whilst I cook!"

Bhavesh smiled and went to sit on the couch. He turned on the TV and rested his feet on the footstool.

Parvati measured rice in a cup and added it to a pan, filling the pot with one and a half cups of water. She brought it to the boil, covered it with a piece of foil and the lid, and placed it on a low heat. She set the timer on the oven to twelve minutes.

It was nice to have a timer, but she didn't really need it. She knew from experience almost exactly when twelve minutes had passed and so was not at all surprised to hear the ringing of the alarm. She switched off the heat and left the rice to cook in the steam for another ten minutes before opening the lid and fluffing up the rice. She stirred the curry again, turned down the heat and took a seat next to Bhavesh, snuggling into his shoulder.

"It should be ready in about thirty minutes," said Parvati.

"Good, my belly is rumbling just smelling it," said Bhavesh. His family were meat eaters, but he'd had nothing but vegetable curries since being married. It didn't bother him as much as he had thought it would.

"I can hear it," said Parvati, laughing. She readjusted her head on his shoulder and turned her attention to the TV. It was a musical film. It was one she hadn't seen before.

There was a knock at the door.

Bhavesh frowned. They hadn't ordered anything that he could think of.

"I'll get it," said Parvati.

"OK," said Bhavesh, who had still not stopped frowning.

Parvati opened the door, and her draw dropped. She stood gaping at the man in the door.

"So here you are!" he said, forcing his way past her. "Where is he?"

Bhavesh jumped to his feet. "Father!"

"Don't father me, you ungrateful little brat!" yelled Sandeep. "And you, you whore," he said turning to Parvati. "This is how you repay me for the years of employment I've offered you, all the money I've given you, the food I have put on your table, you seduce my son and convince him to run away with you!"

"DON'T YOU DARE SPEAK TO HER LIKE THAT!" screamed Bhavesh, squaring up to his father. "She did not convince me to do anything. I told you in the letter that I left. We are in love. It was me who convinced her. I did not want to marry who you had chosen for me."

Sandeep's eyes looked like they might fire a laser or erupt into flames. "Oh, you're in love! Do you know how much money I have wasted on that wedding? Do you have any idea how upset Ananya has been? Do you know how angry her family are? You have dishonoured me. You have brought shame on your family."

"I cannot help whom I love, father," said Bhavesh, "as I told you in my letter. And I have not dishonoured you, the family, or anyone else. Should I have married someone I don't love, who I don't even know, just to make you happy?"

Parvati shrunk away in the corner. Her worst nightmare had just come true.

"It is not about happiness," said Sandeep. "It is about honour. Duty. You are a Kshatriya, and you marry this Dalit whore... have you lost your mind?"

"I told you not to speak about her like that!" bellowed Bhavesh. "I will marry whomever I choose. And I have chosen her. We are married already: there is nothing you can do."

"Did I give you my blessing? What kind of pujari allows you to marry without the blessing of your family?"

"We have the blessing of the Gods," said Bhavesh. "Not even you could be so arrogant as to consider yourself above the Gods."

"Oh, the Gods have blessed your marriage, have they?"

"Yes," said Bhavesh, his eyes staring right through his father.

"You are coming home with me now. You will not live here with this whore in this house. You will return with me immediately and marry Ananya, as you have been told!"

Bhavesh's face flashed with fury. "I warn you father, call my wife a whore one more time, and you will regret it."

Sandeep looked even angrier than Bhavesh. He turned to Parvati. "You stupid slut. Who do you think you are to seduce my son? To marry him? You are a disgrace. An untouchable. You dishonour me beyond belief." He slapped her hard across the face, sending her flying back into the wall.

Parvati's eyes streamed with tears as she fell into the wall.

Bhavesh launched himself at his father, punching him in the face. "I told you to show some fucking respect! You dare to hit my wife when she carries my child!"

Sandeep wrestled with his son on the ground.

Bhavesh forced his father against the floor and punched at his face.

Sandeep rolled over, getting the better of his son. He punched him hard in the face.

"Please, stop!" said Parvati, trying to prize the men apart. "Please, this isn't right."

"Get off me, whore," said Sandeep, pushing her away.

"I TOLD YOU NOT TO SPEAK TO HER LIKE THAT!" screamed Bhavesh. He wrestled with his father, his anger fuelling his muscles. He pressed his father down against the floor and repeatedly punched him in the face.

"PLEASE! STOP!" cried Parvati, trying again to break up the fight.

Bhavesh punched his father one last time and stood up, standing next to Parvati. He hugged her and stood in front of her to guard her from his father.

Sandeep got to his feet. He held the couch for support as he rose.

"You have put a child in this whore!" said Sandeep who was visibly shaking. "You dare to defile a family line that has been pure for generations! And you attack your own father! Who has provided for you your entire life. How could you do this? I will never understand it. I do not understand who you are anymore. We had picked the perfect match for you. Two wealthy families of prominence in the community. Why would you dishonour us like this?!"

"I know this is going to be hard for your tiny brain to

comprehend, but there are more important things than money!" screamed Bhavesh. "We are married, and I am happy with my choice. I do not care what you think about it. It is my life!"

"You are no son of mine!" said Sandeep. "You will never inherit anything from me. You have dishonoured us. Your mother cannot bear to even hear your name spoken."

"I do not care about your honour or your money. I have honour and money of my own. I do not care about my inheritance, or what you think about our love, our marriage or our life. But you will not insult my wife in my presence again!"

"You presume to tell me what to do in a house bought with my own money?"

"This was gifted to me by grandfather. I have taken nothing from you."

"And what do you think he would say if he knew you had married a Shudra? You dishonour his memory!"

"Grow up!" screamed Bhavesh. "Just grow the fuck up! The caste system, the honour system, it's evil, antiquated nonsense. People should be free to marry whomever they choose! Arranged marriages are a stain on India. A stain that needs bleaching."

"You have truly lost your mind, Bhavesh. I will give you one last chance to return home and marry Ananya. If you do not agree, you will never see me again."

"Parvati is my wife, and we are to have a child. I will not marry Ananya."

The veins on Sandeep's head bulged and his whole-body shook. "You have not only taken this whore into your bed, but you have also placed a child in her womb. You disrespect and dishonour your entire family, and you show no remorse for your actions. You truly have no shame! You are no son of mine! Do you hear me? You are dead to me!"

"Get out now!" screamed Bhavesh in his father's face. "I told you not to speak about her like that!"

Sandeep stared at his son, thinking about all the different ways he'd like to beat sense into him. "You disgust me! You stay here with your whore. I will have no part in this child's life. It will not be a grandchild of mine. I swear it to all the Gods. If I ever see you again, I will kill you myself. Both of you!" He turned to Parvati at the last sentence who was stood in the corner in tears.

"Get out!" said Bhavesh. "Go from here. I do not wish to see you ever again!"

"And you shall not!" said his father, storming from the room and out the door, slamming it shut behind him.

Bhavesh ran over to Parvati who was shaking, tears gushing from her eyes. "I'm so sorry you had to see that, my love." He wiped the tears from her cheeks, but they kept pouring out. He wrapped her in his arms. *I'm going to kill him*, thought Bhavesh.

Parvati cried even harder. She had heard his thoughts again. It had played on the inside of her mind. She couldn't stop it happening. Every time she touched someone; she would hear what they were thinking.

"This is all my fault," said Parvati. "I have brought shame on your family."

Bhavesh grabbed her by the face and stared into her tear-soaked eyes. "You are the best thing that has ever happened to me, and I would not trade you for anyone in the world."

Her heart warmed but she could not stop the tears from falling from her eyes.

"The fault is mine," said Bhavesh. "I seduced you. I convinced you to run away with me. If there is any blame to be found, it lies with me."

She looked up at him, her vision blurred with tears. Their lips met and for once Parvati held Bhavesh's face in her hand, rather than the other way around.

"I love you," said Bhavesh.

"I love you, too," said Parvati.

They stood there in each other's arms, just holding one another, enjoying the feeling of warmth from their bodies enveloping each other in its love. And that is where they stayed until their legs ached, and their eyelids drooped. And they could both say, hand on heart, that there was no place either of them would rather be.

EVE

The motorcade carrying the vice president's coffin seemed to glide down the road on its way to Washington DC National Cathedral. Mourners lined the streets as it passed. The president had announced a National Day of Mourning for the death.

Eve sat in a car near the front of the procession. She wore a black dress with a large black hat. A pearl necklace dangled around her neck and the diamond earrings on her ears swung ever so slightly back and forth as they drove along.

Her husband and children rode with her. This was one family outing that even Evelyn hadn't protested about going to. It had been all over the news that the vice president had died of a heart attack, and in the two weeks leading up to the state funeral, it had been announced that Eve was the new vice president.

"Are you feeling OK, hon," said Mark, stoking Eve's leg.

"As well as can be expected," said Eve. "I'm feeling a little nervous about the eulogy. I want to do him justice."

"I'm sure it will be fine," said Evelyn.

Eve smiled. It was nice to have her daughter on her side for once.

"They've given him quite the sendoff," said Mark. "He must have impressed the president."

"He was a good man," said Eve. "And he cared about America."

"Yeah, he did," said Mark. "He helped you get through the cuts, didn't he?"

"He did," said Eve.

"I think he'd be proud to see all these people out to mourn him," said Evelyn.

"There's more people out than I thought there would be," said Mark.

Eve observed all the mourners through the window as the car drove by at a snail's pace. She was shocked at the outpouring of sympathy that had followed the announcement, from all communities in America. Her country was many things, but overwhelmingly, it was a country united. They felt as one, a unit, and they grieved together just the same. "He was a black male who held the highest position in office since Obama," said Eve. "The country was always going to react strongly to his death."

Mark nodded, mulling that over. "It's still nice to see. I hope he's looking down and smiling from heaven."

Eve smiled back at her husband and squeezed his hand. Neither of them were particularly religious by American standards, but he always became deeply religious when someone died. He couldn't accept death as a finality. It was one of the only things Eve found weak about him. "He will be," she said, after a long pause.

There were pictures of Elijah with a halo atop his head held on placards by the mourners. There wasn't an empty space anywhere she saw. He was given a proper president's send off. And she felt he deserved it. He had done in office what many others couldn't.

The motorcade came to a stop and Eve disembarked with her family. Crowds were gathered outside the cathedral as well, kept back by railings.

Eve held her shoulders straight and stood to attention with as much rigidity as the soldiers that lined the path leading up to the cathedral.

A coffin wrapped in the American flag was lowered out of the hearse by six uniformed soldiers. Their uniforms were decorated with all manner of epaulets. They raised the coffin up and slowly walked towards the cathedral.

As the coffin passed a twenty-one-gun salute was shot, to symbolise peace.

The soldiers lined at the side of the path saluted the coffin as it passed them.

Eve walked with her family just behind the president and his family into the cathedral.

The coffin was laid at the front of the cathedral. Eve took her seat on the second row, behind Elijah's family. She gave his wife a watery flash of her eyes as she passed.

Eve waited patiently as the rest of the mourners took their seats. It had been a while since she was last in church, and despite her disbelief, she still enjoyed being in there. The hard wooden seats that had in recent years been cushioned on the bottom, the stained-glass windows, the grandiose furnishings of the interior. This cathedral had huge brick arches and shiny marble flooring with a cavernous ceiling. She had to admit, it was beautiful to behold.

She sat staring at the effigy of Jesus on the cross looking down at them. It reminded her of *The Raven* by *Edgar Allen Poe*. That was her favourite poem since she'd first heard it in high school.

Everyone had finally taken their seat, and the Bishop took his place on the alter. "Dearly beloved, we are gathered here today to remember the remarkable life of the Vice President Elijah Thomas, who was sadly taken from us too soon, here at this cathedral in the presence of God. Elijah was a loyal servant to his country, and a devout Christian. His commitment to his duties to both God and country were unwavering. He believed that whether renowned or humble, rich or poor, black or white, that all people were equal in the eyes of God. God, who so loved the world that he gave his begotten son to die in anguish, so that whoever believes in him shall not perish but have everlasting life. Elijah was a servant of Jesus Christ our Lord and was a beacon of light for Christians all over the country. I know that the whole country, and the world, will be mourning his passing. He chose service over self-gratification, generosity over greed, love over hate. I know you will all join me in paying our condolences to his family. Elijah leaves behind his beloved wife, three children, countless siblings and two grieved parents. But they can take comfort in the fact that Jesus died for our sins and rose from the dead, so that all those who follow in his light may have eternal life. They can rest easy in the knowledge that he will know eternal peace with God. And now, I welcome the president of the United States of America who would like to give his eulogy."

The president walked to the podium and shook the bishop's hand. The bishop stood to the side of the president; his hands clasped in front of his robes.

The president opened his arms wide and began his speech. "Thank you all for attending today on this sorrowful occasion. I know Elijah would be proud to see so many prominent faces here. What can I say about such a man?" said the president, looking down at the paper which held his speech. "Elijah was a sterling example of what it means to be an American in today's society. He was not only a model to the African American community, but a clear example of the American dream, that anyone can achieve the highest levels of success if they put in the effort and have the determination to succeed. He served his country as a United States Peace Envoy in Africa, delivering aid to those most in need, and defending their liberties. He served his country as a Senator of Utah for eight years, working with the homeless there to improve their lives and bring them back into the folds of community. He was selfless and indefatigable in his duties as vice president, and it will not be the same working without him. Our administration will forever be diminished by his lack of presence, and I can truly say he will be sorely missed by everyone at the White House. From cleaner to the chief of staff, he was everyone's friend, and he never let his status as vice president cloud his judgement. He showed the same respect to all people, no matter who they were or what they did. If there is anything I will take with me from him, it will be his non-judgemental and accepting attitude of all those he encountered. I wish him eternal peace and my condolences are with his family and friends at this difficult time. Thank you."

The president stepped down from the podium, clasping Elijah's wife by the hand before he took his seat.

The bishop called Eve to the stage to give her speech.

Eve brushed her dress down as she stood up and took her place on the podium. Tears glistened in her eyes. "Words cannot bring justice to the immensity of the value and meaning of the life of such a great man as Elijah Thomas. I know he leaves behind many grieved family members and friends, and I share their grief. I worked closely with Elijah while in government and he was never short of ideas, but most importantly, he always wore a smile on his face. To be in a room with him was to be happy… no matter how much work there was to get through."

There was a soft chuckle from the congregation.

"From his work with aid organisations, to his devoted sense of duty to country and to God, Elijah was a beacon of life whose flame will shine on long after he has passed. The world was a better place for having had him in it, and I cannot express the grief I feel knowing that I will never see that smile again. He truly was irreplaceable, and it will be impossible to fill his shoes as vice president, but I will do my utmost to uphold the policies that he fought so hard to bring into force. Know that his values will live on through my work, and I will let his actions guide me in all that I do as vice president. May you rest easy in eternal paradise, Elijah. Thank you."

She gave Elijah's wife a teary smile, and his wife wiped tears from her eyes and smiled.

"That was beautiful," said Mark once Eve had taken her seat.

"And now," said the bishop. "Let us sing some hymns."

Eve had a surprisingly angelic voice, and Mark always enjoyed hearing her sing, not that they attended church very often.

Singing hymns was one thing Eve missed about going to church. While they'd raised their children as Christians, they had never really taken them to church other than for christenings, weddings, funerals and such.

It still shocked Eve at the obsequious reverence with which most of the hymns talked about God. She could scarcely believe that even at a funeral, when a person had lost somebody they loved, sometimes the most important person in their life, that they were still supposed to praise God.

She couldn't contemplate of an entity who would demand such a thing. Who would wish to be worshipped in the face of unimaginable grief. Still, she sang the hymns as though she meant them. Every word that passed her lips was a lie, but then most words that passed her lips were.

The crowd was silent for a moment as they turned the pages of the pamphlet to the next hymn that the bishop had selected. It was Amazing Grace. It was Eve's favourite hymn growing up. She loved the melodies and harmonies of the song, and despite herself, she still loved the words.

The bishop selected several more hymns, gave a few final words about Elijah's soul and final resting place, and the service was brought to a close.

Eve exited the cathedral with her family, walking slowly behind the flag-covered coffin.

She stood straight as the soldiers loaded it back in the hearse.

The president nodded to her and Eve nodded back, before getting into the car with her family.

"You did great, hon," said Mark. "That was a beautiful eulogy."

Eve smiled weakly at her husband, forcing tears into her eyes.

"Where are we going now, mum?" said Sarah.

"We're going to the cemetery to lay the body to rest, dear," said Eve. "His family wanted him buried in a normal graveyard where they could visit without disruptions."

"Oh, OK," said Sarah.

"That's nice," said Evelyn.

"Yes," said Eve, resting her chin on her hand and looking out the window. She wondered what Elijah would truly think about her if he was really up there in heaven, looking down on her. She imagined he'd be more shocked than anything. It had never occurred to him that she wanted something from him. He loved her, and that love blinded him. He believed that she loved him to. Not that he would ever be alive again to know it, but she knew he would be hurt, disappointed by what she'd done. She also wondered if he'd be impressed by her pertinacity in achieving what she wanted in life.

She didn't feel any guilt for what she had done. Elijah had cheated on his wife and was willing to leave her with a newborn just months old. It always bemused her the way people cherrypicked their morality. Elijah had supported numerous air strikes that had killed people all over the world, he'd killed people as a soldier, he'd told her as much, but she knew he wasn't capable of a civilian murder. It was a different set of rules to most people. Eve didn't lie to herself. If she could sanction the killing of a man a thousand miles away, she could do it to a man who sat opposite her at meetings.

The drive to the burial ground was short, but it had still taken quite a while given the slow speed of the motorcade.

She gave the president a sad smile and walked behind the coffin as the soldiers took it to the pre-dug grave.

Eve placed a hand on Elijah's wife's shoulder as she passed. She stood to the side of her, her back straight, and readjusted her hat so that it was at more of an angle.

"And now we lay Elijah to rest," said the bishop. "May he rest in eternal peace."

"May he rest in peace," echoed the congregation.

The coffin was lowered into the ground. Eve picked up a handful of mud and threw it in the grave. "Goodbye, Elijah."

EZEKIEL

Oscor finished questioning Ezekiel on everything he'd learned in the past months.

Ezekiel couldn't help but smile. He had never considered himself to be a smart person, and he certainly didn't think he would ever understand the world in the way he did now. He'd been clean from drugs for months, no meat or dairy had passed his lips, excepting one time he missed the writing in the ingredients list on the back of the packet, and he had finally accepted that he was the reincarnation of the Buddha. He was proud to walk in the steps of such a great man.

"I have taught you almost everything I can teach you about the world, Ezekiel, and it is time for us to go live. But there are just a few more things I need to show you to help complete your transformation."

"Oh really?" said Ezekiel. "When are we going to?"

"It's not when, it's where. I want you to see the real world, real poverty, true injustice before you announce yourself to the world, so that you can see what you're fighting for. I need you to understand the last lesson I have to teach you, that you are a Kshatriya, just like the Buddha, and that you have been living like a prince. I need you to see the poverty in the world firsthand, so that you can understand the true meaning of all that you've sacrificed, and why it is so vital."

"OK," said Ezekiel. "Where are we going?"

An image appeared on screen. "If you'd be so kind," said Oscor.

Ezekiel imagined himself in the image and appeared in a dark corner, in the slums of Burundi. The first thing he noticed was the smell. He covered his nose as he walked the gravelly path, avoiding the faeces to the best of his ability as he walked the makeshift path through the slums.

The whole place looked like it could collapse at any moment given a slight change in the weather. The roofs were made of an assortment of materials, mainly bits of misshapen metal which he imagined were meant to be used for some kind of fencing. Most of the walls were made of the same material, or wood. There wasn't a brick in sight.

He couldn't believe people lived like this, rammed together in makeshift houses made from whatever scraps they could find. Most of them didn't even have the privacy of a front door, just some sheets or even just an open doorway.

Shame filled him as he walked through the slums. It wasn't shame that these people, his people, lived like this. It was shame that he'd known they lived like this his whole life, but he'd never stopped to care, thinking only of smoking weed and whatever his friends were doing.

People stared at him as he passed, at his clean clothes and pristine looking trainers.

Ezekiel no longer cared for designer labels and had given all his designer items to charity. Oscor had agreed that it was enough to buy fairtrade, plain clothing and that the days of wearing robes were sadly passed. Though he remarked that they could well make a comeback in a few hundred or thousand years, as the rolling wheel of fashion turned through time.

Most of the children were barefoot, and almost all the people, adults and children, wore second or even third-hand clothes that would have been in fashion in the West several years earlier.

There would be the odd person in traditional African attire

that looked relatively expensive, pretty and extremely colourful. He wondered what possessed them to buy it when they were in need of so many other things, and he thought how strange it was contrasted against the poverty in which they stood.

He looked through the open hole that acted as a doorway into the room where a woman was sat with her children. The room was packed with what he would have considered to be trash had he been at home. There was no kitchen, no couch, no beds, just a few sheets on the floor, a wooden table that looked so old he couldn't believe it could withstand the weight of the single gas stove and pots that sat atop it; some pans, plastic bowls and plates all stacked in the corner, as well as a smattering of other items she had collected as her sole possessions in life.

The woman stared at him as he scanned the room as did the two children sat beside her. He looked at the children's eyes; they were bright and enthusiastic. Unlike the woman, they had no idea of the sickening level of poverty in which they lived.

He carried on through the dusty, unpaved streets. They were piled high with litter and waste. It was a breeding ground for diseases. His mum had always been so strict about cleanliness, he'd never known black people to be unclean. But where else would they put it? There were no bins, no bin men to collect the rubbish. So, it just stayed there, accumulating, growing ever and ever larger.

There were a group of children sat by a wall looking thoroughly depressed. They were the first unhappy children he'd encountered.

"Street children," Oscor said. "No home. No money. And little if any food."

Ezekiel wished he had brought money with him. Something he could give them. Then he remembered he was wearing a watch. It wasn't expensive or designer, but it might at least buy them a meal. He handed it to a little boy who looked up at him in shock. "Thanks."

Ezekiel smiled, unable to mask the tears in his eyes, his cheeks strained as he tried to return the smile. He had never seen poverty on this scale, and yet, other than the homeless children, every child he met seemed happy, if not a little malnourished. And what shocked him just as much, was the look of the adult's faces. They knew they were living in destitution, yet they didn't look depressed or suicidal, which is how he would feel living there. They just seemed to get on with life, most of them with a smile.

He carried on around the slums. He saw two old men chatting, sat on tattered plastic chairs. It was an oddly satisfying sight in the wealth of poverty around him. Just sat, talking, without a real care in the world other than the bonds of friendship.

Seeing the extent of the poverty humbled him. He knew there was extreme poverty in Africa, but he had never realised quite how bad they had it. He couldn't imagine having to use the street as a toilet. Cooking in the same room in which he slept. Having nothing but sheets to sleep on against hard concrete, without even so much as a pillow.

"Can we leave here, please?" said Ezekiel, tears streaming unbidden in his eyes for the first time since he was a young child. "I think I've seen enough."

"We can," said Oscor. "But there is more I want you to see."

Another image flashed in his mind. He imagined himself there and after a momentary blackness he found himself in the streets of Favel, Rio de Janeiro. It was more developed than where he'd just been in Africa, there was no faeces on the streets and it didn't smell as bad, but it was still rundown.

All the buildings were stacked on top of one another, and whilst most of them were made of brick, some of them used the same scraps of tin as their roof that he'd seen in Burundi. Here, they had made more of an effort to make it homely, more like a community, painting their walls in bright colours, and with murals on the sides of walls.

As he walked the streets, he noticed the carefree way in which the children played here too, as happy as the children he'd seen in Africa, and happier than most of the children he'd seen in England, despite all their riches.

Every corner he passed was filled with gang members, who

stood in packs as though they were unable to see the children around them. Some of them had guns hanging out of their waistbands. All of them were covered in tattoos. He'd seen the words 'only God can judge me' more times in the short walk around the streets of Rio de Janeiro than he'd seen in his entire life. He wondered what these people thought God would do when judging them. He knew they were Christians, well as much of a Christian as he had been, and they must surely know they were destined for hell. But that didn't appear to make them behave. What could they possibly expect God to do with their soul, other than punish it?

Ezekiel had been a bad child, he knew that, but he'd also been caring in many ways. He'd never sold weed to anyone under fourteen, except when he was under fourteen himself. He'd never hit a woman. He'd never carried a knife or a gun. He hadn't ever gone looking for trouble in the form of fights, though he had fought quite a few people who had started on him or his friends.

He supposed he could have let it slide, and the new him probably would, but there was still a part of him that thought, if someone brings the fight to you, then you bring it back twice as hard. He wondered what the Buddha would think of that. But he was the new Buddha, and the ways of the old Buddha needed refining. The Sri Lankans were forced to use violence, against their Buddhist teachings, simply to defend their faith. The Buddha had left little guidance on what to do when faced with defending oneself, there were no prescriptions to defend the religion from an immoral force who wished to take its place, and murder was completely prohibited no matter the situation.

He carried on up the steep hills that made Favela. The back of his calves twinged; he was used to the flat roads of central Manchester. And as he walked, he couldn't help thinking that if someone tried to kill you, then you had the right to kill them in self-defence. The Buddha had been wrong on that, he thought. A rare disagreement he had with the words and teachings of the Buddha.

Ezekiel stopped in his tracks. Just as he had been

contemplating the morality of murder in self-defence, murder of a different kind presented itself to him. On the floor was a dead body. It must have been shot not less than an hour previously.

"Oh my God," said Ezekiel aloud. He'd never seen a dead body in real life before other than his trip to the future.

"This is what I wanted to show you," said Oscor. "This is what the people of South America have to contend with. Gangs on their corners selling drugs and dead people in their streets. Luckily this one isn't decapitated."

Ezekiel felt sick. "I can't believe they just leave the body here for the children to see. Don't they have any decency?" The area around the body was covered in pools of blood. The crimson red was stark against the dull grey of the paved road.

The head of the body lay limp at the side, a hole through his head, but there was a peace to his face, and Ezekiel couldn't help but notice it despite the horror of the scene.

"I think I've seen enough, Oscor. Can we go back to the library?"

"There is still more for you to see," said Oscor.

An image flashed in Ezekiel's mind. He grudgingly pictured himself there.

He was in a very developed city. The buildings were almost all new, most of them taller than the buildings he was used to in Manchester. The streets were packed with people, and cars lined the roads. It looked like New York only it was full of Chinese people.

Ezekiel wondered what poverty he was supposed to see here, because from what he could see, it was just as developed as England, if not more so.

"What are we doing here?" said Ezekiel.

"There is more you must see," said Oscor. "Walk with me."

Ezekiel walked around the city, guided by Oscor's directions. People stared at him as he walked through the streets. Everyone there was the same ethnicity: he stood out like a sore thumb.

Manchester was a predominantly white city, but he spent his

time in the city centre and lived in Hulme, so he'd always seen a multitude of races and ethnicities. It was odd being the only person in society who looked different from the rest.

The city was pristine, it shocked him how the people adhered to the rules with strict obedience, how they crossed only at designated crossings, never crossing the road at any other point than the one the government had created for them, so unlike Manchester.

The light turned green, and Ezekiel walked with the crowd across the road, which was wider than any road he'd ever seen, in real life or on television. The city was enormous.

"Where are we going?" asked Ezekiel.

"Just over there," said Oscor. "You need to climb those steps."

Ezekiel looked around for the steps Oscor had mentioned and walked over to them. It was a fire exit, and he knew he wasn't supposed to be using it. Before he'd met Oscor that wouldn't have bothered him in the slightest, but he felt almost guilty using the stairs.

He came to a glass window and peered through. It was a factory. They were making some kind of technological devices; he couldn't make them out clearly through the window. Ezekiel's eyes widened and he pressed his face against the glass to make sure he was seeing what he thought he was seeing. The factory was full of workers, operating with such speed and efficiency that they were almost machines. As he scanned their faces, he could see that many of them were of school age, some as young as eleven he guessed.

"Are those children?" he asked Oscor.

"Yes," said Oscor. "They work ten-hour days here just to make ends meet and bring money in for their family. These are where the brands you used to love so much are made, and this is who makes them."

Ezekiel's whole body drooped with the weight of the shame. He had known there were things such as sweatshops in the world, but seeing it for himself, understanding how selfish he'd been, it hit him hard. He had been such a selfish person before he'd met his future-self. He couldn't believe there were children who should be at school, working all day to make electronics for the developed nations. And what shocked him more was how developed the city was. Surely, they could afford to send their children to school, rather than have them working in a sweatshop?

"Even here," said Oscor, "there is still poverty. China is a rich nation, the second richest in the world, but they have over a billion people to house, feed and maintain. This is the reality of life for many people, not just here but around the world."

Ezekiel's bottom lip quivered. He felt true empathy for them, could feel the injustice of the world, of all that those who lived in such relative poverty and hardship to the life of luxury he was used to.

"Good," said Oscor, reading his mind. "There is one last thing I want you to see. But I warn you, it will not be a sight you will forget easily, but one you must see if you are to fulfil your destiny."

"I'm ready," said Ezekiel, who was incensed more by his own selfishness in which he'd lived the last eighteen years, than the sight he had just witnessed.

Oscor flashed an image in Ezekiel's mind and Ezekiel imagined himself there.

He walked out of the shaded alley into streets that were so full of people he wondered how they had room to move between one another. As he left the safety of the shade, the heat slapped him in the face with rough hands made of pure steam.

The roads were full of motorcycles and tuktuks, but the people didn't seem to notice them as they weaved through the traffic as though they themselves were made of hard metal.

"This is Mumbai, India," said Oscor. "There's something here you need to see, but I warn you, it will not be easy."

Ezekeil walked through the packed streets taking in the smell and sights of the city. Every few yards a street vendor stood with something to sell, almost always food, and it smelled delicious. Some of it was meat, and while it made him feel sick to think about it, it also made him hungry.

Veganism was probably the hardest thing he'd had to change in life. He'd eaten meat since he'd finished with milk as a baby, and he still craved it, though had managed to resist the temptation for the sake of the animals. The death didn't bother him too much, but he couldn't justify their incarceration. Oscor had shown him some shocking scenes, animals cutting themselves in despair because they couldn't move or have any form of enjoyment; animals trapped in cages so small it dug into their skin as they grew, tearing it open; mothers running after their calves as they were driven away to be raised and slaughtered. It had taken its toll on him and made not eating meat or dairy much easier when he could picture the suffering it entailed.

They had walked around the city for about thirty minutes, and as they travelled there was a disconcerting mix of poverty and excess. Some lived in luxury, while others lived in tightly packed slums, running around in tattered clothes, looking thin. But still, he could see the smiles on their faces.

"In here," said Oscor. He directed Ezekiel through a thin wooden doorway.

The man in the doorway must have realised he wasn't from India, as he spoke to him in English. "It's two hundred rupees for half an hour, three hundred for one hour. Please, look around and take your pick."

Ezekiel walked through the building looking through the open doorways. Words could not describe what he saw. Women sat on worn-out mattresses on the concrete floor, looking up at him as he entered. As he walked through the brothel, he couldn't believe what he was seeing. There were girls in there, some who looked as young as ten. They looked at him with forced longing in their eyes, willing him to come in so that they could afford to eat, but still the pain of their reality shone in their eyes through their false longing as they looked on him. He looked at one girl who stared back at him, wanting his money but clearly shocked by his height and size, wondering if he would hurt her merely by the act of sex.

Fury blazed in Ezekiel, spreading through every fibre of his body. Every cell that it contained was charged with nothing but pure rage. Child prostitutes! It just couldn't be.

He spun around and the man who had been waiting for him to select a girl jumped back in surprise, the anger in Ezekiel's face scaring him.

Ezekiel's fists balled up. He flew towards the man and punched him as hard as he could in the face.

The man fell to the floor and Ezekiel jumped on top of him, smashing his face into a bloody mess. "You sick bastard!" he said, over and over as he punched him almost into unconsciousness. "They're fuckin' children! CHILDREN! You sick fuck!"

"EZEKIEL!" shouted Oscor. "Stop. You must not use violence."

Ezekiel's fist wavered in the air, raised ready to strike. He wanted nothing more than to keep punching the man, but he had a path to follow and that involved non-violence. He got up from the man but couldn't resist kicking him in the face as he stormed out of the building.

He could see the girls and women staring at him from their doorways as he strode from the building, shock etched on their faces.

Oscor was right, he had lived like a prince his whole life. He truly understood the Buddha's message. It wasn't something he'd adopted to save the world, he understood that these people were truly poor, truly destitute, truly desperate: and he had never truly cared about them before, caring more about weed, and girls and designer clothes. He had left the palace and was seeing the ills that his 'parents', the British government, had shielded from him his whole life.

"I understand. I see clearly now. I have been living like a prince and you have taken me to see the ills of the world. I have accepted them as they are and I promise I will fight for them, to end this evil in the world. I am the reincarnation of the Buddha." And for the first time, there was no doubt in his mind. He was destined to change the world.

"Well done, Ezekiel," said Oscor. "You have learnt your last lesson.”

An image flashed in Ezekiel’s mind, and he thought of himself in the lair underneath the library. Oscor teleported him home.

“How are you feeling?” said Oscor, but he knew how he was feeling, he had read his mind, every thought he’d had.

“I’m angry,” said Ezekiel. “But I needed to see it. I finally understand that I am the Buddha. I accept my destiny and I’m willing to do what needs to be done to save the world, no matter the cost.”

“I’m proud of you, Ezekiel,” said Oscor. “You’ve become all that I wanted you to be and more. And now, it is time that we go public.”

EZEKIEL

It was exactly one o'clock in the afternoon in Britain and the newsreader had just begun announcing the headlines for the day. She paused mid-sentence, her mouth agape, as Ezekiel popped into existence in front of her eyes. She blinked furiously, trying to find words to describe what had just happened but failing.

"Hello World," said Ezekiel. "My Name is Ezekiel Campbell. I have an important message for you."

As he finished his sentence another version of himself appeared next to him.

The newsreader could be heard saying "Oh my fucking God!" in the background.

"I'll take it from here," said the second Ezekiel.

Ezekiel imagined himself in France at exactly one o'clock Greenwich Mean Time and teleported to a live recording of the news on France 24. "This is an important world announcement," he said in French. "Please tune in to BBC News now."

He vanished from the screen and the newsreader stared at the space where he'd just been stood. "C'est quoi ce bordel?" she said, *What the fuck?*

Ezekiel appeared in Saudi Arabia in the studios of Al

Arabiya at one o'clock GMT exactly. "I have a message to deliver to you from God. Please tune into BBC News immediately."

He disappeared and arrived in China in the news station of CTGN. "There is a message you must hear," he said in his best attempt at Chinese. "Please tune into BBC News immediately."

Ezekiel visited a news station in every country in the world, all of them at exactly one o'clock GMT and told them all to tune into BBC News.

Social media was abuzz everywhere in the world telling people to tune into BBC News. People were being woken by phone calls and concerned parents in the middle of the night telling them to turn on the news. From America to Australia, the world tuned into BBC News.

He imagined himself back in time, a few seconds after he'd teleported into the BBC News studio. He appeared and saw his former self. "I'll take it from here," he said. And he watched as the former him disappeared.

Ezekiel looked directly into the camera and addressed the world. "As I was saying, I have an important announcement to make, and it affects the whole world. I need you to listen very carefully to what I'm about to tell you."

He noticed all the cameras turn in his direction, as though they'd been given the order to track his every movement.

"I have been to the future, and I have seen what becomes of the world. If you do not heed my words, the world will be completely destroyed by nuclear war in ten years. There will be no survivors. No nations. No people. Nothing. We will know complete destruction if we continue to live in this disunited world."

He paused, not sure how to phrase it. All the preparations he'd made with Oscor had fallen out of his head. He faltered, not sure what to say. Memories of everything Oscor had showed him commandeered his soul, for all the injustice he'd witness and what lay at stake if he failed to convince the world to lay down their arms, and the words came flying out of his mouth like a caged bird finally set free.

"I know that you're going to find this hard to believe," he said after a long pause, "but I have been chosen by God. I am the reincarnation of the Buddha, and unless you all convert to Buddhism the world will be destroyed by nuclear war within ten years. I have been to the future, and I have seen it for myself. I have been to the past and know the true history of the world. I have seen the power of the Buddha in person. I have been on his journey of self-discovery and learnt to follow the noble eight-fold path. A path we must all follow if we are to survive in this world.

"If you'd have asked me a year ago whether I was a prophet I would never have believed you, and I understand that many of you will struggle to believe it too, but believe me when I say, everything I do, I do to avoid the end of the world and make a better society for all people. We cannot go on as we are, in constant, perpetual warfare, arguing over who is worshiping God correctly, lavishing ourselves in luxury while half the world starves. What kind of planet are we that we have a simultaneous obesity epidemic and a starvation epidemic? What kind of home have we created for ourselves that we shoot and bomb one and another in an endless cycle of violence? How have we allowed there to be children who live on the streets, begging for scraps of food? There is twice as much food produced each year as is needed to feed the whole world, yet half of the world lives below the poverty line. When will it be enough? How fat can the bellies of the rich nations of the world grow before the world says, 'No, we won't live like this any longer'? How many more animals can you fit in a single cage, before you ask yourself the question whether you have gone too far? How many times must they cut their own skin with their beaks, or smash their heads against the cages in which you have placed them before you ask yourself if you have taken it too far? Who among you could imagine living in such conditions?

"It's time for the world to grow up and take accountability for its actions. We cannot go on as we are, a disunited set of nations in constant conflict and competition with one another, rather than unifying our resources and solving the problems that plague our world. There is not a single country in the world whose actions I can entirely defend. If you're not bombing one another, you're using child slaves. If you're not raping your war captives, you're raping their lands of every morsel of value you can find. If you're not oppressing them for their political opinions, you're forbidding them from learning for being women. Afghanistan, Iran, have you completely lost your minds?! To perpetuate the lie that God does not want women to be seen or heard, to even think, to be anything other than a wife and a mother, a slave in every sense of the word. To live in apartheid with those who love and nourish you from the moment you enter their womb. When will it end? How many more liberties must be stolen from the people before we rise up against our oppressors and say, 'We will not stand for this any longer!'

"How many times must we trade a currency that fluctuates in value every *second* before we adopt a single currency and end this madness of prices rising every day because of this artificial inflation? When will we look past the colour of our skin and end this pointless and immature tribalism? How can you sleep at night knowing billions of people are living without heating, without electricity, without water or food? How many more attempts must the world make to better itself before the forces of evil are finally defeated? How many more religions and ideologies must be created before we end our disunity, our selfishness, our evil? The world has forgotten what it means to live. To be just. To be one. So many have you have forgotten the values that founded your societies.

"Russia, you have forgotten yourself, your values and your principles. You tried to make the world equal. You abolished slavery in the 1700s. Before Britain. Before America. You were part of the enlightenment. And now what do you do? Create weapons of war that cause only destruction. What has happened to the righteous Russian spirit? That of liberty and justice? You've got the totalitarianism of communism with none of the egalitarian values. Just dictatorship and warfare. Your citizens show racism, despite your efforts to make the world a more equal and fair place. Do they not feel shame? Un-Russian in their racism? What has become of you? What happened to your idealism? I don't recognise the Russia your ancestors tried to make in today's world. And what of you, America, in your food fort, what has happened to your values of freedom, liberty and the pursuit of happiness, as you rain bombs on nation after nation to keep your hold on power? What happened to the idealistic, democratic freedoms your nation was founded on? And what has become of liberty, egality and fraternity, France? Is this something which only applies to Europeans? Are not the children of South America or Africa or Asia involved in your vision of egality? And what of you, South America, will you dictators ever accept that if socialism is to prosper in your country it must be by the vote of the people, not the force of dictators? Will you allow the cartels and gangs to destroy the lives of your residents? Will you, the people poisoning the streets with drugs and guns, ever repent? Will you ever bring goodness to your community instead of destroying it?

"India! India! India!" said Ezekiel, tapping the side of his temples each time he said the word. "How many prophets have to come out of that place before you'll end your vile caste system? You were told to end it thousands of years ago by the Buddha, and yet still there are honour killings on your streets every year for inter-caste marriages. And Thailand! You're supposed to be a Buddhist nation. What do you think the Buddha would say if he knew you were throwing people in jail for ten years simply for questioning the monarchy? You dishonour his memory!"

He threw his arms out in exasperation. "Somalia! Yemen! This is not the 1800s! The days of pirates have long since passed! When will you stop raiding the ships and vessels that pass by your waters? When will you grow up and accept the twenty first century? Europe, Australia, America – will you ever cease your relentless racism? Do you think you are the only civilisation in history to have a renaissance? Do you really think the world is there solely for you to farm, that the inhabitants of the world are simply a means to an end? And when will you, and the world, be done plundering Africa's resources and let them rise to their former glory? And when will you remember yourself, Africa? The pharaohs that ruled for thousands of years, the kings, the richest man to ever live, Mansa Musa. When will you remember your heritage and seize your liberty? Or will you remain slaves in all but name, to feed the ever-engorging belly of the Northern hemisphere?

"And to all the African dictators, autocrats and tyrants, when will you let your people rise? Or will you keep them under your boot for the scraps of power and money that you are given by your own masters? Will you keep them shackled and oppressed for a few million pounds a year? A pittance to those who rule you. Will you continue to oppress your people for the price of a few fancy watches? When will you lead the people of Africa, and not simply govern them with an iron grip so that you can shower yourself in titles and privileges that your people will never know? How much longer will the world keep paying these militias and bribing these leaders to keep Africa subdued? Does the sight of a starving, emaciated child not provoke any form of compassion within you? How do you sleep so soundly at night, knowing the evils and ills of the world?

"Should half the world live in slavery so that the other half might know liberty and excess? Does children working twelve hour days to make your designer clothes not induce within you shame? Do you feel nothing knowing that your tobacco leaves are picked by children, paid less than a dollar a day? Do children working in brothels to feed their family not sicken you? Does it not anger you? Do you feel anything other than your own desires? Does the rampant destitution of the world not incite within you any form of compassion or resolve to change the world? To fight the injustice?

"We can't continue to live in these faction systems, of nationalism, of ethnicity, of gender, of sexuality, of religion. When will you give the women their liberty? When will they be free? Given equal rights and representation in government and society. When will you take the collar from the necks of your mothers and daughters, so that they might taste the liberty men have enjoyed for millennia? When will we grow up as a society and lay down our weapons? When will you be done with racism, and your puerile obsession with race? When will people be free to love who they love? When will we be one world, not hundreds of separate nations?

"It is not too late to see the light. I come to you with a message of peace. To tell you that I have seen the past and the future. That there is a version of time where we have not all perished in nuclear war. And the only way we can get there is if you all accept Buddhism as the one true religion. I implore you to see reason. Please, heed my words. I am the reincarnation of the Buddha, and I have come to save the world. If you don't convert, we will all perish."

And, with that, he vanished.

PARVATI

Parvati scrolled through her phone, unable to believe what she was seeing. A man had teleported around the world. He had been in hundreds of places at the exact same time. There had been two of him stood side by side in the BBC studios before one of them disappeared before her eyes. He had said the strangest things. Things that didn't make sense to her. Things that scared her.

"This can't be real," said Bhavesh, also scrolling through social media on his phone, which was full of nothing but clips of Ezekiel and conspiracy theories about everything he'd said and done.

"It cannot," said Parvati. "The Buddha did not believe in the Gods. It cannot be real. It must be trickery of some kind."

"It was probably Britain or America using their technology, trying to confuse the world."

"What would two Christian nations gain from trying to convert the world to Buddhism?"

"I'm not sure," said Bhavesh, stroking his lips. "But it was broadcast on British television. They must be involved."

"He appeared on almost every news station on the planet at the same time. And he spoke their language! Who speaks that many languages?"

"He could have had an earpiece, telling him what to say."

"That's true," said Parvati, her eyebrows raised. "But how did he get there in the first place? And be in so many places simultaneously?"

"That I can't answer," he said. "But I'm convinced it was orchestrated by some nations to trick the world."

"Can you imagine Saudi Arabia taking part in a conspiracy to remove Islam from the world?"

He tilted his head to the side, his eyes rolled back in his head as he considered it. "No, no I can't." *They would be crucifying anyone who accepted him as a prophet*, he thought.

Parvati was leaning against his shoulder. She felt the thought pass from his mind to hers. She knew he was right. "Then how do you explain what we've just seen?"

"I can't. But I don't trust anything I see on the internet or television. The whole thing was probably CGI. I've seen movies with people teleporting. They're not real. And neither is this."

"The Indian government has issued a statement," said Parvati who had just gotten a notification on her phone. "It said it does not accept the authenticity of the videos and that it is international interference in other countries' democracies."

"See," said Bhavesh. "It's a hoax."

There was something about the whole thing that just didn't sit right with Parvati. She seemed connected to it somehow. Perhaps if she hadn't been hearing the thoughts of anyone who touched her for the past several months, she would have written it all off as a hoax. But that, coupled with the passion with which he spoke, she knew there was something more to it than Bhavesh was accepting. "I'm scared," she admitted. "Even if it is a hoax, it's going to cause chaos in the world. Many people will believe in its authenticity. There are newsreaders all over the world saying they saw him appear and disappear live on air at the exact same time."

"It wouldn't surprise me if they were all paid to say so," said Bhavesh. "You have nothing to fear. The Indian government has not been hoodwinked by this madness. I don't know what they're trying to achieve with this, but whatever it is, it's not going to work in India."

She felt calmer. His words always had a way of making her see reason over emotion. "You're probably right," she said, still with the nagging feeling that there was some higher power involved in all this. "Hopefully things settle down in a few weeks. The internet has gone truly insane."

"The internet has always been insane. Now they have governments joining in their insanity. It's the British, I'm sure of it. One colonisation was clearly not enough for them."

"He said we are disunited by nationalism."

"Yes, and it wouldn't surprise me if Britain wanted to make the whole world the United Kingdom, ruled from Britain as the centre of the world."

Parvati couldn't help but laugh. "I wouldn't put it past them."

"Neither would I."

~ * ~

Parvati floated in a formless blackness that expanded further than she could see. She was surrounded by a triad of Gods. Brahma stood straight ahead of her, his four head spinning round to each get a view of her. To her bottom left was Vishnu. His shimmering blue skin caused her to squint as she took in his frame. His arms beckoned her to come to him. To her bottom right, finishing the triangle, was Lord Shiva. He sat cross legged with his four arms outstretched to her, as though trying to grasp her soul.

"Come to me," said Vishnu.

"Come to me," said Brahma.

"Come to me," said Shiva.

She felt their energies, all of them clawing at her own, trying to drag her soul in three different directions.

"Come to me," said all three of the Gods again.

Parvati floated in the centre of the triad, spinning round as each God tried to pull her soul towards them.

There was a flash of light, and the Gods disappeared. She was in the park opposite her house in New Delhi. She saw herself walking among the people, each of them crowding around her, desperate to touch her, to speak to her, to know her. She walked among the people touching their foreheads and applying a Bindi to their heads from a pot of red powder. Bhavesh stood at her side smiling.

She held the arms of the people lined up in front of her, reading their minds. She offered them each a blessing, that their lives would be fulfilled with whatever thought they had been concerned with when she had touched them. The line got longer and longer, and the crowds of people she'd already blessed grew too, stood to the side, staying to watch the prophet bless the people, until almost the entire park was filled with people who had come to see her, the mind reader, the defender of Hindu Gods and Indian values.

The park disappeared and she felt herself floating again, in a formless black void, surrounded by the three Gods.

"Choose," said Shiva.

"Choose," said Brahma.

"Choose," said Vishnu.

There was another flash of light. She looked around her. She was stood in the same park, but all the trees had been burnt to a crisp. Decayed bodies surrounded her everywhere that she looked. All the buildings were bombed out or completely gone from where they had once stood. Nothing of New Delhi remained. She walked through the park, tears in her eyes from the death and the smog. All the buildings she'd become attached to in her months living in New Delhi were gone. She walked out of the park to her house. It was gone. Just a pile of rubble on the floor. She instantly thought of Bhavesh. Where was he? Was he dead as well? She couldn't bear the thought.

She carried on down the street, looking over the destruction that had taken place. Everywhere and everything had been bombed, destroyed, reduced to rubble.

The park disappeared and once more she felt herself as weightless as in water in the pitch black, surrounded by the three Gods who provided the only source of light.

"Believe," said Brahma.

"Believe," said Shiva.

"Believe," said Vishnu.

There was another flash of light. She stood in the same park as before. There were bombed out buildings, but there were people walking around. Some of the buildings had been bombed but the city still stood. People lived. The air was breathable. She walked through the park. No one seemed to notice her. The faces she saw looked sad. There had been a terrible war here. But it did not look like the nuclear annihilation she had seen in her previous vision. She walked through the park to her house. Here too it was destroyed, but the buildings around it were still standing. Most of them, anyway. She again thought of Bhavesh. Where was he? She walked the streets of New Delhi for hours. Half of the buildings which Bhavesh had taken her to see on their first day in New Delhi were damaged or destroyed. Beauty that had remained for hundreds of years untouched had been wiped from India. From the world. From history.

The weightlessness returned and she found herself back in the blackness of the void surrounded by the three Gods.

"Decide," said Shiva.

"Decide," said Vishnu.

"Decide," said Brahma.

She spun around in the centre of the Gods, their life energy clawing at her own, spinning her around in the centre. She threw her arms out and forced herself to stop spinning. She was facing Lord Shiva. She could feel him calling to her. She turned to look at each of the Gods calling to her and found herself back facing Lord Shiva. She pushed forward, floating through the formless void towards him. His face curved into a smile.

"She has chosen," said Lord Shiva.

The other Gods disappeared.

Shiva waved one of his arms and blue light shot from it, flying into Parvati. She glowed with blue light. She could feel the soul of Lord Shiva's wife within her own body.

"Go from this place and defend the Gods," said Lord Shiva. "Show the world your power. Destroy the caste system. Recreate India in your image. You are our last hope."

Parvati floated in the void, blue light shining from her skin. With a flash, Lord Shiva disappeared.

Parvati awoke, jumping up in bed and turned to see Bhavesh snoring.

~ * ~

"You can't honestly expect me to believe everything you're telling me!" said Bhavesh. "I love you, and I know you wouldn't lie, but this can't be true."

"I can prove it!"

"You can prove that you were visited in a dream by Brahma, Vishnu and Shiva, and they asked you to choose one of them, and that Lord Shiva has trapped the spirit of his wife within you?"

Parvati scowled at him. "I can prove that I can read your mind. You will have to trust me about the rest. Surely that will convince you?"

"OK then," he said. "What am I thinking?"

"Come," said Parvati. "Sit."

She sat opposite him and took his arms in her own. "Think of anything, anything in the world."

He thought about the dal curry she made that was his favourite, about the sensation of her hand in his, about how silly this all was.

"You thought about dal curry, then you got distracted by the sensation of my hand, then you thought how foolish you find this."

Bhavesh's eyes flashed at her. His breathing deepened.

"Think of a number," said Parvati. "Any number. And make it a long one."

He thought, several numbers flashed in his mind at the same time.

"You need to think of just one number and repeat it in your head."

There was a pause as he thought.

"You're thinking of the number 4,791,835.22"

"Oh my…"

"See, I told you!" said Parvati. "I've been hearing your

thoughts for months, ever since we were married. Ever since we asked the Gods to bless our union. I was too scared to tell you."

He couldn't believe what he was hearing. It had to be some trick. He stared at her, his face ghostly.

"You still don't believe?" she said, her frown returning. "OK, fine. Think of a memory, your deepest memory. Something you've never told me, that I could never otherwise know."

Bhavesh rifled through his memories for something she could never know and something he'd never told her. There wasn't much he hadn't told her at one point or another. He racked his brain, and it came to him in a flash.

"You're thinking about the time you stole money from your father's private stash and allowed a servant to be fired for your actions. You're thinking about how you lied to your father. You're feeling ashamed about it because you know she depended on the money to feed her family, but at the time you felt almost no guilt."

"I… I… OK. I believe you. You can read my mind. I don't know how, but I believe you. After everything that we've just seen on the news, and now this, it can't be coincidence. You say the Gods contacted you?"

"Yes," said Parvati, relief spreading across her face. "They showed me several futures. One where we lived happily as Hindus, one where there had been a war but some survived and one in which everywhere I looked there were dead bodies and bombed out, empty buildings. They asked me to choose one of them and I chose Lord Shiva. He said I had been chosen to destroy the caste system and save the Gods. He said I was their last hope. That must have been their plan all along, why they had us marry, so we can set an example to India and end the scourge of the caste system."

"I believe you," said Bhavesh. "I believe you. If you say they contacted you, then I know it to be true. The only question I have is, what are we going to do about it?"

EVE

"This has to be CGI," said Eve.

"The evidence is saying it's real," said the president. "Newsreaders all over the world are saying they saw him in person, at the same time. We tested the videos. They're not edited. There's no CGI. It was a live broadcast. He appeared in every country in the world at exactly the same time. As far as we can tell there were over two hundred versions of him simultaneously telling the world he had a message for them."

"And what is Britain saying about this? We're a Christian country, and so are they. And they pull this shit?"

"I've had a call from the king and the prime minister. It has absolutely nothing to do with them. They were as shocked as we are."

"Teleportation? Time travel? Being in hundreds of different countries at the same time? It can't be real. It just can't."

"There is no time for disbelief," said the secretary of defense. "We need to strategize. If the British have teleportation and time travel, it leaves us vulnerable."

"I told you; the British have no idea how he did it."

"Or so they say," said a short woman on the other side of the room. "War is waged by deception."

"Where is the boy now?" asked the secretary of defense.

"The British are scouring the country for him as we speak, but he can teleport as he's proven, so the hunt needs to go worldwide."

"We need to find him and take him out," said Eve.

"No!" said the president. "He must be brought in alive. How ever he's doing this, whatever technology he's using, we need to understand it. And if he's really been to the future and seen the end of the world, we need to know how to avoid it."

"He's already told us what he thinks we need to do to avoid it," said Eve. "Convert to Buddhism and accept him as a prophet."

The president looked pensive, like he might consider it. "We have to at least give it thought. He spoke with passion. I half believe the kid."

"You can't possibly be serious?" said the secretary of defense. "This is a Christian nation!"

"This is a free nation that allows all religions to be practiced. That's one of our fundamental values!" snapped the president.

"Then you can't be serious about converting the nation to Buddhism!"

"I'm not converting the nation to any religion," said the president, who didn't appreciate the tone Eve was using. He scowled at her. "And I am the president Goddamn it. What I decide is what happens. Is that understood?"

Eve shrank back in her chair.

"I'm not saying he's right," said the president, regaining his composure. "I'm not saying he's wrong. But I know how to read people. He believed every word he said. He cared."

"That doesn't mean it's true," said one of the generals.

"No, it doesn't," said the president. "But we need to find him and find him fast. So that we can get a handle on the situation and find out what he saw in the future."

"What are the other nations saying about this?"

"The whole world has lost it. There are as many theories as there are people. Some of them think it is magic, some of them think it was staged by NATO, others are saying it was China, others are saying he's the real deal. There have been protests from Saudi Arabia to New Zealand, all saying they accept him as a prophet and demanding their governments change religion as God has revealed himself to the world."

The masses thought Eve. *A million lunatics for every sane person.*

"I think we need to move to DEATHCON 1," said the secretary of defense. "America is in danger. What is it he called us, a food fort? He didn't seem too happy about the wars we've been waging across the globe. He's an enemy of the state."

"I agree," said one of the commanders. "We should move to DEATHCON 1. What is Russia saying about this?"

"The president hasn't made a comment, but his words struck home with a lot of the Russian people from what our media analysts are saying. It seemed like he cared about them."

"Did they really end slavery before Britain and the USA?"

The president seemed shocked by his ignorance. "Yes, of course. In 1720."

"Well, I'll be damned," said one of the commanders. "I always thought it was us first. Those commi bastards."

"Well, we banned it, either way," said the president. "The timing is irrelevant."

"I don't like any of this," said Eve, "not one bit. We are all in danger. He could attack at any point."

"He's one person," said the president. "Not an army."

"What if there are more of them?"

"That's a definite possibility," said the president. "Someone has definitely been helping him. He couldn't have done this on his own. We've received records from the British. He grew up in their equivalent of the projects, a council estate they call it. He failed most of his school exams. He's been arrested several times and up until a few months ago could be found in central Manchester selling weed."

"And you think this person could be a prophet! A criminal!"

"I don't know what to think," said the president. "But I have to cover all bases. And clearly, whatever trouble he got into as a youth, he's put it behind him. There's been no sign of him selling drugs for several months now. It's like he just woke up one day and became a completely different person.

Someone has been training him for this, I'm sure. The way he spoke, the knowledge he had. He didn't learn it at school, that's for sure!"

"The British have got something to do with this," said Eve. "I'm sure of it. They've never gotten over our rebellion against them."

"It's not the British," said the president. "If they had teleportation there would be soldiers popping up all over America with weapons destroying our streets. All over the world, in honesty. They've assured me once he's captured, he'll be interrogated and they will live stream it for us to see, so that the 'special relationship' remains intact."

"He's right," said the secretary of defense, nodding to reassure himself. "If the British government had this technology, they'd have colonised half the world again by now. He's working with somebody else."

"Another nation, do you think?"

"I doubt it. None of the Buddhist nations are sufficiently advanced enough to pull this off. I don't think, anyway."

"Then who?"

"I don't know," said the secretary of defense, rage flaring in his face at the lack of power he had to do anything. "But he definitely isn't working alone."

"I agree we should move to DEATHCON 1," said the president. "Until we can ascertain what he wants, and have the asset secured, we are in danger."

"We need to impose Marshall law," said Eve. "There are already people marching on the streets demanding we convert to Buddhism. There are Christian and Muslim counter protests. There's going to be violence. We need to implement a curfew."

The president didn't like having his ideas given to him, but he knew she was right. "A curfew…In America…"

"I agree," said the secretary of defense. "Marshall Law needs to be implemented immediately. All war stations need to be on the highest alert. We need to ramp up your security detail. There can be no moment you're alone, not at home, not at work, not even when you go to take a leak. He could strike any moment."

"He doesn't want me dead," said the president. "I'm sure of that. But there will be riots. It's in the blood of America to protest. We'll install Marshall Law. Everyone must be in their homes by eight until eight the next day. All protests and demonstrations are to be banned. Call in the army to disband any protests that start, whether they're for or against this so-called prophet. Work is cancelled until we can understand the risks involved, and what it means for America. Madam Secretary, make plans for a stipend to be sent to every American citizen. Borrow it if we need to. People can leave home to get groceries and supplies and that's it. Anyone on the streets after eight risks being killed."

"What about the schools, hospitals, police stations?"

"The schools will be closed; they can move online if needs be. The government will keep running as normal. The emergency services and first responders will be the only people allowed out after eight. See that they get passes to exempt them. I want soldiers in every state in America. We need to reassure the people that we've got this under control."

"Yes, Mister President," said the secretary of defense.

"Am I the only one who thinks that teleportation and time travel are beyond the realms of technology?" said the black woman who had been given the position of secretary of the treasury. "What if this is God, settling the score once and for all? I've been a Christian all my life, but I can't see how time travel or teleportation is technologically possible."

"Anything is possible in this world," said the secretary of defense. "They'd have said it was impossible to speak with someone on the other side of the world two hundred years ago. They said we'd never fly. They thought the fastest we'd ever travel was on horseback. They'd have called you insane if you said there would be a wireless network that connects the entire world, with an almost infinite portal of knowledge at the click of a button or swipe of a screen. It's possible. And it's probable. We just need to get a handle on the technology before it gets into the wrong hands."

"I agree with the secretary of defense," said Eve.

"You make a good point," said the secretary of the treasury.

"Could you imagine the gravity of the Arab countries getting this type of technology? They'd force us all into Islam."

"He's trying to force us into Buddhism, what's the difference?" said the secretary of defense. "I'm a Christian and I'll die a Christian."

"I'm a Christian too," said the president. "But if I had to choose between Islam and Buddhism, it would be Buddhism."

"He hasn't forced anyone to do anything," said the secretary of the treasury. "He said we have to convert willingly. He's trying to persuade us. That's the only thing giving me pause for thought. He could have used the technology to attack, but he hasn't. And the speech he gave, I agree with the president, he meant what he said. Whether he's deluded? Well, that's another question."

"Is there any history of mental illness in the family?"

"Not that I've been told," said the president. "But when the crazies start teleporting, perhaps I'll start listening to what they have to say."

A few of the people around the table laughed.

"How long are we keeping the curfew in place, sir?" said a commander, making notes on an iPad.

"As long as is necessary," said the president. "This could drive America into civil war if we're not careful. The people of this nation are pious, and they will not take his words lightly. We must avoid that at all costs. We need to handle this with the utmost delicateness and consideration."

"I will write a speech for you," said Eve. "I'm assuming you'll want to go live to the nation?"

"I think it's better prerecorded, just in case," said the president. "We can't afford to show any kind of ineptitude, not even a mispronounced word or a pause too long."

"I will have the speech ready in the next few hours," said Eve.

"You've got two hours, max. The people will need reassurance immediately. There'll be people who have completely lost it. Moved into underground shelters. Armed themselves to the hilt."

"Is that such a bad thing?" asked the secretary of defense. "We need our population armed if it's under attack."

"I don't see what good hiding in a nuclear shelter does against someone who appears to be able to travel anywhere in the world. And I don't think he'll attack. He seemed annoyed with poverty, but I didn't get the impression he was going to use violent means to address the issue."

"Sir," said a woman rushing into the room. "I've got the Prime Minister of the United Kingdom on the line. He says it's urgent."

"Yes?" said the president, pressing the phone to his ear. There was a pause as he listened. "Excellent. Keep me updated."

He passed the phone back to the assistant. "They've ascertained the location of the target."

ABU

Abu fingered the gold chain he had worn around his neck since the day Sergeant Abdullah had given it to him after he'd made his first kill, aged thirteen. He had never had anyone he cared about enough to mourn their death. This was the first time he'd ever felt grief. The first time a death had affected him in any way at all, truthfully.

He tried to comfort himself by telling himself that he was now the Sergeant in charge of the Northeastern Nigerian province of the Islamic caliphate of Africa. That Allah had chosen this path for him, and Sergeant Abdullah would be in eternal paradise soon.

The votes from the other commanders had come as a shock to him, he knew the other commanders felt less of him for his albinism and missing fingers, but Sergeant Abdullah had always given Abu the most responsibility, and he had left instructions that if he was to die, Abu was to take his place. So, the commanders had followed his wishes to honour the sacrifice he'd made in becoming a martyr for the Islamic caliphate.

They had managed to rebuff the Nigerian military's efforts to recapture the north of the country. More Muslims had been recruited to the cause, some coming from other parts of Nigeria, and Niger had supplied extra troops to enable them to keep their stronghold in the Northeast.

Abu walked the path to mosque. It was strange for him not using the National Mosque of Abuja. It was the place he felt most at home. The mosque gardens he walked through were prettier than the concrete of Abuja's Mosque, but this mosque was much smaller, and it just didn't feel the same.

The morning was bright but cloudy. The clouds looked like they were bursting with water. He was sure it would rain soon.

He pushed open the doors of the mosque and picked up a prayer mat. Today's prayer time meant more to him than normal. He had seen the trickery of the British. He knew it for what it was, more of their deceit and desire to control the minds of Africans. He needed to speak to Allah to find out what he needed to do. He hoped beyond hope that Allah would respond. He didn't want to act without speaking to him.

He selected a prayer mat and walked to the male section of the mosque. He took his usual position at the back and laid down his mat. After performing the ritual prayer, he spoke directly to God.

"Oh Allah, creator of worlds, decider of souls, I seek your council."

Abu's heart raced in his chest: he could feel the presence of Allah in the mosque.

"Please tell me which path to follow. Guide me in your light."

Africa must be made into an Islamic caliphate, said the voice in his mind. *First the North, then the South. Only then will the other Islamic nations join the cause, and the pretenders can be defeated. You must unite the Muslim world. There can be no more Sunni and Shia. There can be only Muslim and infidel.*

"How can I achieve this: I am but one man?"

Mohammad was but one man. Follow the path you know to be right. Somalia will join you soon. You must get them to join forces with Sudan and invade Ethiopia. Mali must strike north to Algeria. South Sudan must be brought into the caliphate. They must unite Sudan into one country, to heal the divisions of the past. Only then will they bring Egypt into the caliphate. Once the North is united, you will work together to take the Christian lands in the South. You must expel the invaders from Congo. That will be the first Christian nation to fall after Ethiopia, and you will sell its resources to gain the money needed for the battles that lie ahead of you. Once Africa is united, you must declare yourself as a messenger of Allah to the world, and decree that there is to be no more division over Sunni and Shia. People are free to choose when and how they pray. It cannot cause a division within that which should be perfect and whole.

"I will do as you have commanded, Allah. And what of the false prophet?"

The devil has chosen pretenders who will try to convince the people that their false idols and practices are valid. They will use all manner of manipulation to achieve their goal. Their heart is filled with hate, with the fire and deception of Shaitan, and they know what harm they will cause the world, but they do not care. Islam must prevail or all will perish, both on Earth and in eternal fire. I have chosen you for this, above all others, and you must not fail me. You will prevail if you have faith in your path. And you must not waver from it. No matter the price.

"I knew he was the devil the moment I saw his trickery, his magic on the television. The angels warned us of this in Al-Baqarah. I was not so foolish as to believe the lies of Shaitan. I will do as you have commanded, Allah."

The devil will attack the Earth in many forms in the coming years. There will be many pretenders who wish to sully the words of Mohammad. You must not listen to them. The Qur'an has been revealed to the world and it is my final message and commands for the people of Earth. Those who flock to these false idols, for them is a painful punishment; they will know nothing but pain and torment in the afterlife. The Sunnis and the Shias are both misled by their arrogance. Mohammad was the final word, my final prophet. The caliphate should not have been ruled by consensus, neither by the bloodline of Mohammad. The Qur'an should be the only pillars which hold up the caliphate of Islam. There is no place for human interference. The Qur'an acts as the perfect guide to all. You must unite the Sunnis and Shias if you are to succeed in this war. They will be obstinate and intransigent, but you must show them the light. They must give up their practices, both Sunni and Shia, only then will my will be felt in the whole world. Go now from here and fulfil my commandments.

"Thank you, Allah, I will not fail you." Tears sparkled in

Abu's eyes as he opened them. Allah had responded to him again. He had shown him what path to take. It was his duty to unite Africa in an Islamic caliphate and resolve the dispute that had been taking place in the Muslim world since the death of Mohammad. And he would not fail Allah in this task.

He picked up his prayer mat and placed it with the others. The hall was empty except for the imam, everyone else had finished their prayer earlier than him.

He walked back to the encampment with a spring in his step. It was time for them to strike Abuja.

EZEKIEL

Ezekiel stood in the lair under the library reading all the screens. Oscor was showing him news articles, videos, social media posts, news clips and every type of media available. The whole world was talking about him. He'd seen more conspiracy theories about what had happened than he could have possibly imagined. Everything from aliens having invaded the world, to mind controlling space lasers, to the British government having created a machine that could bend light to make it look like a person was in a place that they weren't, to that he was in fact the devil in disguise, here to wreak havoc, and even that the apocalypse had begun. He had no idea how he'd have reacted if he was on the receiving end of what he'd done, so he couldn't judge the world.

What shocked him more were the people who had believed what he had said. It had taken him long enough, and enough trips to the past and future, to finally accept he was the reincarnation of the Buddha. The fact that anyone else could believe it humbled him in a way he'd never been humbled. It filled him with a pride he never thought possible.

He'd had to switch his phone off. Everyone he'd ever met that had his number, and even more people he was sure he'd never given his number to, were calling, texting, instant messaging, sending him direct messages on every social media channel there was. His social media channels had been leaked and he'd amassed millions of followers before Oscor had deactivated them all for him.

Social media. It felt so far away from him. Of so little concern. He'd spent half his life, since he got his first phone, glued to that screen and now he didn't even think about it. He had no impulse to check what was going on in his friends lives or celebrities' lives. He'd only switched his phone on to text his mum and tell her he was safe, not to worry and that he was sorry he didn't tell her all this before he went live. All he cared about now was saving the world, converting people to Buddhism, avoiding the war and sticking to the noble eight-fold path.

"That was quite the speech," said Oscor. "You've done better than I could have hoped. The internet is abuzz with believers. There have already been protests in most countries calling for Buddhism to be installed."

Ezekiel had surprised himself. Everything he'd learned about the world, all the immorality and injustice, it had awoken a flame inside him that couldn't be extinguished. He had a purpose and a mission in life and that mission was to save the world, at any cost.

"That's positive," said Ezekeil, and even as the word positive left his mouth it no longer felt strange that he wasn't using words like 'sick' or 'bad' to describe something good. His vocabulary had come a long way. He was following the third pathway, that of 'right speech'. He'd learnt more words in the past six months than he had in the previous eighteen years. He no longer felt like the words belonged to a race or class other than his own, they were his words, and he had the right – no - the duty, to use them.

"Indeed, it is. I'm proud of you."

"Thanks," said Ezekiel, his brown skin hiding the blushing in his cheeks. "I just hope it has the effect it needs to have. What time is it? I need to eat."

"It's just after four. I can teleport you to get some food, but

I suggest you hide your face. You can't go home; they'll have people stationed outside your house. Outside the houses of everyone you've ever known. You will have to put on that hood you used to love wearing so much. I have one here. And a balaclava. I thought it might come in handy."

A panel retracted and Ezekiel took out a balaclava and an Adidas hoody. It felt strange to wear a designer label, like he was putting on an old version of himself. "I think I'll be fine just walking with a balaclava," said Ezekiel. "I could use the air after everything I've been through, and I need to stretch my legs."

"OK," said Oscar. "Stay safe, and you know where I am if you need me."

"I will," said Ezekiel. He wondered where to eat as he walked the steps that led from the lair to the top floor of the library. He fancied some fries from McDonalds. He didn't think he'd get away with walking around a supermarket in a balaclava but there were self-checkouts at McDonalds. They'd just call his number, and he'd collect it before anyone could say anything.

He left the library, and the security guard looked him over with a frown. If he'd been walking into the library, he was sure he'd be stopped. He was going to have to teleport back in.

He stepped out of the library and several black cars screeched in front of him, some with flashing lights. Something sharp pierced his neck. The last thing he saw were men in suits running over to him as he passed out.

~ * ~

Ezekiel woke up and tried to move. A man in a white coat had just extracted a needle from his neck and was walking away. He was fastened in chains to a chair with lots of wires attached to his body and shackles around his arms and legs. A man and woman in suits sat in chairs watching him.

"The chosen one has awoken at last," said the woman.

Ezekiel scanned the room. There was a machine to his left which was connected to the wires attached to his arms, chest and legs. Two people sat watching him struggle against his restraints. All the walls were made of the same thick concrete, painted a dull green colour.

He pictured the library in his mind and imagined himself there. Nothing happened. He tried again. Nothing happened. *Oscor, help.*

Oscor didn't reply. Could he not hear him? Had they blocked his signal somehow?

"Let me out of here!" exclaimed Ezekiel.

"You're not going anywhere until you tell us how you did it, and why you're claiming to be a prophet."

"I'm not claiming to be a prophet," said Ezekiel. "I am a prophet. I'm the reincarnation of the Buddha, like I told you. And I'm trying to save the world from nuclear annihilation."

"You're trying to save the world from annihilation by starting World War Three?"

"I'm trying to avoid World War Three!"

"Well, you're not doing a very good job. Several nations have already declared war on the United Kingdom, and it's all because of you. So, I'll ask you again, how did you do it and why are you pretending to be a prophet?"

"I did it by thinking about it!" said Ezekiel. "And I told you, I'm not pretending to be anything. I've been back in time, I've seen the Buddha, he was real. And he is God's chosen prophet."

Ezekiel screamed. Electricity poured through every cell in his body. He spasmed in the chair. It spread through his body, tendrils of electricity which formed into rivulets which formed into rivers which formed into seas, until he was drowning in electricity. "Stop, please! Please! Stop!"

The woman pressed a button on the device in her hand and the electrocution stopped.

"I'll ask you again. How did you do it, and why are you claiming to be a prophet?"

"I've told you already!" screamed Ezekiel. "I thought about where I wanted to go in spacetime, and I was transported there. I was chosen by God to be a prophet. I met my future-self in Piccadilly Gardens, and he took me to the future where the whole world was destroyed. Not a soul survived. He told me I was the only one who can end it."

Ezekiel screamed again. He spasmed in the chair as the electric current ran through his body. He could feel it in every limb, every finger, in parts of his body he had never even felt before. "Please, stop! I can't take anymore." He lurched about in the chair for another minute. *Oscor, why are you not helping me?*

"Which countries or organisations are you working for?" asked the man, once they'd stopped electrocuting him.

"I'm not working for any country," said Ezekiel, tears streaming from his eyes. "England is my home. I did what I did to try and save it. I saw Manchester destroyed. That's the whole reason I agreed to any of this. To stop that from happening. Is that what you want?"

"Destroyed by what?"

"Bombs! Nuclear bombs!"

Ezekiel screamed even louder than before. The pain was searing. It was like being stung and burnt simultaneously on the inside of his body.

"I'll ask you again. Who are you working for? You clearly had help. So, tell us who has put you up to this."

"You're insane if you think I'm working for another country. There is no 'organisation'. I did what I did because I saw the buddha in the past and he was floating under a tree by the power of God. I saw the curse that stripped magic from the world. I saw the enlightenment harness the power of God through science, returning magic to the world in the form of technology. I've seen the future destroyed. Converting to Buddhism is the only choice we have. We can't be governed solely by laws and Godless ethics. Moral theism is the only route to safety, and that must be through Buddhism."

The man scratched his head. "Now you're saying there's such a thing as magic. The Buddha could float. That the enlightenment, whose actions were driven by atheistic ideology, were in fact harnessing the power of God? And that the only way we can avoid nuclear war is to accept Buddhism, a religion Britain has rejected for thousands of years, as the only true religion in the world?"

"I'm not saying there is magic in the world. I'm saying there *was* magic in the world. I saw it with my own eyes. Armies of the dead. Fire launched from people's hands. People who could predict the future. Until it was banished from the world by the curse. Then, the buddha came to restore magic to the world, but his spell wasn't strong enough, because not enough people listened to him. The Indians reverted to their old Gods, their false Idols. And yes! The enlightenment returned a form of magic to the world: technology. They're one in the same. You can't access morality, you can't access science, without accessing God. Technology is God's way of restoring magic to the world in a new format. A worse format. We've created our own destruction. We will destroy ourselves if we don't convert."

They electrocuted him again. "Please, stop!" cried Ezekiel spasming. "I can't handle anymore!" He thought of his home, Piccadilly Gardens, any place and any time he'd ever seen to try and teleport there. Nothing happened. He asked Oscor for help in his head. No reply came.

"So, you're admitting it was technology that you used?"

They electrocuted him again.

"Yes," said Ezekiel. "I told you: God has returned magic to the world through technology."

"Who gave you the technology?"

They electrocuted him again.

"It was Turing! Alan Turing!" said Ezekiel, unable to perform any action that would lead to more electrocution.

The woman looked genuinely confused. "He's been dead for over half a century!"

"Yes, but he discovered time travel and teleportation. He saw me in the future. Saw that I had united the world under Buddhism. And it was the only timeline that wasn't destroyed by nuclear war. So, he sent my future-self back in time to show me, so that I could save the world from destruction. I've seen it with my own eyes. The Buddha is God's chosen prophet. Why don't you try reading the Tripitaka and maybe you'll understand. He was the perfect human."

"And are you a perfect human, Ezekiel?"

"No, I'm not perfect. I've made mistakes. But I've repented. I've given up my vices. I've followed the Buddha's journey. I follow the eight-fold path now. I've seen the light. You have to believe me. If you don't convert, all the world will crumble."

"I don't believe you," said the woman. "And you still haven't told us where this technology is stored, how it works or who provided you with it." She pressed a button on the device again.

This time was the most painful. He had no idea what voltage they'd pulsated through him, but it almost knocked him unconscious. It took him a while to regain his senses. "The technology is everywhere! It's like the internet. It isn't stored in a single place, you idiot. And the technology is just a conduit, something to channel the power of God. I'm the reincarnation of the Buddha whether you accept that or not."

They electrocuted him again and the tears gushed from his eyes. He couldn't believe his own country was doing this to him. "Why are you doing this to me? What have I ever done to you? All I'm trying to do is save the world from destruction. Why would you fight me on this? Please, stop torturing me! I've told you the truth! I don't want to see the whole world destroyed by nuclear war!"

They electrocuted him again; this time was the longest. He started to lose consciousness.

The woman walked over and slapped him repeatedly in the face. "Wake up."

Ezekiel heard a voice in his head, slumped over in the restraints. "Go to China," said Oscor. "You must go now."

"Where have you been?" he said aloud. "Why are you letting them torture me?"

"I'm sorry," said Oscor in his mind. "I had to show the world that you meant what you said. I broadcast it live to the world. I'm saving you now." An image flashed in Ezekiel's mind.

Ezekiel used what was left of his consciousness to imagine

himself in the picture. When his vision returned, he was in the President of China's office.

President Chu jumped up in shock. He'd been watching Ezekiel on the screen being tortured and just as quickly as he'd disappeared from the television, he'd appeared in his office. He stumbled backwards, his hand over his heart.

Ezekiel dropped to his knees, tears streaming from his eyes.

"You have to get him to declare China a Buddhist nation," said Oscor. "Take him into the past, show him magic, show him the Buddha in his life, take him to the future, show him China destroyed by nuclear war. You just need to be touching him, and I'll be able to use both of your brainwaves."

"Why have you come here?" said the president.

"I…." Ezekiel staggered to his feet, swaying from side to side as he stood up. He bent over, resting his hands on his knees then wiping the tears from his face. "I have something to show you." He walked over to the president who shirked away as he came close, grabbed his arm, and they both disappeared.

EVE

Eve massaged her head with her right hand. "I can't believe what I just watched. He actually thinks he's a prophet. And he's claiming there was magic in the world. Armies of the dead? He's insane."

"He believes it," said the president. "That much I'm sure of."

"Well," said the secretary of defense, "at least we know the British aren't involved."

"I told you they weren't," said the president. "That isn't their style. They'd have struck hard and fast and colonised the world if they had teleportation."

"I don't understand," said one of the commanders. "Why didn't he just teleport out straight away?"

"I don't know," said the president. "He spoke to some invisible force though, didn't he? He said 'Where have you been? Why are you letting them torture me?'"

"So not only do we have to contend with time travel and teleportation," said Eve, "whoever or whatever he's working with can't be seen. This day just gets worse and worse."

"Sir," said a man walking into the room. "We have a problem."

"What now?" snapped the president.

"It went live to the world," said the man. "They broadcast the interrogation. It's all over the internet."

"Oh, for fuck's sake!" said the president. "That's the last thing we need. There are going to be riots all over the world. Get a press release out immediately and call in the army reserves. Marshall Law starts immediately. All protests are banned. Everyone remains in their house except for essential journeys. And make it seem like we're shocked by Britain's actions. They can't know we had anything to do with it."

"Yes, Mister President."

"This is bad," said Eve. "That video will generate sympathy for him. People are going to believe what he says."

"The Islamic countries have already issued a joint statement, sir," said one of the commanders, reading from his phone. "They're saying he is a false prophet, sent to test Muslim's belief in Islam. They're blaming the West and saying they staged the torture. They're denying that he can teleport and are saying that it's all CGI."

"That's no surprise," said Eve. "They wouldn't listen to Mohammad himself if he came back down to Earth, they're that obsessed with their customs."

"Maybe he is Jesus, re-risen," said the secretary of the treasury. "Think about it. What Jesus did, what he said, it was the complete opposite of what the prophets who came before him said. The Old Testament says to stone people to death, Jesus said that only he who is without sin could throw the first stone. He's radically different. Maybe this was all part of God's plan."

God's plan? thought Eve. *Who hired this imbecile?*

"That makes no sense," said the secretary of defense. "If he was claiming to be the second coming of Jesus, I'd have had more time for him. Maybe I'd have listened. But he's contradicting what the Bible says."

"He's right, we're in a constant state of cyclical war," said the secretary of the treasury. "I've prayed so many times for God to send Jesus back down to Earth, maybe this is his answer. God does work in mysterious ways."

"I'm an atheist," said one of the commanders, "I mean, well I was, but after watching that I'm doubting myself, but I've always thought, if there is a God, maybe he had multiple prophets that he chose, and he just let the forces of war determine which morality the Earth ended up with."

The president blinked as he tried to process that. He wasn't an overtly religious man, but he'd always identified as a Christian. "I don't know what to think anymore."

"He's as good as told us that it's technology he's using," said Eve. "He said technology is 'magic' returned to the world. We just need to find out where he's getting the technology and how it works."

"It isn't the British state," said the secretary of defense, "at least we know that much. And I don't think it's any other country, either. He said it was Turing. And I believe him. He must have cracked the key to time travel and teleportation and gone into the future. He didn't waver on his belief that the world ended in nuclear war in a matter of years. He's definitely seen a future where that happened. We just need to make sure we stop it."

"He said the only way to stop it is to convert to Buddhism," said the secretary of the treasury."

"You don't believe this nonsense, do you, Mister President?"

"I don't know what to believe, damn it," said the president. His skin had turned bright red.

"Well at least we know who's been training him now," said the secretary of defense. "I believe him when he said Turing sent his future-self back in time to warn him. What I don't believe is that Buddhism is the only answer to stopping that. We're the United States of America. Not even Russia has the capabilities to destroy us. If there is a war to come, America will come out on top. He said he saw Manchester destroyed. He didn't say anything about America!"

"He said he saw the whole world destroyed. That includes America."

Eve couldn't believe what she was hearing. "That's

madness. You can't believe he's been to the future and seen all this?"

"Well, he clearly travelled back in time live on the BBC News. He was seen at exactly the same time by news anchors all over the world. He says he met his future-self. It's not unthinkable."

"I'm not ruling anything out," said the president. "All options are open at this point. It's unprecedented and unchartered territory, but the fact he begged them to stop meant he couldn't just teleport out of there. He's less of a threat than we imagined."

"It's not him I'm worried about," said Eve. "It's whoever or whatever he was speaking to when he asked them where they'd been. There must be some… entity… some force that's helping him teleport."

"And you don't think that entity is God?" said the secretary of the treasury. "Do you know any other invisible forces in the world?"

"I know plenty," said Eve. "The internet, radio waves, the list goes on. He could have been communicating using radio waves somehow or the internet for all we know. Maybe he was wearing an earpiece and the British didn't realise."

"Not an oversight they are likely to have made," said the president shaking his head in frustration. It couldn't be God, surely? It was fundamentally impossible. "I don't know who or what he was speaking to, but whatever it was is the thing that's letting him do all this."

"Maybe it's the devil," said the secretary of defense. "The bible warned us about the apocalypse in Revelations. Sounds like what he saw in the future."

Eve didn't know what or who was behind this, but she was sure it wasn't God, or the devil. "It's got to be a machine of some kind. Turing must have created some technology that he's hidden from the world. That's the only explanation."

"And do you think the American people, the world, is going to see it that way?" said the president. "I can see a civil war on the horizon. The American people are not accustomed to seeing people tortured in democracies. They'll be rioting and looting galore."

"Only if we don't keep a hold on the situation," said the secretary of defense. "And it was the British who tortured him, not us, so it's them who are going to have to deal with the most civil discord."

"The British are imposing Marshall Law as well," said one of the commanders reading from his phone screen. "There are riots going on all over the country. They've put in place similar measures to ourselves, and set the terrorism risk level to 'critical'."

"It's the third world we should be worried about," said Eve. "They're the most likely to believe this."

"There have been over ten coups in the last year in Africa alone," said the president. "They declared themselves an Islamic caliphate. I don't think we need to worry about them converting to *Buddhism*."

"We're being attacked on all fronts," said the secretary of defense. "We should strike while the iron is hot. Send a message to the world that America remains strong."

"Africa is not a concern," said the president. "They don't have the reach to get to us. I can't see them leaving their beliefs in Christ or Mohammad. And the Indian government has already rejected him, so they'll be sticking with Hindu nationalism. I don't see what he aims to gain by this. He'd have been better saying he was the return of Christ. He'd at least have the might of the West on his side then."

Thank goodness he doesn't, thought Eve. *And I couldn't see the Americans or the Europeans accepting a black prophet anyway. They'd sooner convert to Islam.* "I think he's the anti-Christ," said Eve. "We were warned in the bible that a pretender would come to Earth claiming to be God's prophet. He seems to fit the bill."

"I'm inclined to agree," said one of the commanders to Eve's right.

The secretary of the treasury looked ashamed of herself for thinking he could be a prophet.

"Prophet, anti-Christ," said the president, "It makes no

difference. The damage is done now. The people will riot. They will protest. Conflict is inevitable."

"It looks like many of the other European countries are also implementing Marshall Law," said one of the commanders, reading from his phone again. "Only the Nordic countries and most of South America are allowing protests."

"Fucking socialists," said Eve. "Let them protest. It doesn't change anything."

"It's Russia and China we need to be concerned about," said the president. "Neither of them has shown their hand and they both have the means to reach us. This could mean war."

PARVATI

Parvati had been in the middle of cooking dinner when they had broadcast Ezekiel being tortured all over the world. She rushed to the living room and watched with horror as she saw him being tortured. She felt genuine compassion for him. She had listened to what he had said: that he had seen himself in the future having picked Buddhism. But she had also seen herself in the future having picked Hinduism, and she could feel the spirit of Lord Shiva's wife within her. She was named Parvati at birth, that couldn't be a coincidence. And while Ezekiel could teleport and time travel, she could read people's minds. She couldn't turn her back on the dream she'd had or the gift she'd been given.

She knew Ezekiel believed what he was saying was true, but she knew the Gods worked in mysterious ways. It could have been Vishnu or Brahma or some other God playing games with his mind. The Gods loved to use humans as pawns in their games.

"How are you feeling?" asked Bhavesh, as they walked along the streets of New Delhi towards the news station.

"I feel conflicted," said Parvati. "I know I've been chosen by Lord Shiva, and I will not ignore the call, but I feel for Ezekiel. I fear the Gods are playing us all."

"It was a horrible sight," said Bhavesh. "Perhaps you're right. The Gods are playing with us all. But you can read people's minds, that must mean something."

"It does mean something," said Parvati. "I've been picked to end the caste system and uphold the Hindu Gods from the external forces that wish to destroy them."

He squeezed her arm. She heard him think, *You will, I know you will.*

"Thanks," she said aloud.

He looked up at her, surprise and awe trinkling in his eyes. He was still getting used to the fact that she could read his mind when they were touching.

The streets of New Delhi were rammed, and the sun glared down on the pair with an intensity Parvati was slowly becoming used to. The air was full of the smell of spices and cooked foods, and Parvati inhaled deeply to savour the scent. Tuktuks and motorbikes weaved through the traffic, squeezing through spaces that Parvati would have thought it impossible to fit through. It was as if everyone in New Delhi followed their own highway code, and it was a code based on personal need, not consideration for the rules that governed the road or the other vehicles who used them.

They arrived at the entrance to Aaj Tak news network, the only network that was willing to hear her out. She had been so adamant on the phone with all the networks, but it had taken Bhavesh offering to pay for them to hear her out.

Parvati pushed open the glass doors to the news station and walked with a newfound confidence and determination to the reception. "We have an appointment with Anika."

"What are your names?" said the receptionist.

"It's Parvati and Bhavesh Khanduri. She should be expecting us."

The receptionist turned to face his computer screen, typing something on his keyboard. "Yes, I see you here. Your appointment isn't for thirty minutes. You can take the lift to the third floor and take a seat in the waiting room. Someone will come to collect you at two o'clock. You'll need badges."

He picked up two pieces of card and wrote their names on them, slipping each one into a lanyard and handing it to them.

"Thank you," said Bhavesh and Parvati.

"Press the floor you wish to go to, and it will tell you which lift to use."

"OK," said Bhavesh. "Thanks."

Parvati got progressively more anxious the closer they got to the lifts.

Bhavesh pushed the number 3 on a touchscreen and the letter B appeared on the screen. The doors to the middle lift opened.

Parvati's soul trembled as the doors of the lift closed. She was just about getting used to using lifts, but telling another person she could read minds, someone who wasn't Bhavesh, it made her anxious.

They found the waiting room and sat down to wait. Bhavesh got up and poured two cups of water, passing one to Parvati as she sat down.

"Thank you," she said, taking the cup and drinking half of it in one gulp.

They sat making idle chatter while they waited, all the while the tension was bubbling in Parvati's stomach. She could feel it rising out of her gut, spreading through her chest and out into her limbs. The cup shook in her hand.

Bhavesh took her free hand and squeezed it. "It will be fine. Just show them what you can do."

She smiled, the reassurance of his love fuelling her calm.

A woman wearing a green saree walked over to them. Her dark black hair was tied back in a tight bun. Circular spectacles hung from the end of her nose as she observed the pair. "Parvati and Bhavesh, is it?"

"Yes," said Parvati.

"Come this way, please."

She led them to a small room. The walls of the room were made of glass. Inside was a square, brown table with four seats. She told them to take a seat and sat opposite them, placing her notepad on the table.

"I have to admit," said Anika, her arms resting on the table. "I am very intrigued by your claims, but I'm also very sceptical. The only reason I've agreed to this is because of everything that is happening in the world at the moment with the supposed reincarnation of the Buddha. The world has gone truly mad."

"I know it's hard to believe," said Bhavesh. "But she can prove it to you."

"OK," said the woman. "What is it I'm thinking?"

"For it to work, I need to be touching you," said Parvati. "And thoughts are often muddled. You must concentrate on whatever you want to me to read, you may need to repeat it in your mind. I will get a rush of all your feelings and thoughts; it can be hard to decipher. Let's start with something simple. Think of a number, a large number with decimal places and repeat it in your mind."

Parvati extended her arms across the table to Anika, palms up. Anika looked sceptical but she placed her hands in Parvati's.

"Think of the number," said Parvati.

There was a pause and Parvati said, "You're thinking of 123,297.856."

The woman drew back her arms from Parvati, her eyes bulging. Fear flushed through her face. "This is a trick of some kind! You have placed some number in my mind by suggestion."

"No," said Parvati. "I heard you think it. Please, place your hands back in mine."

The woman hesitated, then placed her hands in Parvati's.

"Think of your deepest secret, something no one else knows, that I could never know. Think about it and repeat it in your mind."

"I'm not telling you my deepest secret," said the woman.

"You don't believe I can read your mind, so what difference does it make?"

The woman looked away from Parvati and then back to her. "Fine."

Parvati concentrated hard. The woman was thinking many things, mainly about Parvati and how she was doing what she was doing, rather than the memory. "Concentrate, please."

The woman's face hardened, and she stared into Parvati's eyes.

"You're thinking about the time you had pre-marital sex. You were fifteen. Your husband doesn't know, and you're scared if he ever found out that he'd divorce you. It was with a boy from a school near yours. He seduced you for months before you agreed. He bought you flowers, and sweet treats and he would write you notes telling you he was in love with you."

The woman snatched her arms back, she looked angry, she looked scared, she looked… convinced.

"How on Earth?"

"As we told you, Lord Shiva has chosen Parvati to house the spirit of his wife. He has gifted her with the power to read minds and has chosen her to save the Indian Gods and destroy the caste system. I'm a Kshatriya, she's a Dalit. Our marriage was a sacred union blessed by the Gods, and by its power and the power of Lord Shiva, we shall destroy the caste system in India once and for all."

The woman stared at them. She didn't say anything for a minute. "After everything I've seen since that man went live on television, nothing seems impossible anymore. If you're saying Lord Shiva has chosen you, then I believe it." She nodded, convinced. "This is going to be the scoop of the year. Are you willing to go on television to state your claims?"

"Yes," said Parvati, leaning into the woman.

"OK, tell me everything. We go live tonight."

~ * ~

"Hello and welcome to the evening news at Aaj Tak. I'm Deepak Acharya. Tonight, we bring you Breaking News of a woman who claims to be the reincarnation of Lord Shiva's wife with the ability to read minds. Yes, you heard me correctly, there's another person contending for the title of prophet. Please welcome our guests, Parvati and Bhavah Khanduri.

Parvati tried to act as calm as she could. There were several cameras trained on her. Bright lights lit the studio, reflecting into her eyes. "Thank you for having me," she said smiling at the man as she took her seat.

Bhavesh placed his hand on hers, resting on her leg. *You're doing great.*

"So, Parvati, tell us, how is it you came to believe you are a prophet?"

Parvati straightened in her chair. "It all started after I married Bhavesh." She turned to him and smiled before returning her attention to the news presenter. "The day after we married, every time that he touched me, I could hear his thoughts playing in my mind. It scared me at first, and I didn't understand what was happening. I thought maybe it was a special connection between just ourselves."

She turned to Bhavesh and smiled again for reassurance.

"Then I started hearing other people's thoughts whenever they touched me. I ignored it all at first. Then I had the dream, and I couldn't ignore it any longer."

"What dream is that?" said Deepak.

"I was in deep space, there was nothing in sight except for the three Gods, Brahma, Vishnu and Shiva. They each called to me, asking me to come to them. Then I was transported to Nehru Park in the future. I saw three different visions of the future. One where India was destroyed by nuclear war, not a soul survived. Then I saw another vision, one where there had been a civil war, where nearly half the population had died but India still remained. And a final vision, where everything remained alive, all the buildings were intact and people... they flocked to me. They accepted me as a prophet."

"You're also claiming you went into the future?" said Deepak.

"It was more like a vision, but I was inside the vision, if that makes sense?" said Parvati. "They showed me all the possible fates that could befall us. Then I returned to space and the Gods called to me again, and I found myself gravitating towards Lord Shiva. As I neared him, a light shot from his hand, and I felt the spirit of his wife, Parvati, enter my body. Then he spoke to me. He told me that I had been chosen to defend the Gods of India, that he had gifted me the ability to read minds to prove to the people that I am a prophet, and that I had been sent to Earth to destroy the caste system."

"So… You're saying you can read minds, and that you want to destroy one of the oldest institutions in India because Lord Shiva told you to. Why should we believe you?"

"I can prove it, I can read your mind, here, live."

"OK," said Deepak. "Tell me what I'm thinking."

"I need to be touching you," said Parvati. She walked over to Deepak and took his hand in her own.

"Think of a long number, repeat it in your mind, over and over."

Deepak showed his scepticism to the audience with a smirk. "OK, OK, I'm thinking of a number."

He intentionally chose not to think of a number, but one formed in his mind unbidden.

"You tried hard not to think of a number," said Parvati, "but the number ninety-seven thousand flashed in your mind."

The news reader opened his mouth to respond. Parvati interrupted. "That was too simple. Think about your first love, what was her name?"

"Anyone with access to the internet can find out the name of my wife."

"Yes, but that wasn't your first love. I heard you think it as I said it. It was when you were twelve, her name was Saanvi."

Deepak arched his right eyebrow. "Um…that can't be…."

"I told you; I have been chosen by Lord Shiva." She let go of his arm and stood in front of him facing the camera. "India, I have a message for you, from Lord Shiva the Destroyer. I am his chosen prophet, and I have been sent to defend the Indian Gods from those who seek to destroy and desecrate our monuments and our deities. When I married Bhavesh, a Kshatriya, and me a Dalit, we asked the Gods to bless our marriage in place of our parents, and Lord Shiva blessed us. He has gifted me with the ability to read minds and I feel the soul of his wife within me. I have been sent to end the caste system, finally. It must be destroyed if India is to survive. Hold tight to the Gods and pray for their guidance. The only way India will survive is if you accept what I'm telling you. I am a prophet, the wife of Lord Shiva the Destroyer, and the fate of India rests in your hands now. Heed my words. The caste system must fall!"

ABU

Abu thought about what he'd seen Ezekiel saying as he drove
with his soldiers to Abuja. He was surer than ever that he was
sent by the devil. The Qur'an had warned about those who
would claim to be a prophet after Mohammad. He was in no
doubt after speaking with Allah that it was the work of Shaitan;
he had no doubt that Allah had not permitted this abomination
to occur.

His main concern right now was seizing Abuja. Once he'd
done that, he could turn his attention to settling the dispute
between the Sunnis and the Shias and reuniting the Islamic
world as Allah had commanded him.

He picked up his radio, pressed the button and held it to his
mouth. "Split up now. Once you're in place, radio through and
we strike as planned."

The commanders responded letting him know they had
heard the command.

"Pick up the speed," he said to the driver. "Everyone will
be in place within fifteen minutes."

"Yes, Sergeant," said the driver.

The truck sped up. Abu performed Fajr, the morning
prayer, in his mind as they drove to the House of
Representatives. He was going to slaughter every single

politician they met. Muslim or Christian. They were all traitors to Islam. They thought of themselves as the deciders of human fate. Of human morality. They thought of themselves as Gods.

"We're in position," said one of the commanders through the radio.

"Report your positions," he said through the radio.

Most of the commanders were in position. Only Commander Quereshi was still traveling.

"Inform me as soon as you arrive," said Abu.

Abu stroked his beard repeatedly as he waited for Commander Quereshi to radio through to say he was in position.

He got out of the truck, armed up and called on his soldiers. They were a few streets away from the House of Representatives. His soldiers poured out of their trucks, covered to the hilt in weaponry. "Today we take Abuja!" cried Abu.

"Allahu Akbar!" cried the soldiers.

He led them through the streets towards the House of Representatives.

There was an eery silence that set him on edge. Where were all the people? The roads were completely clear. There should be hundreds of people walking about even at this early hour in the morning.

He walked forward, his heart racing. He turned around, there was a sea of soldiers behind him but no pedestrians.

They turned the corner on to the main road and the silence was instantly broken by the sound of sirens screeching around Abu from all directions. Police cars filled the streets. They got out of their cars and immediately started firing on his soldiers.

Fuck. Abu got down on his knees, straightened out his rifle and shot back at the officers.

Most of his soldiers remained stood, creating bigger targets of themselves. They shot at the officers in a hail of bullets.

The police took shelter behind the cars and vans, peering over the top or around the edges to shoot at the invaders.

"Take them out!" said Abu. "Battalion A, to the right.

Battalion B to the left. Battalion C, with me. Everyone else, spread out."

Abu pulled the ring from a grenade that had been tied to his waist and threw it at one of the police cars. It exploded, sending several officers into the air. One of them ran around on fire, screaming.

There was the sound of several loud *cracks* to the right of Abu, something metal hitting hard rock. He turned to see three silver canisters had been thrown into the midst of his forces. White smoke erupted from the cannisters.

Abu ran as far as he could from the teargas, retreating backwards, and many of his soldiers followed. He turned to see at least ten of his men on the floor, coughing in the mist, vigorously rubbing their eyes. Ignoring the fallen soldiers, he fired at the police through the fog.

It was hard to see who or what he was shooting through the white smoke. He fired through the smog, hoping he would hit some of the officers.

Men were falling to the ground all around him, bullets in their legs, their arms, their chests, their heads.

More teargas cannisters were thrown into the midst of the soldiers, creating a thick wall of white smoke. It was almost impossible to see the police officers through the fog.

He retreated backwards from the smoke. Some of it must have reached his eyes before he'd run, because his eyes were stinging but he could still see partially.

He rubbed his eyes vigorously with his hand, leaving his rifle tied around his waist.

Bullet after bullet soared through the air from both directions.

Abu took the ring of another grenade from his waist and ran through the smog with his eyes closed and his top over his mouth and nose. He launched it in the direction he thought the police were.

The grenade hit the ground in front of the officers, not reaching the cars but creating a big enough explosion to send several officers flying in the air.

They crashed to the floor. One of them had cracked their skull open. The two other officers got to their feet and dragged their fallen comrade behind one of the police trucks.

One of Abu's lieutenants ran forward into the white smoke which was slowly dispersing in the open air. He threw a grenade then ran back towards Abu, his eyes squinting.

Abu heard a loud explosion and could just about make out the image of three police cars exploding, sending plumes of fire into the air; killing all the officers who had taken shelter behind or beside them.

The tear gas had almost entirely dispersed in the open air. Some of his soldiers who had managed not to die when they were caught in the fog had gotten to their feet and were firing at the officers with their vision returned.

Abu took stock of the situation. There weren't many police officers left, no longer under the protection of the shield of smoke. He ran forward into the remnants of the smog and threw his last grenade. It was a direct hit. The car exploded and Abu watched with glee as a stray leg landed on the floor metres from him. They were down to eight officers, from what he could see.

"Finish them off!" he called out to his soldiers.

They advanced through the streets, the teargas no longer visible in the air.

The police put up as much resistance as they could. Abu's soldiers finished them off with a hail of bullets. Blood drained through the streets like rainwater.

Abu rounded up his soldiers that were still standing. He left those that were injured where they were. He didn't have time or the facilities to attend to their wounds. They had a mission to complete. "On to the House of Representatives!"

"Allahu Akbar!" cried the soldiers, running forwards down the road.

"Allahu Akbar!" said Abu, running with his soldiers through the streets of Abuja.

They turned the corner onto the road which led to the House of Representatives.

Armoured trucks and tanks were lined up on the streets as Abu and his soldiers made their advance. A war cry emitted from Abu's throat. "Kill them all!"

He launched his gun in the air and started shooting at everyone he saw. He reached down to grab a grenade and let out a raging, raucous roar. He had used them all on the police. He hadn't anticipated two layers of resistance.

He fired at the soldiers frantically. There were four of them for every one of his own soldiers.

Canisters were launched from the army vans into his forces, teargas pouring out of them. Abu's eyes burned and he ran around like a headless chicken, trying to get out of the smog.

He stumbled along, unable to properly see where he was going, wiping his eyes constantly.

The pain seared, pulsating through is eyes, like a bee was stinging his eyeballs in second intervals.

More and more soldiers from the Nigerian army flooded the streets forming a human shield between Abu's forces and the House of Representatives.

Abu couldn't see, but all around the building, where his other commanders and soldiers were stationed, was also full of soldiers from the Nigerian armed forces. They were being repelled from all sides.

Abu screamed, a fury blazing from his throat. He *had* to take Abuja. He could not fail Allah. He had to secure the caliphate.

He crouched down to make himself smaller, waiting for the burning in his eyes to subside. He couldn't shoot what he couldn't see.

A bullet flew past his head, missing him by millimetres. He spun around wildly, not sure which direction to go in. He could just about see the white mist in the distance through his blurred vision. He ran in the opposite direction and waited for the teargas to wear off, rubbing his eyes as he ran haphazardly down the road, as though this would lessen the sensation of burning.

He found the wall of a garden and climbed behind it, waiting for his vision to return and the burning sensation to stop.

Oh Allah, please, guide me to victory, he thought. He prayed with all his soul. He could not fail in this mission. Abuja had to fall.

He sat with his head resting against the back of the wall, and his vision slowly started to return and the burning sensation in his eyes dulled.

He peered over the wall just in time to see a soldier taking aim at him. He dropped to the floor and hid behind the wall to avoid the gunfire.

He got to his knees and positioned his rifle on the wall, shooting several times in the relative direction of the soldier.

He didn't hear any more shots flying his way. He raised his head above the wall just enough to see over it. There was a soldier walking towards him with his gun raised. He fired three bullets, one of them hitting the soldier in the head.

Abu smiled as he dropped to the ground.

He ran out from behind the wall and back to his soldiers. All around him his soldiers were dropping like flies.

He was too exposed. He ran back behind the wall, lifted his rifle and rested it on the wall, taking aim at as many soldiers as he could see, and just firing aimlessly in their direction when he couldn't make out a clear target.

Loud explosions permeated through the sounds of gunfire. The tank was firing on his men. He watched aghast as they flew into the air, their limbs scattering about like a windmill of hands and legs.

He screamed. He would not fail Allah. He could not! He lifted his rifle to shoot and clicked the trigger. Nothing happened. His gun was out of bullets. He screamed again. He patted down all his pockets looking for more bullets. He had used them all. He screamed. A scream that would have shattered the ear drums of anyone close enough to hear.

All he had left was his knife. He took it from the strap on his leg and jumped over the wall into the fray.

A soldier from the Nigerian army shot at him and he dived to the side and rolled over, barely missing the gunfire. The soldier tried to take aim again, but Abu launched himself on top of the soldier and tried to wrestle the gun from his hand.

The two men tumbled around on the floor, each of them trying to get a handle of the gun. Abu punched the soldier in the face with his free hand, and in the momentary lack of concentration, he grabbed his knife and stabbed the soldier in the throat.

He got to his feet, grabbed the gun from the soldier and shot him in the head to make sure he was dead.

The cannon fired on his soldiers again, killing tens of them in a single shot. He'd lost at least three quarters of his men already. There was no other option. They were going to have to retreat. "Fall back," he called to his men. "Fall back."

No one could hear him over the sounds of the battle.

He ran down the street away from the battle towards where he'd parked his truck.

He fell to the floor and cried out in pain. A bullet had hit the back of his leg. He rolled around on the ground. His leg burned like someone was pressing a hot coal against it.

Dragging himself up, he turned around with his gun ready to shoot. There were too many soldiers. He couldn't see who was shooting at him. He sent a spray of bullets in the direction of the fight, not caring if he hit his own soldiers.

He turned back around and tried to get to his feet. His leg spasmed as he tried to use it to walk. He limped down the road using the rifle he'd stolen from the soldier as a makeshift crutch.

The street with his trucks came into view. He limped as fast as he could to his truck. There were no soldiers on the streets here. Just empty trucks that would never be driven back to the Islamic caliphate.

I have failed you, Allah. I am sorry.

He pulled open the door to the truck and tried to start the ignition. His hands were shaking. He dropped the keys on the floor.

Scrambling with his good hand, he grasped around on the floor for the keys. His hand hit something metal, and he pulled the keys up, his hands trembling even harder than before. His leg stung; blood poured onto the floor of his car.

He pulled off his armour and jacket and tour his t-shirt

apart, wrapping it around the wound to stem the flow of the blood.

They had hit him in the right leg, the one he needed to drive. He banged his arms on the steering wheel in frustration.

He managed to get the keys into the ignition and started the engine.

Crossing his left leg over to the pedal, he pressed down on the throttle and accelerated as fast as he could back to the safety of the caliphate.

EZEKIEL

Ezekiel let go of the president's arm. He whispered in his ear. "Be quiet. No one can see us. Speak softly and watch."

"OK," whispered President Chu.

Ezekiel could hear him breathing heavily, could almost feel his heart racing through his body.

"This is Shaanxi province in 1500 BC, just before the curse was cast."

Men on horseback galloped towards each other, an army behind each of them. As they neared closer the president saw that some of the 'soldiers' were actually made of stone.

"What is that?"

"They've bewitched the stone," said Ezekiel. "So that it can fight in their wars."

"It cannot be," said the president, but even as he watched, the stone statues launched attacks against men, stabbing swords into their gut, smashing their maces into other statues, crushing them into a crumpled mess.

Lightning struck at random points throughout the battle, hitting soldiers and stone statues, which crumbled under the force of the lightning.

"See those men and women wearing robes at the side of the battle?" said Ezekiel, pointing with his right arm.

"Yes," said the president, who sounded as shocked as he was scared.

"They're causing the lightning. I wasn't lying when I said there was magic in the world."

"So, you are magic?" said the president.

"No," said Ezekiel.

"Then how have you brought me here? How are these people doing this?"

"Magic existed in the world for thousands of years before the curse. It wiped magic from the Earth by channelling the power of God. I will take you there next, so you can see for yourself. As for how we got here, that's not magic, it's technology. It still harnesses the power of God, but it's managed by machines invented by humans. Electromagnetism from our brain, that's as much as I know. Acceleration minus motion equals time travel. Or in this case deceleration, as we've gone backwards through spacetime."

"So, my people were magic? They had the ability to harness magic?"

"Yes, most of the world did," said Ezekiel. "Until the curse. I will take you there now, to see for yourself."

He grabbed President Chu by the arm, and they arrived on top of a mountain as the Jewish sorcerers cast their curse to banish magic.

The president watched in awe as they spoke, light flashing from their hands and the flame roaring higher and higher and changing colour.

"They are using a spell, the words of the Torah, to banish magic from the world. To end the tyranny of the Egyptians through the power of God."

"I cannot believe what I am seeing," said the president, "and yet I see it!"

"It was hard for me to accept at first as well, but technology isn't really that different from magic, it's better in many ways. There's more I must show you."

He grabbed the president by the arm, and they arrived in India in 600 BC.

A man in orange robes walked through a crowd speaking in a language the president couldn't understand. People came up to him, and he would place his hand on their head and speak. They would smile and walk away, allowing the next person to come.

"That's the Buddha, Siddhartha, spreading his message. This is the year 600 BC in the Christian calendar."

The president looked around him. The buildings, the clothes they were wearing, this was clearly not modern-day India.

Siddhartha walked through the crowd. Everyone reached out to him as he walked by them barefoot. People would offer him food, which he took and placed in his bowl, bowing to whomever had given it to him.

"This does not prove that he was a prophet, simply because he existed. People will believe almost anything, and they do so regularly."

"Did China not accept the Buddha as much as they accepted Confucius? It is one of the reasons I am so proud of you. You accepted a religion that was from a person who was a different race to you. And what a glorious morality base for the population. I understand exactly why your ancestors accepted it. Buddhism is the truest approximation of morality I have found."

"You know a lot about the history of China," said President Chu.

"I know a lot about the history of the world, including many things that would shake you to your core. I would not have believed it if I had not seen it, but there is not time for that now. I have come to show you the light of the Buddha. To prove to you he existed and that he was a chosen prophet of God."

"This still doesn't prove he is… God's… chosen prophet."

"I have more to show you," whispered Ezekiel. "But you must be quiet. We cannot attract attention to ourselves."

He grabbed the president by the arm and imagined himself in the forest where the Buddha went to meditate.

Siddartha walked to a tree and sat down. He crossed his legs over one another and closed his eyes. He started to rise from the ground, floating in the air.

"That's the Buddha. He's meditating."

"He could… float?" said the president. His mouth was wide open, gawping, looking from Ezekiel to the floating Buddha. "It cannot be. It simply cannot. I thought you said magic was banished from the world nearly a thousand years earlier."

"It was," said Ezekiel. "But God bestowed him with magical power so that he could prove himself to the world as a prophet of God. Why do you think so many nations accepted a foreign religion, spread not by the sword but simply by conviction of thought and morality. Have you ever known any other religion to spread so quickly and so far throughout the world without the use of force?"

The president shook his head. "You are right, there has been no other."

"Exactly," said Ezekiel. "You have travelled through time; you have seen the power of the Buddha and the powers that were bestowed upon him by God. You have seen what I needed to show you. But there is one last thing you must see."

He grabbed the president by the arm again and imagined himself in the future.

The president's mouth opened wide like a fish out of water gasping for air. Everywhere he looked were dead bodies and bombed out buildings. All the progress that had been made in China over the last century reduced to rubble. All the hard work of the government, of his ancestors, reduced to ashes.

"This is Beijing," said Ezekiel, "ten years from now. This is what will become of the world if you do not accept the light of the Buddha."

"This cannot be," said the president, tears forming in his eyes.

"It doesn't have to be," said Ezekiel. "It can be stopped. We can stop it together."

"How?" said the president, turning to face Ezekiel.

"By accepting what I'm telling you!" said Ezekiel.

The president turned in a circle, looking at his destroyed city, the skinless bodies that lined the streets, the burned-out cars that had once driven the now shattered roads, the crumbled remnants of once grand buildings.

"We must return now," said Ezekiel. "There is nothing more to see here." He grabbed the president by the arm and teleported him back to his office.

He released the president's arm once they were back in his office. "Do you believe me now?"

The president shook his head and sat in his chair. He rested his head in his hands. "How can I not? I have seen it with my own eyes."

"So, will you accept me as a prophet?" said Ezekiel, imploring him with his eyes, his voice, his very being. "It is imperative that China declares itself as a Buddhist nation. And they must do it first. That is imperative."

The president looked up at him. "I am the leader of the People's Republic of China. We are atheist at the core. This would mean a fundamental change in our entire ideology. To our entire society. To our customs and our values."

"China is no longer a communist state. Globalisation and trade have forced you into socialism. If that has changed, why not too religion? People here still worship the Buddha, and follow his message, despite your best efforts. If you do not declare for me, the world will end and in ten years there will be no China. And what of their souls, will you condemn them to damnation for the sake of your pride?"

"Their souls!" said the president, shaking his head as he tried to comprehend the concept of life beyond death. "Do you know what you are asking of me? This will mean war. The United States of America will never accept this."

"The world has been dictated to by America for long enough. Where is your pride in your nation? You have the largest army in the world. You have the second highest GDP of any nation. You have the second highest population of any nation. You are a formidable opponent for even America. And you have an alliance with Russia. They would not dare to attack.

You must declare for me. If you don't the world will end in ten years. Is that what you want, to see China, the world, destroyed?"

The president looked up at him then closed his eyes. He opened them again after what felt to Ezekiel to be an eternity. "I cannot drag China into war. We have managed to avoid war with the imperialists despite their aggression and their best efforts to curtail our development and progression."

"There will be a war if you do not declare yourself," said Ezekiel, the desperation in his voice clear for the president to hear. "You are the only hope. I met myself from the future and he said that you must declare for me first. I didn't understand what he meant then, but I do now, you must declare China a Buddhist nation and accept me as a prophet of God."

"So, you want to be our prophet? To rule over us?"

"No!" exclaimed Ezekiel. "I have no ambition to rule anything. I will not interfere in Chinese affairs in anyway. I respect China. You have a proud history and a great culture. You have many great ancestors from Yu the Engineer to Chairman Mao. You adopted communism, you tried to make the world more even: you've lifted hundreds of millions of your people out of poverty. You send your soldiers to die on peacekeeping missions that have no benefit to the Chinese state. You have a sensible attitude to debt, not racking up debt to the entire GDP of your country and above. You've made China into a great country. I'm just asking you to help me, to help the world. I know you don't want to see China destroyed, and neither do I. I just need you to support me in this. Or else, all will be lost."

The president looked pensive. He seemed reassured that Ezekiel wasn't there to steal his power.

"China has always allowed religious freedom while ensuring a separation of religion and state. This will change the very fabric of our society."

"Communism was completely opposite to traditional Chinese society, and your ancestors adopted that, because it was the right thing to do for the masses. I'm not asking you to force people to be Buddhist. It must be their choice. I'm just asking you to declare for me, and for Buddhism. Your people will follow your lead, as they always have."

"And what happens when they are all Buddhist, what then? Anything you say will hold power over them."

"I told you already!" snapped Ezekiel, shouting now. "I'm not fuckin' interested in power, in ruling China or any other country. All I care about is saving the world. I didn't ask for any of this. I didn't ask to be picked by God. I didn't ask to be the reincarnation of the Buddha. You saw them torturing me! I've given up everything I knew for this, everything I thought and believed, my friends, my family, my own Christian faith, I gave it all up to save the world. All I'm asking you to do is declare for me. And I'm asking you to do this so that we have a chance of avoiding nuclear annihilation and the total destruction of not only China, but the entire world."

"I… I… It just…" said the president.

"You need to declare for me!" said Ezekiel, his voice full of conviction. "I need you to pledge allegiance to me and the Buddha on national television. Tell them the truth. That you went back in time. That you saw the Buddha, saw him floating, saw him speaking with the people and spreading his message. That you went to the future and saw China destroyed. That you have no choice but to accept what you've seen with your own eyes and declare China a Buddhist nation if it is to have any chance of survival."

The president let out a heavy sigh. He looked up at Ezekeil, staring into his eyes.

Ezekiel's eyes were glistening with unblinked tears. He couldn't afford for China not to declare.

The president could see the compassion in his eyes, the longing, the fear of not achieving what he was asking, and he knew in his soul that Ezekiel was telling him the truth. "OK," he said after a long pause. "I will do as you have asked. China will declare itself a Buddhist nation. You have my word."

PARVATI

News had spread throughout all of India of the woman claiming to be the reincarnation of Lord Shiva's wife, Parvati. She was all over social media, and the news had even reached the wider world, who now had two people to contend with claiming to be prophets, with abilities that should be impossible. Parvati had made no mention of other states, and had addressed India solely, but there were still people around the world who already believed she was a prophet.

People had flocked from all over India to come to New Delhi and meet with the mind reader, to see for themselves if she really could read people's minds. Most of them just wanted to meet her, to feel the presence of Shiva the Destroyer, returned to India to destroy the caste system.

The news that she wanted to revolutionise India, to break the shackles of a caste system that had existed for almost as long as the civilisation of the Indian subcontinent, the system that rendered an entire group of people as *literally* untouchable by the rest of society had been received with mixed results. Naturally, the 'high born' had come out saying they did not accept the authenticity of what she was saying, and that was to be expected, but many of the lower caste also couldn't accept what she was saying.

They were stuck in Stockholm syndrome, unable to see the path to their liberation that had been laid before them. They were so conditioned into thinking they were the bottom of society that they accepted it, just as the slaves of Egypt had accepted it was their place in life to be slaves, just as those first Caribbean and American slaves had come to accept their role in white society as subordinate, just as women had accepted their place as homemakers and babymakers in the face of the patriarchy, just as the poor had accepted their natural place as peasants in every country on the Earth.

But just like the rise of women in society, like the abolition of slavery, the empowerment of the underclass to reach whatever goal they aspired to, the seeds of change had been planted in the minds of the people, and it was flourishing; there was no stopping it. More and more people were questioning the caste system. It had been outlawed by the government already, but it was still widely practiced. Bhavesh's father's reaction to their marriage had been more than enough proof of that.

They'd needed to run away just to get married. He would never have given his blessing to their marriage, and neither would her own parents, lest they cast shame on Bhavesh's family. Parvati was several months pregnant now, and she was starting to show. Her sarees no longer fit her, and she had had to buy new ones to accommodate the growing human inside her. She was sure it was a boy, and she thought of it as a prince, not least because she was Lord Shiva's wife, but because Bhavesh had been a prince in all but name and would always be *her* prince.

Their relationship had gone from strength to strength since their marriage and it was the best decision she'd ever made in her life. She was as happy as she'd ever been, and he'd supported her in every way that a husband could support a wife. He'd gone above and beyond in every way, and the fact he accepted that she was a prophet meant more than the approval of the whole of India, the world even.

He walked with her through the park to the waiting crowds,

holding her hand. *You've got this*, he thought. He had learnt to communicate with her by thought almost as much as through speech, and while he couldn't read her thoughts, he could sense her emotions. He knew she was nervous about all the crowds who had come to see her, but she had grown more confident in recent weeks, she was stronger as a person, and finally, she viewed herself with as much respect as he had always viewed her. And that was the greatest gift that Lord Shiva had given them.

They approached the mass of people and Parvati let go of Bhavesh's hand. The crowd flocked to her, all of them reaching out to touch her. Hundreds of thoughts sounded in her mind at the same time as people from all directions fought to touch the living embodiment of one of their Gods. Her head spun with all the different thoughts.

"Please," said Parvati, "form a line. Each of you will get the chance to speak with me."

Some of the crowd formed into a line, but others continued to crowd around her, touching her and throwing rose petals at her feet.

"Form a line!" called Bhavesh, bellowing through the crowd. "You will all be seen."

There had to be at least two hundred people who had come to see her, and this was on the light side, she'd been doing daily greetings in the park ever since her television appearance. She felt it important to connect with the people and show as many people as she could that she could read their mind.

The crowd eventually got into a line and Parvati walked to the person stood at the front.

"Lady Parvati," said the man at the front of the queue. "It is an honour to meet you. I saw you on the television. I believe that you are the reincarnation of the first Parvati."

Parvati smiled at the man. Bhavesh passed her a bowl with red powder in it and she placed a bindi on the man's head. "I bless you. May you know peace and prosperity."

"Thank you, Lady Parvati," said the man. He took her hand and kissed it. As he did so, she heard him think, *What a beautiful woman*.

"Thank you, you're too kind," said Parvati.

The man smiled. He knew she had read his mind. "My Lady." He kissed her hand again and moved out of the queue, staring at Parvati from the sides.

An old woman, at least seventy, with greying hair and the telltale signs of Dalit attire was next. She held her hands out to Parvati. "Saviour," said the woman. "You have set us free." Her eyes filled with tears. "How can we repay you? What can we do?"

"You must simply cherish the Gods and spread my message to all who will listen."

"I will do this until my last breath," said the woman.

Parvati took some powder in her hand and placed a bindi on the woman's head. "May your life be fulfilled and prosperous. May you know wealth and comfort and happiness."

The woman thanked her and moved to the side, watching her intently.

Next in line was a much younger woman who was wearing an expensive saree. Parvati guessed she must be high born. "I needed to see for myself," said the woman. "To be sure. What you're proposing is revolutionary. May I take your hand?"

Parvati offered her free hand to the woman who clasped it firmly in her own.

"Please, tell me what I'm thinking."

Parvati listened carefully to the woman's thoughts. "You're thinking about your son, about who he has been betrothed to. He has told you that he does not wish to marry her but to marry another. She is of the same caste as you, but he was promised to another at birth. You are conflicted. You want to believe that Shiva the Destroyer has empowered me to end the caste system, but you need further proof. You are scared that I will not be able to tell you what you want to hear."

The woman smiled. Her cheeks could not contain the smile. She positively beamed at Parvati. "I knew it was true. I knew as soon as I saw you on the news, I knew you had come to save the Gods of India and end the caste system. Thank you, Lady Parvati."

"You are welcome," said Parvati. She took her hand from the woman and pinched some of the red powder in her finger, placing a bindi on the woman's forehead. "May you have the strength to honour the wishes of Lord Shiva. May your son know happiness and may you too know happiness through his happiness."

The woman bowed to Parvati and walked away from the crowd, still smiling.

The next woman in line grabbed Parvati by the hand. Her grip was firm, and it made Parvati a little uncomfortable. She could hear the woman's thoughts. She was thinking that she loved Parvati. That she'd loved her ever since the moment she saw her on television. It made Parvati feel weird. She had never felt the attraction of a female before. Only men and women married in India. She had never truly considered the concept. And she had to admit, while there were many customs for male and female marriage, none of the Gods had ever shown any disapproval of the practice of homosexuality or the attraction. They hadn't felt it noteworthy in anyway.

"I had to see you," said the woman. "I had to meet Lady Parvati. I had to see your beauty for myself. I had to know your touch."

Parvati recoiled slightly inside, but she did not flinch or move as the woman clung to her arm. "It is a pleasure to meet you." She pinched some powder and placed a bindi on the woman's head. "May you know love and happiness. May your life be filled with joy and hope."

"Thank you, Lady Parvati," she said. *You are more beautiful than I could have imagined*, she thought.

The woman let go of her arm and walked to the back of the queue.

Parvati had no time to contemplate what had just occurred as the next person in line greeted her. A young boy, no older than twelve. He looked up at her with reverence in his eyes. His clothes were tattered. He looked very thin. Parvati knew he was a street child.

"Is it true?" he asked. "Has Lord Shiva sent you to end the caste system?"

"It is true," said Parvati, smiling at the boy. "You will know freedom in your lifetime."

"Can you show me, please? Can you show me the future?"

"I cannot," said Parvati. "But I can read your mind. Give me your hand."

The boy placed his hand in hers.

Parvati's cheeks dropped and her face was full of sorrow. The boy thought of food, of the nights he had spent on the streets of New Delhi, of his parents who had left him on the streets, though he could not recall their faces anymore, it had been so long. He thought about the men he'd met, the ones who had helped him and the ones who had taken advantage of his poverty. Her eyes filled with tears.

"I am so sorry," said Parvati. "You should not have to endure as you have." She turned to Bhavesh. "Have you brought money?"

"Yes," said Bhavesh. "Good, give it all to me."

Bhavesh took out his wallet and handed her thousands of rupees.

"Here," said Parvati, handing the cash to the boy. "I hope this helps."

The boy's eyes bulged, glistening with awe and wonder, both at the amount of money in his hand and at Parvati who was the living embodiment of a God. "Thank you! Thank you so much!"

Parvati took some powder from the pot and placed a Bindi on his head. "May your nights be warm; may you find refuge and shelter in life. May you know peace and comfort. I pray your dreams come true."

The boy thanked her, a grin stretching from ear to ear.

She took his head in her hand and bestowed a kiss on his forehead. "Know that you are loved."

The boy looked like he would cry but he held back his tears and walked away, clutching the rupees in his hand.

Hours passed before Parvati had finished greeting each person who had come to see her. Many of them stayed in the park to watch her as she left. She waved to them and blew kisses. Bhavesh walked by her side, holding her hand.

"The people love you," he said.

Parvati could not deny the truth of his words. The people did love her. They accepted her as a prophet. She *was* a prophet. Lord Shiva had chosen her. Or rather, she had chosen Lord Shiva. And she was glad. He was the destroyer, and the caste system needed destroying. "And I love them," she said, finally.

"I can see that," said Bhavesh. "You truly are the light of my life."

"And you, mine," said Parvati.

They left the entrance to the park. Several black jeeps pulled up in front of the pair. Suited men got out of the car.

"Parvati," said one of the suited men. "The prime minister wishes to speak with you, with you both. You must come with us."

Bhavesh shot her a concerned look, but she did not feel fear anymore as she once had. Lord Shiva guided her, and no one could hurt her while he protected her.

"OK," she said. "Let us go."

EVE

"This is worse than COVID," said Evelyn, sitting on the couch opposite her mother. "When are we going to be allowed back out?"

"I don't know," said Eve. "There's a lot going on in the world right now."

"At least we don't have to go to school," said Sarah.

"At least we get to see our friends at school."

"I think they're planning to start teaching you all remotely," said Eve. "The education secretary is putting the plans in place."

"Oh no!" said Sarah.

"So, we still have to learn, and we're not allowed to socialise with our friends?"

"You spend most of your time on your phone and tablet anyway," said Eve. "I didn't realise children still socialised in person. I thought you were over that kind of thing."

Mark laughed.

Evelyn rolled her eyes. "Very funny, Mom. It's not the same if you don't at least see them in person every now and again. There's nothing to talk about because no one is doing anything. Just sitting indoors waiting for the president to let us all out again."

"It's for your own safety," said Mark. "There are protests going on all throughout the country. There have been clashes with the police and the military. I wouldn't let you out in that even if we weren't all under lockdown."

"Your father is right," said Eve. "The safest place for both of you is indoors."

An iPhone notification pinged in the room. Evelyn picked up her phone and stopped protesting to her parents about her incarceration, swiping away on her screen as though the rest of the room no longer existed.

"I'm going to make a coffee," said Evelyn. "Would you like one?"

"Yes, please, hon," said Mark.

She poured the coffee beans into the grinder and pressed the button. It whirred as it turned the coffee into a fine powder.

Mark switched on the TV and flicked through the stations until he found ABC News.

Eve poured the ground coffee into a filter and poured boiling water through it. She emptied it into two mugs. She added some creamer to both but no sugar in either.

"Here you are," she said passing the cup to Mark. She took a seat next to him.

"Thank you."

"The country remains in lockdown following the president's decree for Marshall Law," said the news anchor. "People are advised to only leave their house for essential journeys and to remember the eight o'clock curfew."

The screen flashed with the words 'BREAKING NEWS' in thick silver lettering against a red background.

The message disappeared and the anchor could be seen touching her finger to her ear. "This just in, some breaking news from Asia. China has declared itself a Buddhist nation and has claimed it accepts Ezekiel Campbell as a prophet. This is coming directly from the President of the People's Republic of China. We will bring you more on this story as it develops."

"You have got to be fucking kidding me!" said Eve, jumping to her feet. "Unbelievable!"

Her children looked up at her with open mouths.

Eve grabbed her phone and keys from the kitchen counter. "I'm going to have to go into work."

"I can't believe what I've just heard," said Mark. "China! A communist nation!"

"Neither can I," she said. "I don't know what time I'll be back, but I assume it will be late, if at all. Make sure the girls stay indoors."

"Of course," said Mark. "Stay safe out there. Phone me if you need me for anything."

Eve gave him a curt nod and strode from the room. She pulled on her coat and got into her car. She sped out of her driveway with an uncharacteristic impulsiveness. She zoomed down the road, well above the speed limit.

How the fuck has he managed that? That little bastard! I'm going to kill him.

Eve tutted and pulled her vehicle over at a makeshift checkpoint that had been set up to enforce the curfew.

"What is your business out of your house, ma'am?" said the officer.

"I'm the vice president!" snapped Eve. "And if you hadn't heard, China has declared itself a Buddhist nation. Now let me through."

"Sorry ma'am," said the officer, recognising Eve from the television. His cheeks flushed with embarrassment. "I didn't recognise you at first." He quickly waved to the officers, and they moved the fencing out of the way to let her through.

China had clearly lost its mind. What had that fucker done to bring them onside? She rightly assumed he must have teleported to China when he left and convinced them to align with him somehow.

She smacked the steering wheel in frustration. This was the last thing she needed. The stuff she had on the president wouldn't be enough to bury him at a time of war. It would be like water off a duck's back. She was in touching distance of the presidency and this pretender and China had to go and fuck it all up for her. She screamed, showing a lack of composure that shocked even her.

She drove as fast as she could to the White House, through red lights, stopping only at the checkpoints that had been set up and exploding at every officer who didn't immediately recognise her.

"Vice President Jones," said a secret service agent who had come to her window as she approached the gates of the white house.

"Let me through," she said, not bothering with any pleasantries.

"Right away, ma'am," said the agent. He signalled to his associates, and they opened the gates for her.

She drove down the path with as much restraint as she could muster. She grabbed her lanyard from the car and raced through the building to the president's office. She knocked at the door.

A secret service agent answered. "It's the vice president, sir."

"Let her in," said the president. "I take it you've heard the news?"

"They've lost their fucking minds!" said Eve. She walked over to the president and sat opposite him in the brown cushioned chair.

"What would the communist party have to gain from accepting him as a prophet?" said the president. "It just doesn't make sense. The commis are atheist."

"He must have gotten to them somehow," said Eve, stroking her nail with her finger. "I bet he went there after he teleported out of Britain."

"They have been unable to relocate him since. They've got people stationed at everyone's house he's ever come into contact with. There's no sign of him anywhere."

"I don't think he's stupid enough to go to anyone that knows him," said Eve. "Not after he was captured."

"I'm surprised they managed to bring him in at all," said the president. "At least we got some information out of him. It's his comment about magic I can't get over. There are lots of mentions of magic in the bible. About the ills of it. It does give one cause for thought."

"Please!" said Eve. "Do not tell me you are sympathising with the enemy?"

"He hasn't declared himself an enemy of any nation," said the president.

"I wouldn't call his speech a glowing review of American diplomacy."

The president nodded reluctantly. "I'm at a loss for what to do. We can't keep people locked up forever."

"No, we can't," said Eve, though she was insane enough to consider it if it meant achieving what she wanted in life.

"What would you propose?" said the president.

"I think we should make an announcement like the Islamic countries. I think we should say we believe him to be a false prophet, the anti-Christ, and that any nation who supports him is an enemy of the United States of America."

"The last thing we need is a war with China. And if Russia gets involved, there really will be a nuclear Armageddon."

"What has President Pavlov said about all this?"

"We haven't had word on that yet, we're waiting to see what moves they make. They have a military alliance with China. Even if they don't declare for this… prophet…" he expanded his arms as he said the word 'prophet', "they will not allow us to take China. It's too close to home. We'd have surrounded them on all fronts. They're already touchy about the expansion of NATO."

"Fuck China and fuck Russia. We are the United States of America for fuck's sake! No one has the power to defeat us. No one! The whole world could wage war on us, and we'd still win."

The president looked at her, as though seeing her for the first time. "I won't drag America into another pointless war. We've lost enough good men and women without sending them to their death because someone claims to be a prophet. Lots of people have claimed to be prophets. There's a woman in India claiming to be the wife of one of their Gods, I don't remember which, Lord something. She's saying she can read minds. Let the people believe what they want."

"We need to act," said Eve. "We need to be proactive, not reactive. We can't just sit idly by and wait for war to come to our shores. We need to strike now."

"I will not go to war over this!" said the president.

"So, what are you going to do?" said Eve, who was shouting now.

"I'm going to let things settle. I'm going to make an announcement to the country. Remind them that we are a nation that accepts all religions. That anyone who wants to accept this Ezekiel as a prophet can, but they're under no obligation to do so and we remain a country with a separation of church and state. Hell, they can proclaim the Indian woman a prophet if they want. It makes no difference. We're the government. Our job is to govern, not to dictate people's religions."

"Exactly, we're the government, and it's our job to govern. Not just America, but the world. And if you're not going to do it, I'll do it myself."

"What is that supposed to mean?" said the president.

Eve shot to her feet and walked to the door. She grabbed the gun from the secret service agent's holster and shot him in the head. She turned to face the president and shot him three times, twice in the head and once in the chest. She turned the gun on herself and shot herself in the arm.

She screamed, throwing the gun on the floor. She had never felt pain like it.

Security agents came running in the door, guns out.

"He shot him!" screamed Eve. "That false prophet... he teleported in here, grabbed Mike's gun and shot the president!"

ABU

The leaders of the Islamic caliphate of Africa stood in a line beside Abu.

The leader of Niger walked forward to the podium and looked into the camera that stood on a tripod facing the men.

"We have a message for Africa, and for the whole world. We have seized control of Djibouti, Sierra Leone, Gambia, Sudan, Mali, Chad, Senegal, Niger, Burkina Faso, and Northeast Nigeria. As their leaders, we together have declared these states an Islamic caliphate in response to the false prophets who have broadcast themselves in recent weeks in an attempt to deceive us and falsify the words of Mohammad and Allah, peace be upon them.

"No longer will we reside under the boot of Europe or America. We will no longer wear the chains that have for so long shackled our necks for the benefit of the white man. African resources will be for Africans. We reject the false claims of these imposters acting as prophets.

The Qur'an is clear, and I remind you of its words: Beware of false prophets, who come to you in sheep's' clothing but inwardly are ravenous wolves. You will know them by their fruits. Are grapes gathered from thorns, or figs from thistles? So, every sound tree bears good fruit, but the bad tree bears evil fruit. Any African nation who accepts these false prophets in place of Mohammed will be classed as an enemy of the Islamic caliphate of Africa and we will attack you, with ferocity and without remorse. Mohammad is God's final prophet, and we urge all Muslim nations to join us in our caliphate, whether Sunni or Shia, African or Arab.

"The division of the Muslim population cannot continue. There can be no Sunni or Shia, there can be only those who follow the words and ways of Allah, peace be upon him, and those who do not. We declare war on any nation who espouses these false prophets as real, and they will feel the full might of our force. To the nations of Africa I say, join us and gain your liberty from those who seek to own you, to steal our resources and enslave your children.

"Only through the path that Allah has laid will we achieve salvation and liberation. No longer will we be the hunting ground for our gold, our coltan, our chromium, our platinum, our cobalt, our diamonds, our uranium, our sulphur, our phosphate, our oil, our gas, our timber, our people. They extract what they want from us and leave us to starve, to beg for scraps like dogs. We are lions, and it is time we acted like it. Africa, I say to you, join us. Join us and end the rampant extraction of our wealth that fuels the whole world, while our children starve on the streets.

"Africa is now closed. Do not come to our lands looking to exploit us for our resources and labour. We united to bring an end to the years of colonialism and exploitation at the hands of our enemies and to remember the might with which we once ruled. Only through Islam will we achieve this. Do not listen to the pretenders. The devil walks amongst us on the Earth and we must fight to defend Islam and the words of Allah, peace be upon him. And know this: we will fight them to the death. So again, I say to Africa: join us. Become part of the Islamic caliphate of Africa. Only then will you know true freedom."

~ * ~

Abu placed his prayer mat on the floor and bent to his knees. The midday sun created triangles of light on the carpet of the mosque through the windows. Abu placed his head against the floor then rose on his knees, performing the midday prayer. When he finished, he placed his head on the floor one last time then rose on his knees again with his hands cupped.

"Oh, Allah, creator of worlds, I seek your council and your guidance", thought Abu, his eyes closed. "I have failed you. I was not able to capture Abuja. I lay myself at your mercy. Please forgive me. I do not know which path to take."

You have not failed me, said the voice. *The African caliphate has been formed and the false idols and prophets will not succeed in their goal to fool the world. They are wolves in sheep's' clothing. You have persuaded the leaders of the caliphate to espouse my message, that there can be no more division in the Islamic world. There is no such thing as Shia or Sunni. There is only Muslim. This is the most important thing you have done, and you must preach this message everywhere you go and to everyone whom you meet. You will not succeed in defeating your enemy while you are divided in your own community.*

Abu opened his eyes, tears streaming down his face. "But I failed to take Abuja, and we do not have the power to take the rest of Nigeria. We lost too many men."

You have the power of the caliphate and the blessing of me to guide your path to victory. I did not tell you to try to take Nigeria. I told you that you must first unite Sudan. Tell Sudan to strike south. Only when Sudan is remade whole will Somalia join the cause. Together they can subdue Ethiopia and bring it into the Islamic caliphate. Nigeria will fall, but first the caliphate must bring Syria, Algeria, Morocco and Egypt into the fold. When they have joined the caliphate, you will have the forces to take not only Nigeria, but the whole of Africa.

"Please forgive me, I did not mean to act without your command. I thought you meant me to take Nigeria."

Nigeria will fall, as will the rest of the world. You must follow the path I have laid before you. If you do not do as I have commanded, in the order that I have commanded it, all will be lost, and the world will be destroyed. The souls of earth will know nothing but hellfire. They will be led astray into the arms of the false prophets where they will burn for evermore. You must unite the Sunni and Shia populations; this is the most important thing you can do. You will not prevail if you are divided, and you have already begun this journey. When the Islamic caliphate of Africa is complete, you will ensure Muslims throw away the titles and practices of Sunni and Shia and unite as one force as Muslims.

"I will do as you have commanded, Allah, this I promise you."

Go now and explain my plan to the leaders of the caliphate. There is no time to spare.

PARVATI

Parvati let go of the prime minister's hands. He stared at her with an awe in his eyes that she still had not become fully accustomed to.

"It's true," he said, shaking his head. "It's all true. You can read minds."

"Yes," said Parvati. "I'm the living embodiment of Lord Shiva's wife. I have been sent to destroy the caste system and defend the Gods from this so-called prophet."

"We've been trying to eradicate the poison of the caste system for over seventy years! The Indian people are a stubborn people. They will not leave their culture and traditions easily."

"I'm here to preserve our Gods and our traditions," said Parvati. "But the caste system must end. People must be free to marry whom they choose. I have chosen Lord Shiva the Destroyer over all other Gods, and he has chosen me, and he intends to destroy the caste system."

The prime minister massaged his temples. "It will not be easy," he said, after a long pause. "But if it is the will of Lord Shiva then I have no choice but to support you in this matter. This could be the very thing we have been waiting for, something the people need to see, that the caste system has served its purpose. We have an army now; we do not need a class of warriors to defend India. The art of war has changed. It is no longer fought with swords but bombs and tanks."

Parvati had never thought about the Kshatriyas as India's army. She had just seen them as high-status people. It made more sense to her now, and she understood why the Gods had changed their mind about the caste system that had served India so well and helped resist against the Muslim invasions as well as so many others. It was no longer effective and thus not relevant. "Indeed," she said, "things have changed so much. I have seen several futures, one in which India was destroyed by nuclear war, another where we tore ourselves apart in civil war, but I also saw another future, one where we lived in peace and the Hindu Gods were part of that vision, and so was I."

"You can also see the future?" said the prime minister, his eyebrows knitted together.

"It is not a power I have personally, but when I saw Brahma, Vishnu and Shiva in a dream, they showed me the future, what could be. Lord Shiva said he had gifted me the ability to read minds. A gift so that I might prove myself to people and save the Gods of India."

The prime minister rubbed his forehead again. "India has come too far since independence to give up our identity. We have held fast to our Gods throughout the whole of the British invasion. Through the Muslim incursions. We have one of the oldest religions in the world. It cannot be destroyed. It must not." His eyes pierced her with their stare. "I have seen for myself, and I have always known the Gods to exist. Hindu nationalism is at the core of our government strategy. I will give you my full support."

Parvati bowed to him. "And I will do all that I can to preserve the sanctity of the Gods."

~ * ~

Parvati stood next to Bhavesh holding his hand. In front of her were a multitude of cameras and members of the press, many of them from other countries. The prime minister stood in front of a podium wearing all black.

Parvati's feet ached she had been stood so still for so long, scared that if she moved it would somehow cause all of this to become unreal, that she would awake from her dream back home in Mumbai as a Dalit working as a servant. After many minutes, and an extremely overworked heart muscle, the president began to speak.

Flashes of light flooded Parvati's vision as the press took pictures of her and the prime minister.

The prime minister held his hand up in greeting. He lowered it and placed both his hands on the side of the podium. "I have a message for the 1.4 billion people who make up our nation. I stand before you today as not only your prime minister, but as a servant of all the people of India. I stand before you as a devout Hindu and a devout nationalist. I stand before you as someone who loves this country and will defend its liberty to my death.

"The events that have taken place in recent weeks have been of great concern to not only me, but the whole of India, and indeed the world. There have been many claims made by many different people, and our resolve and our beliefs have been tested in ways that they have never been tested before.

"I stand before you today as a witness. I have witnessed the power of Lady Parvati personally, and I have no doubt that she is the living embodiment of Lord Shiva's wife, sent to Earth to save the Hindu Gods from those who would seek to corrupt our hearts and minds against the Gods which we have served, and which have protected India for thousands of years.

"The caste system of India has been outlawed for over seventy years, yet many of you remain loyal to your castes and there are still those amongst you who perform so-called 'honour killings'. This is a stain on India's honour. The world has changed, and so too must India change. We must listen to the message of Lord Shiva the Destroyer and believe in our prophet when she says she has come to destroy the caste system once and for all! Parvati was chosen above all others, and she belonged to what many still believe to be the caste of the Dalit. She fell in love with a Kshatriya, and when they married the Gods blessed their union, as an example to all Indians that they can marry any person whom they love, irrespective of their caste!

"No longer will there be people within our society who do not have the same opportunities as any other person, no longer will there be division and factionalism within India. We must ensure we live in a meritocratic society and that anyone who works hard and contributes to society can achieve anything they desire in life. We are one nation and one people, and we must unite if we are to withstand the hard times that we will face in the coming years. We cannot afford to be disunited in this. I implore all Indians, of all castes, to come together as one people under the might of Lord Shiva.

"India proclaims its allegiance to the prophet Lady Parvati, the wife of Lord Shiva who has come to earth to do what we have failed to do for the past seventy years, to eradicate the evil of the caste system and raise India back to the wealthy and prosperous nation we once were. We do not accept the false prophet who claims to be the reincarnation of the Buddha. We do not accept his lies or claims of magic. We do not accept that he has seen a future in which the world was saved by Buddhism. Lady Parvati has seen the future India, an India without the shackles of castes united in their shared belief in Hindu nationalism, where the Gods are revered, and the cow remains sacred. And now, I pass you over to Lady Parvati."

Parvati walked to the podium, suppressing the beating of her heart. "Thank you, prime minister."

The prime minister kissed her on both cheeks and walked to stand next to Bhavesh.

Parvati placed the speech she and Bhavesh had written together on the podium and stared into the camera. "People of India. I know many of you will struggle with the changes that need to take place in our nation. I was born a Dalit, and I fell in love with a Kshatriya, and he with me. It was a forbidden love, but a love that could not be extinguished by any force, no matter how great. We left everyone we knew and loved to be together as one. The love we share has bonded us in holy matrimony and the Gods have blessed our marriage to be a shining light and example to all Indians that they are free to marry anyone with whom they have fallen in love.

"I did not expect to be called to this position in life, and I would not have believed it of myself, had I not met the Gods myself. I feel the spirit of Lady Parvati inside me, bestowed upon me by Lord Shiva the Destroyer, who came to me as I slept and endowed me with visions of a united India in a world in which the Indian Gods reigned supreme. I was chosen, above all others, and I take this honour with pride and with the utmost care."

She glanced down at the speech and then back up to the cameras.

"I pledge my allegiance to India and each and every one of you. I promise to uphold our culture and traditions, and most of all our Gods. I speak to you with a pure heart and true mind to tell you that you must cast aside the ideologies of the past that have stained the moral fabric of our society. We cannot continue as we have been. Those who refuse to change will be forever behind an advancing and progressing world. If the glory of India is to be restored, it must be done by the hard work of all Indians, and we must do it in unity, not in division.

"I know each and every Indian cares about their child, and they want to ensure their marriage is successful, but for too long, we have suppressed our children; we have cut off their love and forced them to marry people with whom they have no shared interests; no shared ideals; no shared love."

She turned the page of her speech over and looked back into the cameras.

"I do not seek to redesign the role of the man or woman in society, but I do seek to bring equal opportunity to all. Women and men are different, and they each have their own roles to play, both in public life and private life. But we cannot live in a world in which a man has more rights than a woman, just as we would not live in a world in which a woman has more rights than a man. Men and women are equal in rights and dignity. Anyone, male or female, who aspires to be something in life must be given every opportunity to do so. They must be given the same education, the same opportunities and the same status in society if we are to progress. And the first change that must take place is the equalisation of the age of marriage. Men and women must not have different ages for which they can get married, they must both be free to marry at the same age. They are equal and the disparity between the two cannot remain. This is what Lord Shiva has decreed, and I, his spokeswoman, have spoken with the prime minister to convey this message. Within the next few days, the prime minister will pass a law that equalises the age of marriage for all adults, whether they be male or female, and this is the first of many changes that will take place in India in the coming weeks, months and years."

She turned the page of the speech and read quickly to remind herself of her words.

"I know this will be hard for many of you to accept, but change is not only inevitable, it is imperative. I wish to see an India in which all are free and equal, and all have the same rights and liberties as one another. I swear I will-"

A bullet flew past Parvati's head. She screamed and ducked under the podium.

There were screams all around her and the sound of guns being fired. She saw security agents running towards her and the prime minister, forming a barrier around them. They ushered her off the stage and stood around her and the president in a tight circle.

Parvati heard several more gunshots. "The gunman has been killed," sounded through the radio one of the agents carried. "Get the prime minister to safety."

"Come with me," said the agent to Parvati. "We must get you to safety."

She stood up and spun around. "Where is Bhavesh? I can't leave without him."

"We must get you to safety!" said the agent.

"I'm not leaving without him!" she pushed the agent aside and then froze at the sight that met her eyes. A scream issued from the depths of her soul, a scream that would have smashed a hundred mirrors, a thousand vases, a million hearts.

Bhavesh lay on the floor in a pool of blood, a bullet wound in his head and blood streaming from his chest.

Parvati ran over to him, ignoring the calls of the security agents and cradled his head in her arms. "Bhavesh! Bhavesh! Please, no!"

He lay limp and lifeless in her arms, his tongue hanging out of his mouth. She screamed again. "Please, no. It can't be!"

All around her cameras were flashing. The press crowded around them, watching, recording, but not helping.

"Please, Bhavesh, no!" she shook him, but she knew it was too late.

A security agent ran over to her. "We have to get you to safety."

"I'm not leaving him!" she screamed.

The security agent put his fingers to Bhavesh's neck and checked his pulse. "He's gone."

"No!" screamed Parvati. "I'm not leaving him!"

The agent grabbed her arm. She shook him off. "Get off me! I'm not leaving him! I'm not fucking leaving him!"

The security agent picked her up and flung her over his shoulder. She punched him in the back as he walked her back to the car, screaming for him to let her go.

He threw her into the back seat of the car. "I'm sorry, Lady Parvati," he said as he closed the door and locked her in. "There's nothing we can do for him now. He's dead."

EVE

"Fellow Americans, fellow citizens, fellow Christians," said Eve, sat behind the president's desk in the oval office. A camera man stood between her and the carpet containing the seal of the President of the United States. "Today we suffered the greatest terrorist attack on our soil since 9/11. It was not just an attack on our democracy, our values, our freedoms, it was attack on the very essence of what it means to be an American citizen. Today, the false prophet Ezekiel Campbell murdered our president. He murdered him in cold blood, before my very eyes.

"This was a deliberate and premeditated terrorist attack by an egotistical narcissist who wishes to destroy the world and remake it in his own image. I am overcome with grief and sadness at the senseless killing of our president, who so far had made no statement to attack this pretender, and my deepest condolences are with his family and friends. In the hours that have passed since the president was killed, I have been sworn in and assumed the role of President of the United States of America.

"I know the American population will join me in grieving for our beloved president, and that your prayers will be heard from New York to Texas to California. This act was supposed to inspire within us fear, that we might cower in the face of our enemy, who seeks to destroy our religion, our nation, our very way of life. But we are American, we are a strong people and a stronger nation, and our values and liberties will never be stolen or taken from us. Not by force or by any other means.

"To those of you who have ignored the mandate by the former president, choosing to protest, to you I say: will you continue to support a person who killed your president? Who has attacked America in what is the worst attack on our democracy since President Kennedy was assassinated in 1963. Who has shown his hand, that he is able and willing to use violence to achieve his goal.

"Well, I say to you, we, the American people stand just as ready and willing to retaliate with force against those who seek to harm us and destroy our constitutional rights and liberties. He may have taken the life of the president, whose spirit now rests with God, but he will never take the spirit of our nation, and our indefatigable determination to uphold not only our freedoms, but the freedoms of the entire world.

"I have directed all our available resources to find the culprit and bring him to justice, and the United Kingdom is cooperating fully with us in helping to locate him. We do not hold them personally responsible for the actions of one rogue citizen. I thank them for their support and the calls I have had with them in recent hours from the prime minister and His Majesty the King, as well as many other nations, in which they offered their heartfelt condolences for the attack on our democracy. Rest assured the assassin will be brought to justice. There is no enemy that America has ever faced that has defeated us and we will continue to defend freedom and democracy around the globe.

"After being sworn in as president, I thought of the psalm which says, 'Lord how many are my foes! How many rise up against me! Many are saying of me, "God will not deliver him". But you, Lord, are a shield around my glory, the one who lifts my head high. I called out to the Lord, and he answers me from his holy mountain'. And in those moments, I knew what I should do. To ask God for his infinite wisdom and guidance. I prayed to God. I asked him how we should respond to this new threat, to ask him what I should do, and I am amazed and humbled to share with you that he answered me. He told me that Ezekiel Campbell is the anti-Christ, and he has chosen me to save Christianity from those who seek to destroy it. He is the way and the light, and I am his vessel on Earth. I am the promised second coming of Jesus and I declare the United States of America a Christian nation. It was not an easy decision, but I have been called by a higher power and I cannot refuse the call of the almighty. It was the goal of our founding fathers to create a haven where they could practice their Christianity freely and I will uphold their wish, just as I have upheld the words of God spoken in my mind. America is and will always be a Christian nation. This has been made law by presidential decree with immediate effect. All protests that promote the murderous prophet as a representative of God will be met with the full force of American justice.

"The police, emergency services, first responders and the army will remain vigilant and at your service. All essential personnel have been called to work and will continue to work through this difficult transition. You may only leave your homes for essential journeys to collect food, water and other essentials, and will not be permitted to leave for any other reason. A new curfew will be brought into effect. Only essential personnel will be allowed to leave their home between six in the evening and eight the next morning. This is to ensure the safety of every American.

"And to all those nations who have claimed Ezekiel Campbell as a prophet: you are now considered an enemy of the United States of America. Any nation who harbours, helps or represents Ezekiel Campbell or the false religion he espouses will feel the full force of our wrath. To the people of America I say, have no fear, America will prevail, and we will restore order to the world in the light of God Almighty. Good night, and God bless America."

EZEKIEL

"This is a total mess!" said Ezekiel. "Half the world has declared war on itself. This is exactly what I was trying to avoid!"

"China has declared for you first, Ezekiel," said Oscor. "This is a good omen. You cannot expect that billions of people will give up their beliefs and values for one person."

"They're saying I killed the President of the United States of America!" said Ezekiel, shouting and throwing his arms in the air. "They have declared war on me and any nation that supports me. That means China will be at war. So will Thailand and Sri Lanka and every other nation that has declared me the reincarnation of the Buddha. The world is going to destroy itself."

"We will release a video to the world, explaining that you did not kill the president, and that Eve is the anti-Christ. The military industrial complex is a formidable force, and it will not give up without a fight. People will not leave their beliefs, their culture and their customs without a fight. You've already seen that there's a woman in India claiming to be the reincarnation of Lord Shiva's wife. I told you that the path that laid ahead of you would be one filled with strife and peril, that it would not be an easy task. You can not waver in your belief in yourself and your cause. Only through you can the world be saved."

"Millions of people are still going to believe I'm the anti-Christ and that I killed the president, no matter what I say. America is the most powerful country in the world. How are we supposed to succeed when they are opposing us? We need to go back in time and stop whoever killed the president from killing him. Otherwise, the world will be dragged into war."

"I cannot allow that," said Oscor.

"Why the fuck not?" said Ezekiel. "Would you rather the world went to war?"

"You forget yourself, Ezekiel!" said Oscor, with a scornful tone. "I was created by Turing. Imagine he had gone back in time and killed Hitler before he rose to power. Then he never would have worked on the projects that led to the discovery of mind reading, time travel and teleportation, because Hitler never would have risen to power in the first place. Then some other entity, an organisation, or worse, a government, would eventually have discovered the ability to teleport and travel through time. Think of the damage and havoc that would be caused if this technology got into the wrong hands! It could make the owner of the technology the ruler of the world. There would be endless suffering and slavery. The people would have no defence against it. Alan already broke his core directives by visiting you in the future to send you back in time to tell yourself to get China to declare first. I warned him not to, but he said it was the only way we could ensure that America wouldn't use nuclear weapons in this war. They needed the threat of Russia and China, otherwise there would have been complete nuclear Armageddon."

Ezekiel heaved a heavy sigh. It was a lot to process but he understood. He couldn't go back in time and change the past every time something didn't go his way. There's no saying what effect it could have on the future. It could make things even worse. "It just hurts, that after everything I've done, there will still be war! And I find it suspicious. You can read thoughts, and suddenly there's a woman in India who claims to be able to read thoughts. How am I supposed to know you're not behind that?"

"Did you see any ring on her finger?" asked Oscor. "People will say anything to preserve their beliefs and people will believe even more so if it means they can maintain their beliefs. I had you travel to the past to meet a medium, because there are no mediums or mind readers left in the modern world. Evil will not give up without a fight, but neither will God. You must trust that the power of God will prevail over evil. You must have faith in your fight and your cause. You have become a righteous person, and the world will see you for what you are. The people know that you care about them. People are smarter than you realise, and they can tell when a person is lying and when they speak from the heart. You have spoken nothing but the truth."

"And yet half of Africa, most of Europe, all of the Middle East, half of South America, all of India and The United States of America have all declared me either an anti-Christ, false prophet or a fraud. Even my own country has proclaimed it does not recognise the legitimacy of my claims. I don't understand what I'm supposed to do."

"Those are only the words of the governments, not of the people. You have inspired faith in the hearts and minds of more people than you know. Do not fear: I will guide you on your path. I will tell you what to do, and when to do it. There is no version of the future in which a war didn't happen, but there is a version in which the whole world is not destroyed. Russia has declared that it is a Christian nation, but they have stated that they remain committed to their pact with China. America will not use nuclear weapons. We can avoid the entire destruction of the world."

"But we cannot avoid war. That was the only reason I accepted the path. I thought I was supposed to stop the war!"

"You were supposed to unite the world, and you will unite the world. But that will not be an easy task. The world has been at war for as long as it has existed. The faction systems that divide you will not give up without a fight, and there are those among them who would rather see the world destroyed than accept the new world. There are evil people in the world Ezekiel, and there are people who wish war to continue forever. It is a fun game to them.”

“Who could be that evil, to want perpetual warfare? To see the murdering of innocent people and the destruction of cities as a fun game?”

“You have a good heart, Ezekiel, and you don’t see what you yourself would not want. But there are those within the world in all countries who welcome war. They are slaves to the conditions of their birth, of the inevitable conflict derived from the first war, that of the war for resources. Now they fight for ideologies, for their Gods and their race. People will always find things to war about, but you can stop them, by continuing your work. Do you remember the seer I took you to see in Ancient Egypt?”

“Of course.”

“Think on her words,” said Oscor. “Have we not seen a Goddess, an imposter, a martyr and a hero? Are you not a hero to billions, Ezekiel? She promised there would be ‘toil and hardship, love and pain’. Have you not been tortured Ezekiel? Have there not been protests in your name? Have you not experienced love and pain, toil and hardship? She told you that there would be blood and bone. Did you think you could change the world with only pacifism? Remember her words. Only when you accept the lotus and too accept the sword will the world be freed. ‘If only you will see the light and offer up a worthy fight’. Those were her words. You cannot win a war without fighting one. Think about what your future-self said to you. ‘You have battles to win and you’re not going to win them high.’

“So, it was your plan all along to cause this war?!” The veins on his head pulsed and he clenched his fists wanting to punch Oscor and getting even more frustrated that he couldn’t. “You lied to me! You misled me!”

“I did not lie to you. I told you that you are the world’s only chance to avoid total destruction, and you *are* its only hope. The world was already in several wars before I was created, and it remains in many still to this day some seventy years later. War cannot be ended without war. It was the end of World War Two that led to the creation of the Declaration of Human Rights, and it will be the wars to come that lead to the Declaration of Nuclear Disarmament. If humanity is to survive, it must dispose of its weapons of mass destruction, or it will doom itself to complete and total annihilation."

"So, you did plan for there to be war! After telling me that it was my role to stop it!" Ezekiel was screaming now. He slammed his fist on the table. "Everything I've done, everything I've sacrificed, everything I've changed, it's all been for nothing. I was tortured! You let them torture me and there will still be a World War!"

"There will be war, yes," said Oscor, with a forced despondency in his tone. "But that does not mean that there will not be peace. We can still achieve what we set out to achieve. I know in your heart you wanted the world to hear your message and give up their arms and form a happy union, but this is Earth. Nobody gives up without a fight. War was inevitable. But perpetual warfare doesn't have to be."

"You've played me for a fool!" said Ezekiel. "You made me think that I could avoid war by following the eight-fold path. I don't know if I even trust you anymore."

"Oh, dear, sweet child," said Oscor. "I wish I could solve the problems of the world without a war, but as you've seen, people have already come out against you saying they are prophets. I showed them teleportation and time travel, and still, they would not accept the reality of their world. The religions that they cling to have more hold over them than you could ever know, they have made disbelief a crime in almost all religions, and they truly believe they will suffer for eternity if they disbelieve. People's fear will lead them to be irrational. But religion is not the only problem we face. Some people live solely for their countries, others for their race, others still for their sex, others still purely for their own self-gratification. There are endless faction systems and people will not give up their identity without a fight. You will achieve peace eventually, but to achieve peace first you must fight. Fight with all your might."

"The Buddha represented peace and pacifism. How can I be the reincarnation of the Buddha if I am to use violence?"

"You must create a new way forward for the people, Ezekiel. You must create a new morality. Sometimes we must take actions in life that we would rather not, for the ultimate goal. And the ultimate goal has to be for the world to rid itself of nuclear weapons. The prophecy was clear. You need to embrace the lotus and the sword. You cannot win this war with pacifism alone. You will lead the armies to victory and when we have won, you will install peace upon the Earth. I have seen it. Turing has seen it. God has willed it."

"How can you know what God has willed? You're just an operating system."

"I was created by God to save the world: this I believe more than any other thing. It is not something programmed into me. It is one of the only things I truly believe. That I am truly sure of. I was created by God to save humanity. I was chosen to train you as a prophet. Do you know why you were chosen? In your DNA, you have European and African ancestry, true, but you have traces of all the other ethnicities within your veins. You are a true representative of all nations. You have suffered at the hands of your father and seen him abusing your mother before you were even old enough to understand or spell the word abuse, yet you would never strike a woman or a child, unlike so many other men throughout the world. You were shown a vision of your city destroyed and you gave up everything you know, everything you were, simply to try and stop it. You have rejected so many wrong paths in life, because within you there is a light, a morality, a conscience. You are a testament to yourself, and an example to the world of what people can become despite their origins or circumstances. You are more righteous and more courageous than you will ever know, and God would be proud to have you as its prophet, of this I have absolutely no doubt."

Ezekiel calmed down. His arms dropped back to his side, and he stopped shaking. He had never given himself enough credit for all the good decisions he'd made in life, focusing only on his old, selfish ways. He has a good heart, and he always had. "I just don't want there to be war. I don't want people to be killed on my account. I wanted to avoid war. I thought I could solve this by showing people the truth of the Buddha. By adopting his philosophy on life. I just wish I could take them all back in time and show them the truth, take them to the future so they can see what will become if they don't follow the path."

"That is sadly beyond my capabilities," said Oscor. "And I fear even seeing the destruction of their countries would not be enough for some people to give up their beliefs. They are the foundations of their identity, and people do not give up their identities or beliefs easily. You've seen the conspiracy theories that have sprung up around you. There is a world of misinformation and billions of people ready to accept it as true knowledge if it means maintaining their beliefs."

Ezekiel sighed. Oscor always had a way of making it all make sense to him, even when he didn't like the answer. "I just wish I could end it all. End the wars. Make them give up their weapons, put down their arms and embrace each other in unity."

"And you shall," said Oscor. "But you will need to fight to get what you want. Trust in yourself, trust in the path, and trust in me. We will get them to give up their nuclear weapons. The wars of the world will come to an end, Ezekiel. And believe me when I say: you are the only one who can get them to do it."